Rules For Dating a Bookshop Owner

S. C. Gray

ISBN: 9798549317963 (Paperback)

Any references to historical events, real people, or real places are used fictitiously. Names, characters, and places are products of the author's imagination.

Book Design by Lauren Yates/Arete Graphix
Book edited by Kristine Hutchinson

Printed in the United States of America

First printing edition 2021

Published by Gray Publishing Co.
Hampstead, NC

Rules for Dating a Bookshop Owner

Dear book lover,

Tell me—Is there anything more wonderful in life than a good book, a cup of coffee steaming in hand, sitting cross-legged on a comfy sofa with a cozy blanket and your dog curled up nearby in the peace and quiet of your home? My answer would quickly be *no,* if you ask me. I mean, minus time spent with my husband and kids, of course. But I *have* to say that, right?

All joking aside, before you dive heart first into *Rules for Dating a Bookshop Owner*, I wanted to thank you now, not later, for picking up this little yet *big* project of mine. For years, I've had *this* book inside my heart, tucked away. This year, I decided to act on the overwhelming feeling of wanting to write it.

I will say, writing this book was one of the hardest things I've ever done. But that's the challenge: the hours upon hours spent tucked away in some corner in a coffee shop somewhere in town... it all led to words I never thought I'd get to write—THE END. So many obstacles stood in between this short message and those two words. But, here we are.

There are so many people I want to thank that played a role in making this novel a reality. Without the amazing people I'm about to acknowledge, I would have never had the time, strength, or persistence to write these pages. So, here we go. Have your coffee ready?

First and foremost, Bobby Gray. Even though you say you're scared to read this book (because I think deep down, you're scared it may make you cry real tears, and we all know you only cry those while watching *Keeping Up with the Kardashians*), I'm writing this message to you in case that you will, one day, read it.

It's been a year. But when I first sat down at our dining table a year ago and told you I was going to finally write this book, you looked at me and said, "Okay." I'll never forget it. Like, it was no big deal. You said it like you had no doubt I would actually do it. Like it was any other crazy project I've dived into over the years, and you were right there with me, beside me. You had my back.

As always, you have been the one steady and constant thing my heart has held onto for twelve years now. You are why Bishop, the book lover in this novel, exists. You're why so many things in my life exist. You gave me two beautiful boys and a beautiful home to raise them in. You gave me the courage and confidence to know I would always become a writer if I wanted to. I have been able to write in the most stunning home library. I love my library room so much—best anniversary gift ever.

You've pushed me to understand how love really works and why love worked for me in the end. You taught me to be brave, and never have I been alone with you in my life. I love you more than anything my heart will ever have the chance to love. Thank you for always being the one thing my soul could never live without.

To my children, Wyatt Porter and Lincoln Alexander. Thank you for being the sweetest gifts in the world. Thank you for being so good to me, for being so sweet, kind-hearted, and easy on me when I felt like life was so out of control and busy. Thank you for being patient each time I have asked for five more minutes of quiet, yet you understand when I ask for just one more hug and kiss before bedtime. You both give me the best kind of wrinkles at the corners of my eyes because all I can ever do when I'm around you both is smile.

To my mother. We are more alike than we care to admit. And I think finally, after writing this book, that I'm okay with that for once in my life. Your stubbornness became mine, but also your heart and good intentions became mine as well. I know you are so proud of me. I love you.

To my father. Seeing you for the first time this year in ten years so you could meet my children was one of the greatest gifts I've ever given. To you, to myself, to my kids. I couldn't let the time pass for it to one day be too late. The act of forgiveness wasn't for you or me. But for them, and that time I got to see you with them was one of the most meaningful moments I've ever had. And I love you, too.

To my sister, Krys. Your carefree spirit sets you apart. Although sometimes we agree to disagree, our travel adventures, our days spent rapping in the car on the way to college, sharing bags of Ramen in our small two-bedroom apartment with three dogs we weren't allowed to have, surviving on $1,000 a month, just trying to get by—those days are some of the best days of my life so far. I love you.

To my mother-in-law, Melissa. You raised the most wonderful man, and every time my husband is kind, loving, warm, gentle, and a good father to our children, I think of you and Mike and all the work you two put in to make sure he turned out semi-okay. I love you guys so much.

To my best friend, Kate, and my first reader. You're too good for me, and I don't deserve you. Remember about twenty years ago when we were on that beach near Los Angeles? Back when my parents were trying to let me fulfill my dreams of becoming famous, and I was about to secure an agent, had an offer and everything, but I turned it down against my parents' wishes because they wanted Krys to be famous, too? I think deep down, I wanted that to be you and me. Looking back, it's all so silly now, but I mean, when are we going to get our big break? I adore you.

To Meaghan, megalodon, mega-millions. Thank you for keeping me sane in the square when, at times, I felt like I had no one else I could tell my biggest secrets to. You, at times, took on my sadness, so I didn't have to hold it all in. Thank you for being there when all I really, truly needed was just a listening ear.

To my amazing family and friends for standing by me and supporting this novel. Doug, Heather, and Mckenzie, I'm so thankful for you guys. And, I love you.

To my TWC family, I am so filled with gratitude for our time together. To Ruby, my girl, and Rupp, the only dog I know who can read, I love you and you two are the only reason I come to work. Dr. Mathew, thank you for giving me a place I don't mind coming to everyday for the past six years. It's a pleasure working for you, and I never take it for granted.

Special thanks to Tracie Hilsman for allowing me to partner with Birch Hill Candle Co. to make the most amazing candles for the book. You've always been a friend to give the most sound advice. I adore you.

To Rachael Somplasky, for nudging me years ago to start selling books again. Look where it all led.

I'm so thankful to all of the bookshops that will offer my novel in their amazing stores. To Zelle at Zia Boutique, Jill of Coastal Home Store,

Thunder Road Books, and the amazing Inlet Blue Market. You've made every dream come true by carrying my book. Thank you, Debbi and Alli, for welcoming me with open arms. You ladies are a vision and I'm so thankful I took a leap of faith and picked up the phone that day.

Thank you to Taylor Salvetti for sitting with me and telling me all the ins and outs of coffee shop life. Casablanca was such a beautiful spot to sit and write, and when you're lucky enough to work there, you're lucky enough.

To the amazing book lovers I've met because of our mutual love for pages: Shelly Porter, Kate Czyzewski, Samantha Freeman, Shea Breier, Christina Holfelder, Brittney Lyon, Dell Gray, Renée Blankenship, Nikki Ojakian, Michelle Walker, Kelsey Whitney, Laura Paredes, Leona Abarca, Breanna Critcher, Michelle Zelyez, Maureen Casey, Holly Miller, Crystal Kirby, Kirsten Kirk, Jennie Barhydt, Lara Eisel, Katie Miller, Amber St. Pierre, Jackie Zepeda, May Madelo, Emily Wilkinson, Brittany Bumgarner, Shemri Harris, Amy Rowe, Lena Lawson, Bethany Williamson, Katie Finnegan, and SO many more of you. I love chatting with you about all things books. It makes my day.

To the *endless* book bloggers, Bookstagrammers, and readers. Go into this novel with the open heart I wrote it with. I hope when you read this book that means so much to me, you smile, laugh, and cry just at least once. I hope, by the end, you love it. Thank you for the hype-up, every post, every share, and every sweet comment this year surrounding this project. It was such a pleasure getting to know you all. Your endless passion for this book has amazed me since the beginning, and I'm forever indebted as you help me reach so many more readers.

To every single customer of Porter Co. Book Shoppe, I love you, and you make my dream come true every day. Owning this bookshop is one of my best adventures in my life, and a true honor. To those that preordered this book, believed in my work, and have been on this journey with me... it meant the world.

Thankful to no end, Kristin McCauley. The behind-the-scenes genius behind Book Porter. Thank you for being a good friend to me after all this time, for driveway conversations, for being open to every crazy request of mine. Your talent and my ridiculous love for picking out fabrics has created the most amazing partnership, and I thank the heavens every day for Laura Lobdell pairing us together.

To the many author mentors that gave me countless pieces of advice over the last year, I don't know how to repay you.

Kristy Woodson Harvey, you are the epitome of all an author is meant to be. You're an even better friend. You are *the* goal, and I cannot wait to sign books next to you. Thank you for all of your endless encouragement. It meant everything to my soul, and I am beyond grateful.

Annalee Thomasson, our lovely coffee dates are why this book is sitting in these hands right now. Courtney Walsh, Shawn Maravel, Amy Lea, A. J. Banner, you ladies are an inspiration, and every bit of your success is deserved.

Thank you, Arete Graphix, for spending many, many months listening to my crazy ideas to create the most amazing book cover there ever was.

To the Get Social Podcast and all the others that have me on as guests to share this story, you're amazing, and I love you!

Ann Vestal, thank you for playing with me in the sunshine and producing some of the most memorable photos I'll ever have the privilege of taking.

To my amazing editor, Kristine Hutchinson. You made writing this novel exponentially easier than it should have been. You took a load off of me when I needed it most. I will always be so grateful for you. Ready for Book #2?

To our outstanding service members, veterans, and their families, we are all so thankful for your sacrifices. They do not go unnoticed.

Lastly, it's important to mention the men that fought alongside my husband while deployed to Afghanistan all those years ago, time and time again. To those that have been by my husband's side this year, the hardest year, and for answering my phone calls back in March. Thank you. For reaching out a month later, when it truly meant everything. For checking on me, too. I know this book won't do your service justice, but this novel was written for *you*.

Most don't know, but this year has been difficult for Bobby, for our family, and if I could carry just half of the weight for him... if I could take away just half of his pain, I would. But, I can't. I've tried, and I can't. So, instead, I wrote a book for him to show the world that his service wasn't for nothing. To show that I understand, if only just a little. That the sacrifices meant everything, and that they always will.

This book is dedicated to him.

S. C. Gray

Rules For Dating a Bookshop Owner
A Novel

S. C. Gray

S. C. Gray

PART ONE
The Beginning of a New Forever

S. C. Gray

Rule Number One

Never show up at closing time.

Books are one of the best things this life has to offer us. Don't you find that to be true?

Careful not to trip over the haphazard stacks of putaways, I look out of the front window at the sky, the lightest hues of gray moving just over the brick walk-up across the street. I head to the front of the bookshop and begin to gather my things, searching for my keys, wherever those damn things are, and turn to walk out into the crisp, cold evening.

The forecast calls for light snow tonight. The stoop of the bookshop is lit with the prettiest strands of lights, connecting some trees to the black and white striped overhang just outside the store. Especially during the holidays, they are a nice addition.

I bend to pick up Piper, my thirteen-year-old Dachshund. She's been with me since what feels like the beginning of time, when my life truly "started." Back to when I was truly on my own. We're a team, her and I. Two peas in a pod. A pair. Where I go, she goes. She's one of the best parts of my life. Around here, they call her the "Book Pup."

She makes a small grunt and gives me a little side-eye, knowing I'm about to subject her to her favorite kind of torture—the cold.

I reach for her little sweater and pull it over her head, the one she pretends to hate but really loves because it keeps her a little warmer than if she didn't have it on. She can be stubborn—kind of like her mom.

I bend over to be eye level with her, conscious that her neck must hurt after a long day of constantly looking up at a ninety-degree angle. Her short legs are an unfortunate genetic fault, but an adorable one nonetheless. She's constantly looking for me, begging for snacks, asking for me to throw Bunny. I'm very considerate as I stoop to her level.

"Listen, I know it's cold out there, but do you want to stay here all night with all the creepy creaks and shadows, or do you want to come home with me? Your choice."

She's ready to get home just as badly as I am, but she hates the biting weather. I give her a look, raising my eyebrows. Her ears perk up, and she begins to wag her tail.

I kiss her little black nose and rub underneath her chin, knowing she will always pick coming home with me, even if it is cold.

She sighs heavily. She seems to think she works as hard as I do. In the near dark, I can see her beginning to shake, even before we head out the door, already dreading the piercing cold. Life is hard being the Book Pup.

I've been here in this storefront, my bookshop called Turning Pages, for a little over eight months now. Every time I close the vintage Dutch door, squeaky hinges and all, (with a gentle reminder to myself to get that light above the door fixed) I take a step back in awe of all the pages and spines I can see through the window, slightly faded from the sunlight.

The vines have been growing for years up the side of the brick building, now painted black and white. They inch toward the sign above the door that reads "*carry a book, carry a friend*." Every bit of this storefront screams *cozy*.

For a quick moment, I stop, taking a deep breath, to thank whatever cosmic force brought me here. Whatever it is—I don't ask any questions. The minute I start to think to ask is the minute it all will stop making sense.

Benny, my landlord, handed me the keys after I put most of my life savings down to cover the first year's worth of rent.

"Do what you can with the place. I'll see you next year." And just like that, he was gone. It was almost too effortless. So, I painted the walls, cleaned up the fireplace, threw down some rugs, and dusted off the built-ins.

This is the place I get to call "work." A little bookshop off Main in the most quaint and lovely plaza smack dab in the middle of Salter's Ridge, Maine.

And it's all mine. For now.

At first, I thought by putting all that money down, I wouldn't have to worry about much for at least twelve months. I thought that by taking care of the biggest expenses, which are the building and space (utilities and insurance included), my dream of having this bookshop would be possible, a reality. In hindsight, hopefully, I would be able to keep sales up enough to at least make *some* profit. Eight months in, and I'm still in the "honeymoon phase" with this place.

I'm doing well enough. Being a small bookseller is hard these days. With all the online shopping options, I knew it would be no easy feat. And Amazon. Don't even get me started on Amazon. What about that pesky little Target aisle no one can stay out of?

Serious question: Can anyone *really* walk into Target as a book lover and *not* take a quick stroll over there? Even the carts ride smoothly and quietly. They're so sneaky. I'm convinced it's a brilliant ploy and marketing scheme, so we don't realize until two hours later while standing in the checkout line how full our cart has become with a bunch of random shit we don't need.

I've tried with all my might a few times to skip the book aisle in Target. It's comical to think my urges can be resisted.

I can't imagine the excuses some women come up with to wander away from their partner, only to end up there, the most desirable spot in Target... "Scotty needs some new socks! I'll be right back..." Next thing she knows, she's in the checkout line trying to conceal a charge on the credit card, hiding receipts and all other evidence of her shopping spree.

Thankfully, I'm single. Very single. It's a choice I love making. Who wants to be thirty years old and hiding their book hauls? It's honestly no way to live.

Lately, though, I've been thinking about the months to come and what it all means for the shop. During the winter months, sales could always slow down with everyone bundling up inside. But for now, with the holidays rolling in, sales have started to increase again. And to those gifting books this season, I am thankful.

People still love to read and hold a physical book, this I know. The reassurance has been a Godsend. It lessens my anxiety just a bit. The holidays are my absolute favorite, and there is nothing better than this season. My little gift-wrapping station behind the register confirms my feelings.

I have my natural linen ribbon and brown crafting paper on their respective spools, and a fresh mini Christmas tree on the counter next to them with nothing on it but a small strand of clear battery-operated lights. This shop is what dreams are made of—my dreams.

I've always loved the holidays, something I attribute to growing up in an Asian household, where you could find a decorated Christmas tree in the front window lighting up the living room, you know, at Halloween. Looking back now, I can see how that could have been confusing to the average trick-or-treater.

You see, my mom, Priscel, a petite and dark-skinned Filipino who, like every other Asian woman in the '90s, had gained her United States citizenship when she married my father while he was stationed in the Philippines, has never truly become that *Americanized*. She still rolls lumpia on the weekends and makes a big pot of Sinigang for family dinners. She still has every single piece of furniture she bought when she first married my dad, all in pristine condition. And no shoes allowed in the house, of course.

She has the biggest and kindest heart. Well, unless you're me.

My mom and I have always had this love|hate relationship. But she did

19

give me an appreciation for the holidays. For that, I am eternally indebted to her. And trust me, she keeps tabs.

Anyhow, having that tree up at Halloween was literally one of my favorite childhood memories. Looking back, we were no different than the family next door. Well, except for the tree.

Ready for our walk home after a long day of doing inventory and organizing shelves, I grab Piper's leash, secure the door behind me, leaving the ginger jar lamp lit on a table near the door to illuminate the front window.

I place the key in the lock, mentally preparing myself for a walk on the coldest night of the week, bundled up in my gently used tan J. Crew peacoat. Turning the key, I spin around with my tote full of books heavy on my shoulder, happy it's time to head home, which is a short five blocks away from the shop. Long days call for tall drinks. Today is no exception if I'm being honest.

As I move to start my walk home, I'm met with the scare of my life as I run face first into what must be the hardest chest and set of abs that currently exist on planet Earth. I might as well have run straight into the brick building I just locked up. Ouch!

"What the fuck!" I *accidentally* let it slip out of my mouth before I understand what's happening. I almost dropped Piper's leash and was losing control of the big ass bag on my shoulder. Why do I pack it with so much shit?

"Whoa, I am so sorry!"

I look up to see standing in front of me a guy I've seen around a few times before. I just can't quite place him. Maybe at the coffee shop in the square? Passing by the bookshop window?

Well, h e l l o.

I blink several times like I have a damn bug in my eye, although all the bugs have been frozen dead for months now. My body is always deceiving me.

I bend to check on Piper reflexively, and on the way up, I realize I pause and hold my stare a second too long, right at his hips. I notice the way his jeans are hanging nicely on them. Ahh... he smells so *nice*. Wait, what am I doing? This position is very assumptive—palm to forehead.

I stand up straight again, looking at Piper. Rest assured, she has not just dropped dead from a heart attack as I have. I hold my hand to my jacketed chest, huffing and puffing white clouds into the crisp night. I reach up and tuck a piece of fallen hair behind my ear.

Once I am semi-confident this man is not about to kidnap me—as portrayed in the fantastic movie *Taken*—I pull my coat tighter around my shoulders. I look up again to see a set of the most striking hazel eyes, complete with long dark eyelashes that seem to flutter as fast as my heart is beating.

"Gosh, I'm so clumsy. Are you okay?"

He instinctively grabs my shoulder gently with one hand, concern in his eyes.

"I was in such a rush, hoping I'd make it to the bookshop before it closed." He points his finger up at the sign above the door, trying to catch his breath. "I just ran five blocks to get here and was really hoping I could grab a copy of *War and Peace*. Looks like I made it in the nick of time."

He's still breathless, a little calmer now, and his mouth pulls into a long smile, exposing his straight, white teeth. A smile I'm about to destroy. Too bad, because he's kind of cute in his own way, his dark brown hair pushed back off his forehead.

You see, I love owning this bookshop. It's been a dream of mine for as long as I can remember. I gave up everything to have it. But the one thing I've learned is that a hard day's work must end sometime. You know, boundaries. And that "some time" for this girl was three minutes ago. I grip Piper's leash tighter. Momma needs tequila.

Now annoyed because I'm late for my solo drinking date, I will gladly let him know he's approximately ninety seconds past closing and indeed did NOT make it in the nick of time. I snap my fingers once, jerking my fist across my shivering body.

"Oh damn, looks like you just missed the train," I say with a slight smile on my face, my eyelashes fluttering with the same sense of urgency as his. "The train has left the station."

I would feel bad, except, who the hell thinks it's okay to show up at closing time, on a FRIDAY, in the twenty-first century? If this is something you do, a word from the wise: cut it out.

"Sorry, I'm heading home. Door is locked. We are closed. I'm off to my 'house of friends'."

Fridays are always so busy at the shop, especially when I am by myself. If you haven't had the pleasure of making a Casamigos margarita at the end of a stressful day, I highly suggest you drop what you're doing and head to a liquor store, pronto. I hold up the keys in my hand, giving them a little jingle. All hail, George Clooney!

He seems a bit thrown off. I roll my eyes so far back that I feel something detach inside. I give him a wide smile, once again, mouth salivating at the thought of the fresh limes I'm about to soak up. And the salt. Oh, that salt.

Having to spell it out, I say, "Sorry, you'll have to come back tomorrow."

Thing is, I know for a fact I do *not* have a copy of *War and Peace* in stock. I'll have to order it. Why don't I want to tell him this piece of information? I'm not sure... Maybe I have a ridiculous urge of wanting to see him again tomorrow... Maybe I think he's just a smidgen kind of sexy with that hoodie and those fitted jeans and... Jesus, what is wrong with me? I'm an asshole.

Since having to lay off Sophie for the winter, a part-time employee I hired a few weeks into my lease, I've had to do all of the sourcing for the shop recently. I've just done inventory and organized all the shelves the past month all by myself. I know what's currently on them. With times changing and so many folks ordering books online, opening the storefront had not been the easiest start, I'll admit. It has been a lot of work.

I also have this ridiculous urge to make this guy, who probably uses his amazingly good looks to get him everywhere and everything in life, suffer—just a little. Don't judge me.

He reluctantly gives the widest grin, and my insides melt as I notice he too has fine lines at the corners of his eyes, the same ones I've taken to when I look at myself in the mirror every morning while getting ready for work. Me and my wrinkles—we also have a love|hate relationship.

I look up, and he seems now a bit disoriented and completely lost as to why I haven't opened the door back up for him. I wonder how long he's going to keep staring at me like that before saying something.

As if on cue he says, "You're kidding, right?"

He chuckles, confirming my thought, shoving his hands deep into his pockets for what I assume is warmth. Or maybe he's clutching them. Hard to tell.

I turn quickly, seeing he's used to getting his way.

"No, I'm actually not."

His smile quickly drops away. Yes. Mission accomplished. He bends over slightly to make sure I see him. Oh yes, I see you, hoodie guy.

"I *just* watched you lock the door. Can't you just open back up for two minutes, and let me grab the book? Then I'll gladly be on my way. Like we never met." Once again, there's that unbearable smile. I wish he would stop doing that.

"Considering you basically just broke my nose trying to break in here to get a copy of the most pretentious book ever, I'd say it'd be pretty damn hard to act like we never met."

I try organizing my thoughts, as my brain seems to have turned to a mincemeat pie at Thanksgiving—a disturbing mixture of brown shit that should never, ever be put together in the form of an edible dish.

Annoyed with myself, I can't seem to think straight. Which is weird because I just met this guy, thought he would mug me, and now here I am acting like a meet-cute just occurred. Inwardly, I roll my eyes again, this time at myself. Get. It. Together. Campbell. Harrison.

Quickly, I break eye contact, and I look out to the road. Which way is home again?

"Listen, I really, *really* need that book. I have this thing that's...." He bends his knees slightly and holds his hands together in a prayer-like beg. "It's kind of dumb, kind of important."

I quickly hold a hand up to stop him.

"You listen, Hoodie. I'm not opening the shop back up. It's cold, and me and Piper here have a date."

He frowns.

Now, he's starting to get it. He looks down at Piper and whispers, "Who's the *lucky* dude, Piper?" I give him a *"how rude"* scowl, and my mouth opens to say something, but he beats me to it.

"I'm pretty sure the owner of the place would be pretty upset to know you turned away a customer."

Now that's a stretch. Here he is, after closing and begging to be let in. Can he not read a room? Or, in our case, the sidewalk?

Now laughing, inside and out, I side-swipe him very methodically, dragging Piper along, but of course, at the most inconvenient time, she plants her feet.

"Fine, stay with him."

I look up, a craze in my eyes. I'm about to ditch the leash and leave her here with her newfound friend, Ryan Reynolds' stand-in. I give Piper one more tug, and finally, she lets up as I avoid his unreasonably large biceps. I bet he has to eat six eggs a day to keep up with those.

Just then, I notice him taking a look at the keys in my hand.

"Look! Over there, the cutest dog!"

I turn quickly to look for a baby, as he tries to grab the keys from my hands, thinking this is a joke. I pull them back as quickly as I feel his hand trying to take them.

"Major look..." He says, disappointed he wasn't quick enough.

"You mean *made you look?*" I ask, scowling and thinking, *God, what an idiot.*

He offers a confused look.

I start walking away from the building. I'm currently unaware if I'm even going the right way toward home. In all honesty, I don't care. I just desperately need to remove myself from this situation.

Something tells me this guy is trouble. And the kind I really don't have time for at this particular moment in my life of vowed celibacy from all things *men.*

Like pretty eyes, hooded sweatshirts, nice arms...

When he moves it forces the faintest waft of... Damn, he sure does smell amazing. What is that, hazelnut and cinnamon? Maybe I *have* seen him at the coffee shop.

"Hey! Are you serious?" I hear him call at my back.

I can tell by his tone of voice he's in disbelief. I have walked away, leaving him on the stoop. Without the book he just ran five blocks for.

Like that was *so* far for him to run. He's fooling no one in the shape he's in. I mean, come on. I bet he has a 26.2 decal on the back of his car. I'm the person with the 0.0 sticker.

"I don't believe this. I'll be back tomorrow," I hear him yell. "And when

I am, I'll want to have a chat with your supervisor!"

Okay, I think to myself. "Can't fucking wait," I say out loud. Insert just *one* more eye roll. And my eyes are actually hanging from their sockets at this point. He's both handsome and annoying.

A block away now, I begin to talk to myself in the way people do when they know there is not a soul to hear them, but they still know in their heart of hearts they are in deep need of some meds. Like, the psychiatric ones.

"And when you do pop back in, I'll be sure to point you toward the suggestion box. And then, I'll sic Piper on you," I say to no one in particular. Piper perks her ears up, even though I have a slight feeling she won't listen.

Feeling somewhat defeated after that conversation, I remember my other friend, José, is waiting for me at home. I pick up the pace. I don't want to be late for my "date."

S. C. Gray

Rule Number Two

A dog always knows.

Saturdays are always the busiest days for the shop. I try to get there at least an hour early by default to start the day without feeling rushed. That extra time of blissful quiet in the morning is golden.

I hook Piper to her leash, open the front door to the outside, and step out of my five-story building. The street I live on is quiet, as is most of the town this side of Maine. The town is about five minutes from the shoreline, the definition of quaint. I'm within walking distance of the harbor. The buildings are historical, the trees are mature. It's just wonderful.

My neighbors are all older than I am, most choosing Salter's Ridge to retire to. But, some have lived here on this street their entire lives. I feel lucky to call this place home.

This morning, I'm in extra layers. It's been unseasonably warm around this part of the country for this time of year. Or so I'm told. Nevertheless, I'm still cold. Coffee in hand, I'm ready to face the day ahead. I decided for my signature look today to make it easy on myself—one less decision to make.

I went for a black and white striped tissue turtleneck tucked into light-washed jeans topped with a black sweater, leaving my turtleneck visible underneath. I have on my favorite white sneakers. The look is finished off with my favorite J. Crew trench coat. I love a great coat.

This one, in particular, I picked up at the thrift store next to the bookshop. A sweet lady named Mrs. Leo owns it. Not to be confused with Ms. Cleo, the late and great fortune teller.

I reach into my tan leather tote for my cable knit gloves and hat before heading down the brick steps. Piper is already three steps ahead of me, in such a rush to get to a place where there is warmth. White clouds appear before us as we exhale.

Light snow is falling, and it is unbelievably beautiful outside, the beginnings of a winter wonderland that covers the bushes and the bare branches of the trees lining the street. Piper hates walking in the snow, but to drive to work with such a short commute would be ridiculous.

The walk to work is honestly one of the highlights of my day, most of the time. Piper seems to think otherwise. But this morning, I'm caught off guard by an overwhelming feeling that I sometimes take a whole list of things for granted. I've been dwelling over this more so recently. Today, it's at a fever pitch.

The first thing on that list would be the joy of an eight-minute walk with Norah Jones crooning in my wireless Apple EarPods. There is literally no other voice on the planet that brings me more joy, which is why as soon as I arrive at the shop, she instantly connects to Bluetooth through the hidden speakers I had installed the week I moved in.

The piano, the snare drums, the saxophone. Oh, the happiness it brings me. The benefits of music in the morning are everything. The boosted immune system, the lower cortisol levels, the inspiration to be more creative. It's so *good*.

The second thing I love about my short morning commute is this lovely younger couple I pass by every so often. They are always walking their dog, a wonderful black lab I yearn to reach out and touch each time. Do people actually pass by a dog and ever *not* feel this way?

But as they pass, one female of the duo religiously refuses to make eye contact with me as I say good morning to them, squeezing past on the narrow sidewalk. Mostly, I talk to their dog, of course. But the one woman, she couldn't care less who I'm talking to, so long as she doesn't have to walk into the frozen, wet grass next to the sidewalk.

Her poor partner, always white-knuckling the leash, screams with her bulging eyes, "Help! Shit, lady. Please help me. She's the *worst*." It's quite alarming, the amount of emotion seeping from her gaze. This is where Piper comes in. And this is what I enjoy the most about this part of the walk.

It's almost as if Piper senses the desperate plea from this poor woman because at this very moment, each time without fail, she tries to detach herself from her leash and narrowly attacks the mean partner's obnoxious snow boots. You know, the ones with the fur. She barks as loud as her little lungs will allow. Almost like she sees a wild bunny. I'm half-tempted each time to let her go.

You see, Piper's eyes have gotten worse with her old age, so I don't dare try to correct her. Of course, this may not be the nicest thing I've ever allowed Piper to do, letting her semi-attack this lady, but I think it gives both this passing stranger and me some hope that those who do us wrong will suffer, if even just a little. Plus, I think the lady loves to see her girlfriend squirm and almost slip off the path as Piper does her thing. Who am I to take away what little joy they have left?

————

Not all of my neighbors are in despair. During the spring, the walk to work is refreshing. The breeze pushes the trees that line the street this way and that, which forces me to put my hair in a wispy bun.

I enjoy the flowers that folks plant in their beds, with the brightest shades of purples, pinks, and yellows. The wide cedar boxes under tall windows are always filled with hanging jennies and begonias. These are some of my favorites.

I sometimes find Mrs. Harrison, my next-door neighbor, gardening in her small front yard behind the black metal fence. It seems to be her happy place. She dresses in her worn jeans with ever-growing holes in the knees and wears her fantastic gardening hat tied under her aging chin with a thick black ribbon. I love that gardening hat on her.

She lifts one of her hands in a kind hello every time she notices Piper and me leaving the house to head to work, glass tumbler in the other. No matter the time of day, I suspect there's not just sun-made tea in there. I wave back, silently envying her and her seemingly simple life.

But right now, it's deathly freezing, with temperatures that seem to have fallen ten degrees since we left home. My hands are frozen to Piper's leash, even with gloves on, and it puts me in a mood very opposite of my springtime daydreaming.

After a few minutes, I turn right toward Main, and a short time later, I arrive at the shop's stoop. I immediately forget it's forty degrees outside, instantly feeling a sense of gratitude toward my day ahead.

I think to myself—*I'm about to spend my day surrounded by books and folks who love them.* I give myself a little inward smile, switching Piper's leash from one hand to the other.

I reach into my bag, fishing around for my keys, thinking to myself for the thousandth time that this bag is unnecessarily too big.

Breathless like I've just run a marathon in fourteen layers of clothing while chasing a short-legged Dachshund, I find them and pull out the one for the door to pop into the lock. Suddenly, I hear someone walking up behind me, and instantly notice a familiar reflection in the foggy vintage glass of the shop's door.

Shit, he's back. He *actually* came back.

He begins to talk before I've even have time to turn around, and as I do, I almost slosh my precious coffee all over the pavement. I hear him take a deep breath. Goodness, there's that wonderful hazelnut smell again, and I'm sure it's not the coffee.

He looks me in the eyes. "Listen, I think we got off on the wrong foot."

He extends his hand, presumably to shake mine. I look down and then take a sip of my best friend, caffeine. I can be stubborn—something else I inherited from my mother.

"My name is Bishop. Bishop Graham. We met last night."

He gives his widest smile, and now I'm feeling torn. I'm quiet because I am suddenly thrown by how exponentially more gorgeous he is in the daylight. He continues as if I've missed a beat and have zero clue who he is.

"I showed up at closing last night. You were late for some date, and you wouldn't open the shop..."

Date? Oh yea, José... I interrupt him.

"I know, and I'm sorry about that..."

I'll be the first to admit, maybe it wasn't my finest hour.

I decide giving him a slight grin won't kill me. I reach out my gloved hand to shake his, and when he smiles back at me, I notice a little beauty mark just above his lip, almost completely hidden by his scruffy five o'clock shadow. I have an unreasonable urge to kiss it.

Whoa, what is happening?

Knocking myself from my own reverie, I finally say, "My name is Campbell. Campbell Harrison... and this is Piper."

I point down to her and notice that she hasn't barked at him for the second time since meeting him. Not once. That's strange because she hates everyone. At least, at first. He reaches down to pet Piper on her raggedy blonde head, and I feel my ovaries twinge.

"Once again, Bishop, you've come at the most inopportune time because guess what? We're not open yet." I made a little tisk sound. "You can't seem to get it right, can you?" I give him a sly smile. "Come back in an hour." I move to turn back around.

He looks off in the distance, disappointed. I squint a little, noticing I don't have my glasses on. Shit. Did I forget them at home? God, he looks so familiar. "Do I know you?" I ask.

He snaps his attention back to me.

"I'm pretty sure I'd recognize you and gladly avoid you at all costs if we had met before and I didn't *need* that stupid book from you." His apologetic plea now turned sour, and he's lost that charm in his eye. He gestures to the sidewalk. "I guess I'll be back. For a third time."

As he turns to walk away, pushing a lock of fallen hair off his face, I feel a stitch of guilt knowing he has walked here twice now, in the cold—all for a book I don't actually have for him to purchase. Understanding I may be taking things a little too far, I call out to him quickly because even I know my limits on being a jerk. I'm *very* mature for my age.

I take a deep breath, "Bishop, wait." I lower my shoulders, raised in unrealized angst.

He stops walking, a little too quickly if you ask me. Almost as if he was expecting me to stop him this time. He slowly turns back around, and I swear. Is he *laughing*? Who does he think he's fooling here?

I decide to let it go, letting him have this one victory.

As he walks back, I look him in the eye, glancing over him quickly. His relaxed light-washed jeans and snug black Adidas hooded sweatshirt are a cozy look on him. His white broken-in sneakers crunch the salt on the sidewalk as he continues back toward me, success and achievement written all over his face. We lock eyes.

I know his game. I invented this game. One could say I'm an *expert*.

"Let me open up really quick, turn on some lights, and you can come in," I say reluctantly.

I turn around and grasp the keys hanging on the door, feeling a rise of heat at the back of my neck, sensing him now looking me up and down. I immediately thank myself for putting on a cute outfit this morning.

I give the old heavy door a good tug, and it squeaks in hesitation. I need to break out the WD-40, stat. I mentally add that to the list of things that I need to tend to... if I can find the time.

As I pull open the door, Bishop reaches his hand over my head and grabs the inside, allowing space for me and Piper to walk. I look up, my eyes saying a surprised *thank you* because my mouth can't. I reach over to the left above the lamp to switch on the lights for the rest of the shop.

Bishop walks in behind us, and I'm suddenly aware that if he were indeed a serial killer or kidnapper, inviting this man in, good-looking or not, may not have been the best of bright ideas I've had.

Am I looking to star in the next episode of *48 hours*? That show is so good... I turn around, only half-serious, with a smile on my face, and ask, "Bishop, are you a serial killer?"

He lets out a small chuckle but then quickly realizes I need an answer. His smile drops. *Good*.

"Campbell, I'm not a serial killer." His smile returns. "If I were, I would have offed you last night before you had a chance to run your mouth a second time."

His eyes fall to my lips, and I'm filled with a sudden rush. I draw a thin line across my lips.

Touché.

I move through the shop with ease across the worn-in rugs and low-lying tables covered in books to drop my large tote on the front of the cash wrap. The heavy bag lands with a loud thud.

You see, it's filled with tons of bullshit I *think* I need for my day. You know, like six types of lip balms, my water bottle, advanced reader copies from publishers that I have yet to unload at home, Piper's dog treats. And snacks. Lots of snacks. Two pairs of sunglasses, for *all* the sunny days here. Poo bags. The keys I can never find.

I honestly feel like I need one of those luggage bags with wheels on them or that ridiculous rolling backpack some folks tote around on college campuses, of all places. The idea is very practical, but the look of them makes me actually laugh out loud when I think about it.

If you are an adult currently using one of these hilarious contraptions to lug your junk around, I loudly applaud your bravery and outstanding ability not to give two shits what other people think of you. I, for one, lack this characteristic and would not be caught dead with one. I'd much rather break my back and develop osteoporosis. Can you picture it? Me, hunched over, all for the sake of vanity.

I unleash Piper, giving her a little scratch between her ears before she shakes, her collar jingling, and runs to her toys near her bed under one of the tables in the middle of the store. The shop isn't that big—just one floor, one room. But it's cozy and has the space to offer just enough books for keeping the doors open these past eight months.

As I stand back up from petting Piper, I realize Bishop is standing right in front of me. Almost forgetting why he's here in the first place, I move around him quickly, leaving him standing there alone.

"What a great shop," I overhear Bishop say with genuine interest. He looks around. "You're lucky you get to be surrounded by books all day. My grandfather would have loved this place," he says as an afterthought. His grandfather?

He puts his hands in his pockets as he moves to a table just in front of the counter, one that displays psychological thrillers and mysteries—some of my favorites. "I've passed by a few times, but I've never stopped in." He looks in my direction.

Oh, I would remember you, Hoodie, I think to myself.

Then, I hear Bishop ask, "What was that?" And I realize I may have actually just said that out loud.

Quickly moving on, I say as I walk behind the counter, "I actually own the place." I turn my computer on and select a Spotify channel for the day. Norah Jones Christmas, of course.

"Well, I own the *bookshop*. I lease the building." I look up to gauge his reaction to this admission. His face is hard to read. He thinks on it.

As if he needs reminding, I say, "I know last night you said you wanted to chat with my supervisor." I give a small smile. "Here she is." I volunteer a slight wave, almost embarrassed by my childish behavior.

Just when I think I may have taken things a bit too far, he gives a little laugh. "That's cute, Campbell." He points a finger my way and moves over to the counter where I'm standing. He lifts his elbow onto the counter and rests his chin on his fist. "I'm actually quite relieved I don't have to throw your pretty face under the bus like I was planning to."

He removes one hand from his pocket and runs it through his shaggy, unruly hair. I feel his demeanor change from confident to nervous. Interesting. He shifts his feet.

"Look, I know you must be very busy. I'll just go ahead and grab that book if you'll just point me in the right direction. And then I'll be out of your hair." The thought of him leaving just yet throws me into panic mode. Quick, Campbell. *Say* something.

"About the book. I actually don't have *War and Peace* in stock at the moment," I say in hesitation. "I'm going to have to order it. Another thing I could have mentioned last night." My eyes squint in an apology, raising my eyebrows.

He looks at me in disbelief, and in hopes of keeping the conversation light, I say, "I would have told you last night at the door had you not tried to murder me."

He smiles and chuckles. "Again, with this whole 'kidnapping' fantasy of yours. Someone needs to get laid." He pauses and looks at me, not unlike someone who is starved. "I almost think you want me to take you home."

My body goes still. Why does he have to have this whole Paul Walker thing going on?

"In a non-creepy way," he feels the need to add.

I notice his eyes crinkle at the corners again, and in that instant, I crave to know more about him. Who is this guy standing in the middle of *my* bookshop? What gave him those wrinkles at the corners of his eyes? Was it happiness? Grief? These are thoughts that cross my mind when talking to someone new.

Another thought crosses my mind.

"What do you need the book for anyway? You said it was stupid. I take it you aren't reading a 1,200-page book for leisure."

"Some of the guys at the station bet I could never finish a book of that size." He rolls his eyes. "I'm almost scared to see if they're right."

"Station?" I ask, curious now.

"Oh, yeah. I'm down at station seven. I'm a firefighter."

Oh shit, now *that* makes sense. *That's where I know you from,* I think to myself. The station he works at is right by my home. I don't dare offer up this information.

Working to break the awkwardness, he moves to say, "All right, I guess I can prove my ability to finish the world's most pretentious book next week. I'd love to order it from you if I'm able to. Gives me a reason to come back in. You know, to see..." He gives me his most hopeful grin.

Suddenly, I wonder where Piper is before I look down. I don't see her in her bed in the middle of the store anymore. I move to the front of the counter, hoping she didn't sneak out the door somehow. I notice Piper at Bishop's feet, front paws on his knee, stretching up for him to pet her. He reaches a hand down to touch her head. I purse my lips.

"Weird, she usually hates everyone. At least at first." He looks up at this comment and straightens back up, so we are at eye level.

"Kind of like her owner?" His smile reaches up to his eyes. Mine does the same. And now I solidly know why Piper doesn't bark at this charming man.

S. C. Gray

THEN.

The loft we used to share was small. It was on the second story of a small apartment complex. It was located in the middle of the city, and within walking distance to a restaurant we would venture to on the weekends by foot, sometimes by bike. It used to be nice, the things we shared. We split the bills, and we went on short trips together to visit family. Everything was always "together." Until it just wasn't.

"Where have you been?"

I sat at home for two hours after work one evening, waiting for him to show up. He strolled in high, and even a little drunk after joyriding around town in a car that wasn't his.

"I was out with some friends, Campbell. Chill," he responded nonchalantly. He took his jacket off at the door and walked straight toward the stairs, avoiding making eye contact with me.

Now, this is how it always is. Fighting, yelling, and screaming until one person completely destroys the other. It's been months of this. And, it's getting worse.

"Why are you lying to me? I know you were out with *her* again."

I accuse him, and I know in my heart he will deny it. He always does. He doesn't think I have proof. I actually never had proof until tonight. Tonight, it's different.

"What are you talking about? You're fucking crazy. You know that?" he yells at me over the banister. And before I know it, I'm going up the stairs too, chasing after him as I always do in the hopes that maybe I will be wrong about what I have in my possession, but sadly, I'm not.

"I saw your text messages to her on the iPad. Your phone is linked to it. How could you be so stupid? It was too easy to find."

Now he turns around and is in my face in the blink of an eye.

"What did you just say?" he asks.

His eyes are pitch black. I'm two steps below him on the staircase, but I have the upper hand.

"You're disgusting. How could you do this to me? To us? I've done everything for you! I've let you come live with me, and I let you meet my family. My mother loves you!"

"Your mother loves everyone, Campbell. Give me a break."

"Were you with her tonight? Tell me the truth," I beg.

I feel like I'm going to be sick. I can hear in my question how pathetic it sounds. I want to know the truth, but then again, I don't. If I know the truth, what will I do with it? It will be the end of us. And I just can't fathom that. Not yet. Not when we still have so much left to do together.

"Yes. Yes, I was with her tonight."

He spits out the words like they mean nothing. And before I know it, I'm raising my hand. My fingers connect with his left cheek. And again, over and over. Something like blacking out is where I'm headed, and I don't understand what is happening. I don't understand how we got *here*.

He was with her. *Again*. Because I'm not stupid enough to think this is the first time. The distance between him and me is where she sits. She's been there, stagnant for months. It's only now that I've had enough because I have proof. I've seen it with my own eyes. It's not just a hearsay rumor anymore.

He turns around and I grab his shirt and try to pull him back, and by doing so, he almost stumbles back down the steps. He gains his footing and walks into the room we share. *Shared.*

"How could you do this? I've given up so much to be here with you. I should have listened when everyone told me you were trash. You and her both! I hate you! Get out of my house!"

At the landing of the bedroom above, he takes some of his clothes out of the dresser we share. *Shared.* Together. I move past him, take a frame that holds a picture of us, and throw it against the wall, shattering it into a million pieces.

"I never want to see you ever again."

"I honestly don't care, Campbell. We've been over. This is not news!" he shouts.

This admission throws me. Years of my life have been wasted down the drain. And he doesn't care?

"You are so selfish! You only care about yourself. You don't care about me. That much is clear."

He reaches over and grabs my arm, likely to leave a bruise.

"You're damn right. I don't care about you. All you do is nag. You constantly accuse..."

"Do you hear yourself right now? You're upset because I nag you? You've been *cheating* on me! With my best friend. Get the fuck out!"

When he finally lets go of me, I hold my hand to my arm, feeling the effects of his grip on it.

"Hopefully, you treat her better than you treat me."

This throws him over the edge.

"She's nothing like you!" he spits.

Anger and rage crawl up my neck, enclosing me in the room in this small apartment. By now, the neighbors are banging on their side of the wall, telling us the cops will soon be at the door. We are a domestic violence situation waiting to happen, just like all the other times.

Rule Number Three

Never, under any circumstances, dog-ear pages of a book, borrowed or otherwise, to mark where you left off.

I will be the first to admit, when I was a bit younger and naive, I too took pages in my hands, folded down the triangle edge, and used this form of massacre to pick up where I left off the following day. And don't get me wrong, I agree. This type of mutilation can be very effective and seemingly useful.

But as I've gotten older, as my once-supple skin ages next to my eyes, and as my brain starts to max out on the amount of absolutely useless information it can carry, I've begun to understand that bending the corners of pages because I can't find a damn bookmark nearby is honestly one of the most selfish things I have ever done.

I left the house early this morning to head to Luca's for a coffee before heading into work, nonchalantly looking to my right as we left in an attempt to see if I could spot Bishop at the firehouse next door on my way out. But, nothing.

Ever since he told me he worked at the station next to my house while ordering his book for him, I've been mindful when checking the mail out by the road or when walking Piper. I've made sure my hair was brushed, I wasn't in pajamas still, and that I had lip balm on. You know, normal adult things I skip out on most days.

Placing an unused napkin between pages 136 and 137, I close up my current read, and slip my book into my homemade book sleeve, keeping it safe until my next round of binge reading on the go.

I work on finishing up my pumpkin spiced latte, leaving nothing but foam on the sides of the cup, layered from each sip. I push the cup forward on the white quartz countertop and I rise up from the coffee bar, pushing the rattan counter stool back a foot.

The atmosphere here at Luca's is light and airy, and I feel like I'm on vacation when I visit each morning. The snow outside has melted away, the sun is shining, and the weather is warming up for what will surely be a beautiful day. For now, at least.

I take a deep breath, inhaling the smell of freshly ground coffee beans, and look around. Luca's is one of my life's simple pleasures. I'm so thankful for this little coffee shop. Especially Anders, a good friend in town, who also happens to be the head barista here.

Anders and I could gossip for hours and hours about all the interesting people in town that come here for coffee. Take old man Langston for instance, a local farmer who tries to chat up every female he comes in close enough contact with, to no avail. He's the worst, but like Anders always says—we can't imagine a Saturday morning without him.

Luca's is our neighborhood coffee shop that's been around since the dawn of time. It's the only coffee shop in town, actually. Some time ago, Anders approached the owner, Cale, with the idea of doing a full renovation on the building, inside and out. Two years later, Cale is still grateful and Luca's is not only known all around the state for its coffee, but it's also *the* place to have a local business meeting. It's the place all the college kids head to around 1 p.m. once they've woken up for the day. There is no place in town cooler than Luca's. That's not really saying much since there isn't much in this town, to begin with, but you catch my drift.

Years ago, Anders tapped into his brilliant inspiration gathered from all of his travels up and down the west coast to coffee shops across Seattle, San Francisco, and Newport Beach, all while exploring the idea of maybe moving back in with his parents at the ripe age of thirty-one. Since the renovation, he's become a staple here at the cafe.

Anders has ideas. He has insight. He has business sense that makes him worthy of being a successful coffee shop owner himself one day. I push him to think about expanding his horizons all the time. But I know I'm wasting my breath.

He recently convinced Cale they could roast their own beans in the back for the freshest coffee along the east coast. He helped them sift through a catalog of coffee companies, owned by fresh college grads, green from all of their wisdom collected over the last forty-eight months. He helped find the single most eco-friendly sourced and curated coffee beans.

The floors are now an esthetically-pleasing black and white geometric tile, and the walls and ceiling are covered in white shiplap. The natural light here is to die for.

There are palms in natural wicker baskets in every corner, and original art that hangs on the walls. There's a massive chalkboard that lists all the pastries for sale, fresh out of the oven that morning. Above the chalkboard is a sign in bright pink neon that reads *"sugar is not just for a cheek."*

For me, this coffee shop is my sanctuary. I come to sit for forty-five minutes every morning before opening the bookshop if I can help it. I head in around 7 a.m. at opening, pull out several books from my worn-down tote, spread them out on the countertop at my spot at the bar, and get into the right frame of mind to start my day— surrounded by good people, good coffee, and good books. Anders always has my cup steaming hot, waiting for me in my favorite white mug when I arrive. He just gets me.

Luca's is my jam, it's my niche. I was so thrilled to find out when I first moved here that I knew I had already found my *place*. It's where I come for complete peace and serenity. My little spot in heaven.

During the spring and summer, Luca's has outdoor seating under fantastic black and cream umbrellas with tassels that hang down around the edges, washed-out teak tables for two and four, and all of the wooden chairs are mismatched, but still look like they were meant to be placed together. Everything flows here so beautifully.

They have a dog bowl, never without water, by the front door. The benches have throw pillows on them for goodness sake. This place is a treat in the middle of one of the country's smallest towns. I look all around me, thankful for this little slice of paradise.

I finish my morning ritual, reaching for my bag and my coat.

"Are you leaving already?"

"Yeah, I've got to head to the shop and open up."

I've got so much to do this week, including making a call to my mom. Something I always dread this time of year. She plans a huge get-together every year for the holidays. This year, as always, she plans on hosting it at her house. Back home. With her new husband. I'm all but thrilled.

Thing is, I'm very happy for her. She finally found a good guy. But, get-togethers with my mom are exactly like every other huge get-together in the movies.

Tyler Perry's *Why Did I Get Married?* Insane.

The Family Stone. Awkward.

Meet the Parents. Hilariously comical.

If you haven't watched these movies, I highly recommend them.

Anyhow, I try to get out of the Christmas dinner at mom's every year. But, I keep going back. Mostly, for the amazing food. Inside, I despise the days approaching. The dinner. The get-togethers. It's just all so much. And to insert the gathering at a time that is supposed to be all twinkling lights and carol-singing. Well, it just seems a bit too cavalier if you ask me.

"Hey, what's on your mind?" Anders asks from across the counter.

"Thinking about visiting Priscel is giving me anxiety," I confess.

"So don't go."

"I have to. If I don't show up, that would be worse than enduring the damn dinner. The aftermath of that would be World War Three. And plus, we know I'd never miss a chance at Sinigang and her egg rolls. Come on now."

"Bring all the wine. At least you'll have Lou with you."

My sister always makes things better. I think ahead, imagining it now, trying to make the best of it.

"You're right. It's just one day. And, if I can make it through all I already have, then I can make it through one dinner with my mom."

"You're a survivor, Campbell. You're not going to get up."

"Um, I think you are saying that line wrong. I think it's 'I'm not going to *give* up'." Destiny's Child, the world needs a comeback right about now.

He stands back to think about it, turning his head slightly downward.

"No, that can't be right."

I roll my eyes, we giggle, and I hold up a wave of goodbye. "See you later, Anders."

On my way out the door, you can imagine my complete amazement and utter demise when I glance up to see a face I recognize, and seem to be haunted by, heading in. My downfall is coming. Someone is out to get me. *No, nope, never. I refute it...* I inhale a deep breath and let out a sigh.

"What. The. Hell," I say out loud to anyone and everyone.

I can hear Anders behind me giggle a bit.

"Well, hello there, stranger!" he says in the most charming bravado, giving that killer grin I've become partial and impartial to.

Bishop. It's fucking Bishop Graham.

"Are you stalking me?" I ask as he walks in and closes the door behind him.

The breeze from outside floats in before he secures it. I'm surprised at myself for feeling a sting of excitement at the chance of getting to talk to him again. He looks... beautiful. In the back of my mind, I'm reminded I have been half-mindedly looking for him. Everywhere.

I haven't seen Bishop since he ordered his book from the shop a week ago. And even though I've tried hard to look for him, I also have dreaded the moment we would come face to face again. You see, it's hard for me to remain professional when he looks at me...

Like that.

"Has my book arrived yet, Campbell?" he questions, reading my mind.

"As a matter of fact, I was going to call you today once I got to the shop to let you know it did, in fact, come in. I clearly could not make it that far today without you impeding on my territory. So, here we are."

I hold my hand out as if to show him the coffee shop that is mine and mine alone.

One secret I let Anders in on was the strength I did not know I had by having Bishop's phone number and not texting him randomly on one of my drunken tequila nights while home alone this week. When he gave me his information over the counter, it gave me a sense of overwhelming excitement. For what, I'm still a little hazy over.

At night, I would ask Piper if she thought it was a bad idea to text a guy I just met at the shop with something more than just book talk. What I would say, I hadn't gotten that far yet.

She'd just look at me, curl herself back into a ball of wiry fur, and sigh. She acted like I was making a HIPAA violation and I realized at that moment I needed more *human* interaction. Piper was becoming very judgmental.

"You do realize there is just one coffee shop in this town, right?"

Bishop chimes into my thoughts, breaking me from reminiscing on my pitiful lifestyle and the lonely chats I have with my dog and pushes his hair back. He looks past me, trying to read the menu over my shoulder. He looks back at me.

"I come here every morning after I have a shift, Campbell. The coffee is shit at the firehouse. It's funny, I've never seen *you* in here before."

"Yes, Bishop. I do realize that this is the only coffee shop in town. I do live here, remember? However, this space. This coffee shop. It's peaceful. It's so *good*. And you're killing that vibe as we speak."

I roll my eyes so far back in my head, I feel as if a seizure is inevitable.

"You sure do roll your eyes a lot," he says.

"Yeah, I know."

The audacity.

"You might have never seen me here before because I get up early. I get here at the crack of dawn so I can get to the shop early before my day gets hectic. It's the happiness that kick-starts my morning."

I'm starting to become annoyed with this banter. It's exhausting me. And I'm already vitamin-D deficient.

"Want to have a cup of coffee with me?" he asks, interrupting me.

"Excuse me?" I stammer.

I look at him, trying to read his eyes, gauge if he's joking. Surely, he's kidding, right? I stumble over what to say next.

"What, still dating 'José'?"

I think he might be serious, but he chuckles like his request is no big deal. He's no Dane Cook. Now that guy, he's funny.

"Have coffee with me, Campbell. It won't kill you." I hear him whisper, "It might kill *me*..." and I'm appalled. I glare his way, daring him to say one more word.

He gives me a suggestive hand toward the nearest table and starts to walk to the front toward Anders standing at the register near the bar. I can slightly overhear Bishop telling him he'll have a large coffee, black. Then, I lose all supersonic hearing as I watch Anders leaning in to seemingly whisper something to Bishop. From behind, I can tell he has all the confidence in the world that I will have a seat with him. The nerve of this guy.

Thing is, I kind of want to.

This is my chance. My thoughts bring me back to my parents, to old friendships, and to how I promised myself that coming to Salter's Ridge would help me move past my hurt regarding those relationships. Is this a step in the right direction? I can't be alone forever, right? I've made some new friends here in town. What's one more?

This is my moment, to have coffee with a guy I have yet to stop thinking about since the night on the stoop when I thought I was being kidnapped by him.

I hesitate, knowing if I sit with him, it'll open so many doors. And maybe it'll begin to close other doors too, perhaps. I could always use a little nudge when it comes to moving on from my past, not that moving a thousand miles away wasn't enough. It is what it is.

I look over to see Anders, who's been eavesdropping this entire time. He nods to me, telling me to stop messing around. Another nudge. Something is telling me to run. Something is telling me to leave it be. A part of me wants to dive headfirst. But something is also telling me to take this man by the hand, get the coffee with him and never look back.

Rule Number Four

Life is short. Eat the damn cookie.

Bishop returns to the table I've just claimed, working hard to balance his black coffee in the crook of his arm. I spot a latte in my favorite white mug with a small saucer underneath in one of his hands, and a plate with two coconut macaroons in the other. He sets the plate with the cookies on it in the middle of the table and I eye him suspiciously.

"What are you doing, Bishop?" I ask. "And what is this?" I point to the plate in between us.

I look up at him standing over the table, a concrete-shaded light hanging above us. He's wearing faded blue jeans and the bottom of his hoodie hangs over the top of them. I try to maintain a modicum of focus, but my left eye starts twitching. Why must my body always deceive me?

"I'm having a cup of coffee with you. Mostly, though, I just wanted to see Piper."

He smiles, reaches down, and gives her scraggly head a solid rub. He thumbs over his shoulder. "My guy Anders let me in on your regular order. Pumpkin spiced latte, splash of caramel. He said you like the art on top." He smiles. "I also thought maybe you could use a little 'sugar' before you head into your workday."

Something tells me by his smirk, he's not talking about the cookie. He motions to the macaroons and nods to Anders in a *thank you*.

Okay, stop it. That is seriously the cutest gesture.

"Anders is actually *my* guy, Bishop," I offer a small grin but add, "so, back off."

I raise my eyebrows, my petty stake on Anders missed by all. But, it is a nice change of pace that he thought to ask Anders what I like to drink. Smooth. One point for Bishop.

He licks his bottom lip subconsciously, and I feel my palms start to sweat. I'm not sure why I feel so nervous. It's just coffee with some guy, right? The guy just happens to be very catching, and thoughtful. Huh...

As he takes a seat at the table, I look over to Anders, giving him the evil eye and silently thanking him as well for this moment he just created. Anders knows coconut macaroons are my absolute favorite.

The ones here at Luca's are made in the back of the house by our local treasure that Anders found, Jean Paul, a sweet little baker whose parents still reside in France.

Jean Paul will be the first to tell you his recipe for the macaroons. I'm sure he leaves something out at each telling. I know this because everyone says they never turn out just like they'll find at Luca's. It's one of the things that keeps everyone coming back. Maybe folks think one day they will be able to gather all the clues and be able to create what Jean Paul does.

Anders knows these coconut macaroons are the key to unlocking the padlocked door that is my heart. I stop to take a deep breath. I'm trying to soak in this very moment. I look up from my cup of coffee.

"Thank you. For this," I say in all sincerity as I lift my cup slightly.

Since the moment I met him, I knew Bishop was something different. I just didn't think different would be a *good* thing. You know, with the whole murder scenario and all.

Bishop just gave me two things I really needed this morning: more caffeine and a chance to stop with all my shenanigans, stop resisting my attraction, and get to know him a little better.

This is our what? Our third or fourth time meeting like this? Time is short when you look at it on a linear scale. No true love ever says years down the road, "I wish I had met you later in life…" —unless you're serving some sort of prison sentence.

I hate to admit it, but Bishop is mighty easy on the eyes. He's got this ruggedness about him. His hands look rough with what seems like years of hard work. There's something confident and mysterious about him. And let's face it, it's not like there are a million guys to choose from in this small ass town, I've come to notice. Not that I am really looking, but you know what I mean. Which is one of the reasons why I moved here in the first place. To get *away*.

"You're not the easiest egg to crack, Campbell. But something tells me you already knew that."

Bishop eyes me and takes a macaroon off the plate between us. He brings the cookie to his mouth, stops just in front of his lips, almost in a teasing maneuver. I move my eyes away, looking out the window into a bush. As he takes a bite of his cookie, I look back to him and raise my eyebrows in anticipation, waiting to hear what he thinks of it.

"Wow, yep, that is amazing." He devours the entire cookie in less than two bites. "I'm going to have to ask them for the recipe."

"HA, Good luck with that. Everyone in this town has tried, I hear. No one can shake the tree that is Jean Paul."

I get a small laugh out of him, and he moves his hand to grab his coffee and takes a large chug. I notice several small scars across his knuckles.

"I'm always up for a challenge."

He wiggles his eyebrows up and down. Is he referring to obtaining the world's most secret recipe, or me?

"So, Campbell. What is a *horrific-looking* girl like you doing in such a beautiful place as Salter's Ridge?"

Sarcasm at its best. I like it.

"Um, I, personally, would like to think I'm a little easy on the eyes. Even if it means that the eye is lazy. And possibly looking at someone else completely and entirely different."

He laughs so hard I think he might fall from his chair.

"I'm kidding. I actually moved here about a year ago. To start over, I guess. I really needed a change."

I try not to think of what that *specific* change was, lest I start having a panic attack right here in the middle of Luca's.

"One day, I pulled out a map and dropped my finger. It landed here."

Even though 1,000 miles away from North Carolina doesn't seem far enough some days. I gesture to our surroundings like I was meant to be dropped into a stunningly designed coffee shop in the middle of nowhere. I mean, I spend as much time here as anyplace else, right?

"Why did you need a change? Did you kill and bury someone? Are you on the run, Campbell?"

He's joking again, but it actually doesn't feel too far from the truth. I mean, I didn't murder anyone. Obviously. No matter how much I wanted to. But I definitely needed to escape *someone*. And something. Escape that entire draining life I was living. I let my gaze fall away to the floor.

"That might be a conversation involving a glass of wine, Bishop. Not a cup of coffee," I say looking up into his eyes.

For the first time since sitting down, I *really* look at him. He seems to feel the change in the air, in the conversation.

"Already planning date number two, are we? I, for one, personally like to take things slow, Campbell. Not sure about you... but I'd like to get in a few good-quality conversations before being invited into your home where we both know you'd attempt to swoon and seduce me."

He does this subtle wink thing and I'm melting.

"Very funny. But I'm serious. It's a long story of how I ended up here."

"Great." He sits back in his chair. "Because I'm out of commission the rest of the day. I just got off a shift. I've got nowhere to be. I've got the

61

patience for 'long'."

I lean forward a little in my chair, holding my coffee cup with both hands to warm them.

"Why do you care, Bishop? We just met. Don't get me wrong. You seem like a great guy. You say you've got the patience of a Saint. You're the town's *hot* firefighter. The girl with a bad attitude and baggage is usually not everyone's *go-to*," I say, now starting to wonder what's in it for him.

"Number one, I'm not the town's 'hot' firefighter." He laughs a guttural laugh. "What does that even mean? And number two, everyone has their *thing*, Campbell. You're not the only one."

"Oh yeah? Well, then what's your *thing*?"

Two can play at this game. He looks at Anders and bites the inside of his cheek. Maybe, he too has something he is running from. He better not be trying to turn Anders as his gossip, too. He's the holder of *my* secrets.

Now, it's his turn to look out the window. They really need to cut down that bush.

I break the silence, taking the hint he doesn't want to discuss it right now. "Look, although that all sounds nice and appetizing, divulging all the horror stories that are *my* past... I've got a bookshop to run, books to sell, and customers to tend to." I look at my watch. "Shit, I really need to get going." I take one last quick sip of my coffee, another amazing cup for the books, and grab my bag hanging from the back of my chair.

Bishop gazes up at me with his hazel eyes. I look at them. I mean, I *really* look at them and notice specks of gold in them. He is so damn good-looking.

Bishop steels into my thoughts. "Hey, there's this place down the street I've been meaning to try. Their Instagram feed looks amazing. I think it's called The Bodega. How about we continue this conversation there? Tonight? I'm free."

He looks at me and I feel the effect of his magnetic pull.

"Fine."

Truth is, I've seen their feed as well and have been curious. I am such a sucker for a pretty cocktail. I better take the bait before he changes his mind.

"I'd love to go with you. Can I meet you there after I close up? I'll have to take Piper home and drop off my things. I'll change and see you there?"

He gives the biggest smile I've seen him give since meeting him.

"Great, I'll see you there around six?"

"Perfect." And with that, I move to head out, but not before turning around and grabbing the last cookie off our plate.

"Nothing like a little sugar to get my day started."

I look at his lips, teasing him, just a little, and take a bite.

Just like that, I'm off to work with the biggest smile my cheeks have felt in years.

S. C. Gray

Rule Number Five

Stop and smell the pages.

After having coffee with Bishop, I walk as quickly as I can to the bookshop with Piper at my side. Her legs are moving as quickly as they can manage. She looks back to scowl at me, saying, "Slow down, lady. I'm at a disadvantage here..."

As I approach the store, I begin rummaging through my bag for those god-forsaken keys again. I find them by reasonable deduction based on the sound of them clinking around. I really need to start clipping them to the side of my bag.

I pop the key into the lock, open the door, and drop Piper's leash as she runs off deep into the shop with it trailing behind her. She appears again in record time, clutching her stuffed bunny in her mouth, one she's had since she was a puppy. One ear has been ripped off, and all the stuffing has been pulled out. It's tattered and dirty, but it's her favorite. I reach down to remove her leash from her collar. She looks up at me expectantly.

"What, baby?" I pretend like I don't already know what she wants. "Are you ready for another day of helping mommy sell some books? We've got lots of work to do."

She drops her bunny at my feet. I give in and pick it up. I toss it out past a few tables in the middle of the store. She chases and grabs hold of it, and heads off to curl into a ball in her bed. She turns around two times, and then once more for good luck, before plopping down with an audible 'hmmm.'

By the time I've walked around the counter, removed my jean jacket, and put my bag under the register, she's already lulled herself to sleep. Some people take long-term sedatives to be able to do that. Cue the envy.

I turn on my computer and the Bluetooth connects to the speakers above. My Taylor Swift acoustic station begins to play throughout the shop, starting with *August*. Honestly, is there anything better than Taylor, post-Scooter Braun scandal?

Today, I've got a laundry list of things I've got to take care of before the weekend arrives—first thing's first. I file through my emails. I immediately spot something that brings joy to my morning already. *Penguin Random House* has just released its spring|summer 2022 catalog with projected new releases. I make a mental note to request a few advanced readers' copies.

The sheer amount of amazing books I have access to before they come out is enough to want to keep the bookshop open and thriving. To get to read books *before* they are released is an actual dream come true. It all started when I first posted to my Instagram about a book I was reading. I gave a raving review, the publisher saw it after I tagged them in the photo, and they asked if they could send me more books in exchange for more honest reviews. Granted, it takes a lot of hard work and time to blog about books. It's basically a full-time job. But it was something I truly enjoyed back then.

Advanced readers' copies are one of the many perks of being a bookshop owner. Who doesn't love free books? Now, if I could just keep up with my "to be read" list...

I scroll further down and see an email marked *urgent* from Benny. Benny is the owner of the building I lease for the shop. I don't know much about Benny, but I do know any email from Benny would seem urgent to me, considering this is only the third time I've heard from him since signing the contract. The subject line for the email: Lease on Building 2-B in Salter's Ridge.

I continue scrolling, leaving the email unread.

I immediately have a sense of anxiety rush over me. Benny's note could be a reminder of my contractual agreement to clean out the air filters in the space, which is highly unlikely, or it could be an email regarding the upcoming end of the lease on the building, which is a conversation I have been avoiding having with him for weeks now. It's been at the back of my mind for way too long. The lease is up in less than four months. This is *more* likely the reason for the email...

It also is the probable reason for two new wrinkles on my forehead.

When I first reached out to Benny about renting out the brick stone building ten months ago, I did so intending to only stay here for a year, thinking that those twelve months would give me enough time to figure out my next steps for the shop. I thought twelve months would give me time to see how a bookshop would do in this small town, first of all. Second, months down the road, I gathered from locals stopping in that something of a bookshop was really wanted and needed around here, as there was hardly anything standing to offer the town anyway, other than Luca's, thanks to Anders.

Being here in Salter's Ridge has me realizing that maybe, just maybe, I was right to leave my old life behind and start over. To build something for myself that wasn't attached to my old life in the least bit. The shop has been doing surprisingly well these last few months. I've been making enough money to stay afloat and then some. Which is the goal, right?

My savings are miraculously back to where they first started before I decided to move here. With the holidays quickly approaching, I can only anticipate that sales will skyrocket, especially because I've established a great lineup of amazing and loyal customers. I've already made plans to ask Sophie if she would like to come back and help out on the weekends and punch in some inventory during the week. There just aren't enough hours in the day. I am really needing the help again now that I'm off my feet.

Granted, the first several months in the space were absolutely terrifying. I hardly made any sales while people were still finding out who I was, where I was from, and what the hell I was doing here. I started becoming known as *"The Book Girl."* Folks seem to really enjoy the shop so far, which has been a feeling I cannot begin to describe. I feel like I've found my spot, a place to belong. These four walls are my second home. A lifelong list of worries dissipated when I grabbed my footing after opening this bookshop.

Months into the lease with Benny, I realized this shop was something I need in my life. I started thinking that I would never ask for anything from anyone ever again if I could just extend the lease.

That being said, when I signed the papers, it was with the clause of only having the building for a year, while Benny was off doing his retirement thing overseas, traveling through Southeast Asia with just a passport and backpack. That's how he explained it anyway. I picture it now, the male version of *Eat, Pray, Love.*

Wait. Isn't that already a book or something? Drink, Play...?

Anyhow, I haven't heard from him much since signing the lease. He's a bit unconventional as a landlord if you ask me. He's stayed to himself, giving me my space. When he showed me around the building, he even loved on Piper, patiently waiting as I checked the place out. That said a lot. Maybe he didn't think there was much harm that someone with a little dog could do in his building while selling books.

The conversation, my asking Benny for a lease extension, preferably one that would be open-ended, has made me anxious at best. I have no idea what he will say. After all, he doesn't seem to really *need* the space. It stood empty for years, from what I understand. And when I found it and reached out, he seemed relieved to be able to fill it with any sort of business. I saw the listing on a whim, and just by happenstance, Benny was free to meet with me while I was here checking out the town. When I explained I wanted to open a bookshop, his eyes grew large. He smiled wide and basically handed over the keys, no questions asked.

In just two weeks, we settled on a lump sum for me to pay upfront for the space. I wrote out the check, the space was cleaned out, and Benny welcomed me with open arms. It was almost *too* easy.

But in my heart, I know the longer I put off the conversation, the closer I get to possibly being out on my ass with 5,000 books in tow. My apartment couldn't hold half of that until I figured out my next step. I need to talk to Benny. And soon.

I put the thought in the back of my mind once again, promising myself to answer his email tonight after dinner with Bishop, and move on through the rest of my emails. I do a quick scan, and there isn't much else of importance.

I take a sip from my glass water bottle on the counter, infused with mini cucumber and fresh lemon slices, you know, for glowing skin or whatever it is these bloggers are pushing onto people these days, before walking over to switch on the OPEN sign in the window. I pull open the top half of the Dutch door to allow the day's light breeze in. Have you ever had the pleasure of propping open a Dutch door? This feature adds so much character to the storefront. It's amazing. And I adore it.

Sometimes, folks passing by see the door open and stop in for the first time out of pure curiosity. It's days like these I come to be thankful for. The simple pleasures in life, like a crisp breeze through a Dutch door, are all around us. We just have to be open to seeing them.

———

The day passes by without too much excitement. I had a handful of customers come in to pick up orders they placed, and I am always so thrilled when I hear from a person or two who say they found me through a friend in town who recently stopped in and loved the place.

Over the past few months, I've worked really hard to curate shelves that hold not just new releases but those that shelve vintage finds, a few classics, and some that just bring happiness to folks. The self-help section seems to grow weekly these days with each shipment coming in, and with a handful of pretty coffee table books, these four walls are a sanctuary in the making for me, and seemingly the rest of the town too. I shudder to think in a few short months, it could all be gone.

Hours into my day, I checked off all the boxes on my to-do list. I hustle to close up the shop—the front door is shut, the dog bowl brought in from outside, the lights dimmed, and my favorite table lamp is on. I now have Piper on her leash, and tote up on the counter. I'm almost ready to head home to get ready for dinner with Bishop.

I'm about to shut down my computer and tuck it snugly into my bag when I hear someone open the door to the shop and pop their head in. Insert premature eye roll|butterflies before I even turn around. I think back to when Bishop first showed up at the shop at closing time a week ago. A week later, and I'm still feeling like...

"Hey, lady! Have you seen Mrs. Leo lately? She's looking good in her ripe old age."

I look up to the sound of a familiar voice. Damn. Not Bishop, but still a pleasant face.

"Sienna! Hey, dear! Speaking of Mrs. Leo, I need to stop in there soon. She always has the cutest things," I say, turning around to reach out my hand and walk over to her.

My post lady is *the* best. Her mail route is hardly a mile long, the perks of working in a small town, she says. Every evening before closing, she opens my door and brings in my mail instead of putting it into the black metal mailbox mounted to the wall just outside the front door. The thing is halfway covered with ivy at this point anyway.

I appreciate Sienna. She knows how to deliver mail. She's timely, kind, and efficient. She's nothing like my old mailman, the old jerk he was. He always went on and on about how he was retiring. He finally stopped bringing mail altogether. Gosh, he was a real piece of work.

I think Sienna enjoys chatting with a friendly face at the end of her day since she walks in silence for most of it. I can't say I mind her stopping in either. She's been part of my routine for almost a year now and has become a staple during my day at the shop.

"What are you up tonight? Any big Friday plans?" she asked, laced with sarcasm, as there is virtually nothing to do in town.

I smile wider than the state of Texas. "Well, I actually think I have a date."

I can feel it in my face. It sounds almost like a question, even to my ears. To be honest, I'm not sure what tonight is with Bishop. Maybe it's just another basic conversation between two people like it was this morning at Luca's.

"A date?! With who, Piper? She doesn't count," she says laughing.

"No, you asshole. There's this guy I met. His name is Bishop."

Now I've piqued her interest. Small town gossip is hard to come by around here. Nothing much ever happens that is of interest, so people have to make shit up most of the time to get by without keeling over from boredom. To Sienna, this is surely the most exciting thing I've ever conversed with her about.

"He came in last..." I begin to explain.

"Wait, *YOU* are who Bishop *Graham* is taking to The Bodega tonight?!" I scowl at her. My eyebrows nearly touch each other.

Number one, why is that surprising? Number two, I guess gossip isn't as hard to come by as I thought. Number three, why does she know about me and Bishop? I search her face for more information. Two seconds go by, and she can't take a hint, apparently, so I have to spell it out and drag it from her.

"Sienna, what have you heard? How do you know about Bishop and me?" I move closer to her, and I feel my face getting warm. "Is it hot in here?" I haven't even put my coat on yet...

Has Bishop been telling people about our coffee "date" this morning? It's been like, what, eight hours?

"Evans told me about it at lunch today."

Evans is Sienna's husband, who I vaguely recall happens to be a firefighter as well. He must work with Bishop, there being just one station in town and all. And if he, Evans, told Sienna about it at lunch, Bishop must have told Evans right after leaving Luca's.

"I guess Bishop had to take something back to the station this morning after finishing up his shift. He mentioned he was taking some girl to dinner tonight. The entire station obviously closed in on him and made him spill the beans. Those guys have nothing better to do than stand around and gossip. We all know they aren't usually rushing off to put out any fires. Those poor guys are usually without exciting moments."

She eyes me up and down very dramatically.

"Apparently, Bishop has been non-stop thinking about you. Says he thinks he's 'met his match'."

She wiggles her eyebrows up and down and hands me a small, bundled mail stack (most likely all junk), and heads to turn back toward the door to leave. A letter addressed to Benny, with a large red stamp on it, catches my eye: URGENT. What is with all of these urgent things popping up? I toss it to the side. Hopefully, I'll see him soon. Or at least hear from him.

"Wait, are you kidding me? You can't just drop that bomb on me and leave! What else have you heard? He didn't say that! Did he?"

I need more. Bishop has been telling friends of his about me. I wonder what he's been saying. Can't be much. We've seen each other only a handful of times now. Most of which has been spent with him trying to steal my coffee spot and me trying to redeem myself with the universe for being an asshole. And what does he mean by he's "met his match?"

Sienna turns back around with a giggle.

"Why don't you ask him? It would probably be better coming from Bishop himself. I'll let you go. Go get ready for your *date*."

With the sun close to setting just behind her outside the shop, she winks over at me and waves goodbye. I smile with wonder, and with that, I grab Piper, my larger-than-life bag, and walk out behind Sienna. I close the door with a firm push, turn my key in the lock and rush home so I can stand in front of my closet for fifteen minutes because we all know I won't have a damn thing to wear tonight.

I do notice a smile on my face the entire time because tonight, I *do* have a date with a guy named Bishop Graham, and he happens to think *I'm* his match.

S. C. Gray

Rule Number Six

Make eye contact with those you speak to. You'll learn a lot about a person by the way their eyes shine into yours.

Walking toward The Bodega, the night is slowly becoming chilly. I squeeze my arms tight around my stomach. I have an overwhelming number of butterflies floating around, and I can feel the nerves starting to sink in as I approach the outdoor patio area to the right side of the restaurant.

Outdoor lights zigzag above the alleyway, and palms are scattered about, giving way to the summer vibes it's portraying, even in the cold. I almost forget I'm in Salter's Ridge in the middle of absolute nowhere and not in some faraway destination like Punta Cana.

I cautiously walk on the gray cobblestone, doing my best to avoid tripping over my clumsy feet strapped into these ridiculously high wedges. I search a sea of faces, looking around to see if Bishop has arrived before me. I curse myself for reaching for these shoes tonight, but I do feel cute. Beauty is pain. It is also a mother fucker.

I opted for a crisp white long-sleeve backless linen blouse, complete with a tie at the small of my back, just above the pockets of my skintight jeans. Classy, yet sassy. I haven't had a chance to wear it until tonight. Shit. Did I remove the tag?! I twist my neck and pull my arm to the back of my shirt, near the bowtie, to see if I can feel for one.

Relieved when I don't feel a thing, I reach in the back pocket of my jeans for my phone to text to see where Bishop is, but he beats me to it. I see him raising his arm in a wave. He calls out my name, and I nod to him. He's already seated at a back table. There is music playing in the background over a speaker probably hidden in one of the palm trees.

As I begin to make my way toward him, I notice his brilliant white smile from across the patio. Good lord. Please do not let me bust my ass in front of all these people.

Bishop, now moving around our table toward me, places his hand on the small of my back, just barely touching the exposed skin there. He smells of a fresh shower, and he bends slightly. He touches my cheek with the lightest kiss, his lips a soft luxury on my skin. A slight shiver runs down the entire length of my spine.

"You look absolutely beautiful, Campbell," he whispers into the nape of my neck.

I melt right then and there. I'm thankful for the high bun I pulled my hair up in. Here we are outside on the patio, and I'm burning up, even with this crisp breeze blowing tonight.

"You don't look so bad yourself. Who knew you could clean up so nicely?" I say as I pull away, eyeing him up and down.

I want to ask him to leave right then and there and head back to my place. I have no shame. He looks and *smells* yummy. I try to remain composed, you know, as a lady would.

He's dressed in a simple white long-sleeve button-down shirt, wearing navy slacks with his shirt untucked. His white sneakers make for more of a casual look, dressing down his business attire. He looks wonderful. He's not in his usual hoodie and jeans.

He pulls my chair out, gesturing me to sit down, and as I do, he moves back to his side of the table. I look him in the eyes. I have the strongest urge to reach across the table and push his hair off his face so I can get a better look at him. His hair is on the brink of falling into his eyes.

"If I had known we were going to get *dressed* up, I would have worn a different outfit."

I automatically think back to the little body-con number I passed up for a little bit of comfort.

He looks at me from across the table before turning his phone over so the screen faces down. I appreciate the gesture and smile inwardly. I hate when I'm out to dinner with someone and they're on their phone every other minute.

"You would look amazing in a paper bag, Campbell." The way he says my name stirs my insides, dissipates the butterflies, replacing it with a tornado of angst. "And besides, I like a girl who doesn't feel like she has to wear a short dress to impress a guy. Natural beauty and a little bit of class can go a long way these days." He smiles and asks, "Why do girls do that anyway?" He shakes his head ever so slightly.

I smile wide, thrilled I didn't go with the body-con. "Well, I'm glad we came out tonight. I really needed this."

This week has been swamped with customers, and emails that needed answering. I organized all the tables in the shop to accommodate new shipments in anticipation of a busy holiday season. So much has gone to new homes. I'm filled with appreciation at the thought of it.

In the moment, I remember the conversation I need to have with Benny, feeling slightly dreadful at the thought of having to sit down with Bishop and try to push it out of my mind.

Just then, as if she knew I needed her to release me from my thoughts, the waitress comes over and hovers near our table. Bishop refuses to break eye contact with me.

"Hey, guys! Welcome to The Bodega! My name is Leena, and I'll be taking care of you tonight. What can I get started for you? Drinks? Appetizers?"

I look up with a smile, my mouth watering just thinking about it, and jump to ask for the cran-mango|basil margarita on the rocks with salt on the rim. I'd been stalking their Instagram page when I had some downtime at the shop, and everything looked amazing. Especially their cocktails. I'm a sucker for a good cocktail. Who isn't? I've been craving one of their drinks all day. From the looks of things, they seem to be very popular.

The patio area is beginning to get full, and the voices of the restaurant's patrons get louder than the music, just shy of being *too* loud. The sun has set, replaced with a brilliant black sky and golden stars glimmering above us.

I look up at Bishop, wondering if he's forgotten the waitress is waiting on his drink order, and begin to think he may not answer her at all. He looks up just then.

"I'll do a ginger ale, please. Thank you." He smiles and looks back at me quickly, then moves down to the menu. "Want to try out the guacamole platter?"

I look up at the waitress and then back over to Bishop.

"Sorry, are you not drinking tonight? I can get something else. I just assumed..."

I think back to the Instagram page we discussed. Am I the only one that zeroed in on those cocktails?

Bishop lifts his chin to the waitress, then back down to me. "No, no, don't worry about me. Get your margarita. They look amazing," he says.

I'm thankful. I'm also curious.

I give the waitress an approving smile and tell her we'd love to share the guac and some salsa as well. She gives a reassuring grin, tells us it's a great choice, and moves from the table, leaving us in our silence. I look up at Bishop, urging him to explain.

When he doesn't elaborate but instead sits there and ponders over the menu, I understand that I have to be the first to talk.

"So, not drinking tonight, huh? Need a clear head to have dinner with me in case you need to make a run for it?"

I hesitate with a laugh, trying to keep things light.

He lifts his chin, studying my gaze. He brings his fingers up to his mouth, drumming them along his lips. Is he taunting me?

"Not at all. Although, I must say, a clear head has not been possible since the moment I met you. And trust me, I've tried."

One side of his mouth lifts up, revealing a small dimple I never noticed before now.

"And to answer your question. No, I actually don't drink anymore. Or should I say, as much... long story."

"Well, I just got off a shift."

I grin, using his line against him. I lean in and touch his hand, the one holding his menu. Softly, I say, "I'm off the rest of the night. I've got nowhere to be, Bishop. I've got the patience for 'long'."

I think back to our conversation at Luca's and how I avoided explaining how the hell I ended up here in Salter's Ridge. Honestly, I didn't think I'd end up having an opportunity to continue that conversation with him. I almost expected a text from him today, one that said he needed to cancel dinner plans tonight.

When that text never came, I couldn't help but ask myself why I have all the confidence in the world now, which took forever to gain back, but when it comes to him, I think I'm not worthy of a date plan following through. I need time to process this. What is it about him that makes it all so different?

The waitress comes back with our drinks, breaking me from my self-sabotaging lack of confidence. She sets down our plate of chips, salsa, and guac in between us, and takes our dinner order.

As she walks away, I take a sip from my overflowing glass, salt washing away down the side, feeling thankful the drink is as good as it looks. They even added a little sprig of rosemary coated in sugar to give it the illusion of a Christmas tree. God, I love the holidays.

I take a chip from the platter and Bishop does the same, moving to dip a chip in the guacamole, licking his lips in approval. He raises his hazel eyes, hooded with satisfaction. Hints of goat cheese and fresh lime make this the best guac I've ever had.

"So, Campbell. Let's just get to it." He clasps his hands together in front of himself, placing them on the table. "Twenty questions."

"Oooh, games. I love a good game."

"Listen, there's a lot you don't know about me, Campbell. There's a lot from my past, especially my time spent in the military, that I'm still working through and unsure of expressing and talking about. Hell, I'm still scared to admit things to myself, things I can't speak aloud, and I'm terrified that when you start to get to know me, you may not like what you see."

He looks down with what I perceive as disappointment.

This is not where I thought this was going. This explains his rough hands and the scars on them. I try hard to stay focused on the conversation, but my mind is racing. First off, I had no clue he was in the military. How would I? But that makes sense, I guess. I can see that in him. Second, here we are, on this beautiful night, the two of us together. And he thinks I may not like what I *see*. What does that even mean? What else is he holding back? Something like worry plagues his face now. I calmly reach across and place my hand on his one more time, this time leaving it there. He lifts his face to meet mine.

"Let me be the judge of that, okay? So far, you have been the one constant thought on my mind since the night we met. You know, after I was sure you weren't a kidnapper."

We smile at each other.

"I've enjoyed our small moments together so far. I don't wish that to go away any time soon. It's just been a short amount of time. Let me figure out if I like what I see." He seems a bit unsure as I say this, so I add, "So far, I adore you."

"I promise, I know I come off as an asshole, and somewhat, slightly, *very* judgmental..."

He gives a slight laugh. But I remain serious, looking into his eyes, hoping he sees my compassion and empathy.

"I think I have a really good ear when I need to. And maybe you just need someone who will listen."

He lifts my hand and moves his mouth down, surprising me with the lightest kiss on top. I bite my lip in awe. I want to hear his story now more than ever.

"I want to get to know you when you're ready. Whether it's here, at dinner, playing a game, or at home, on the couch. I need the good and the maybe not so good. But don't feel like you have to rush that conversation, Bishop. We have all the time, or at least, I hope we do."

His lips lift at the corners, aging his face with wrinkles in the best way, thankful for a pass tonight and relieved he won't have to disclose *all* the history of his past.

As he said at Luca's, we all have our thing, and sometimes, it's nice to know we are not alone in our struggles. We are never alone. There's always someone who has gone through it before we have, and we are never the last person to go through it either. I just hope he knows that with me, he's not alone at all.

———————

"Bacon or Sausage?"

"Are you kidding?! Bacon. Is there any other answer to that question?"

We start off simple, but the question I really want to ask is floating in the air like a poison we can't see.

Bishop laughs and says, "No, of course. It's always bacon."

"Where did you grow up?" I ask, curious because I can't tell if his accent is a mixture of two places or just one.

"I'm originally from upstate New York. Lots of my family are from around here, though. Aunts and uncles, and my only living grandma. She's what brought me back here, actually. When my grandfather passed while I was deployed overseas, I couldn't stand the thought of her being alone. As soon as I was released to come home, I came straight back, and I ended up staying longer than planned, but it led me here."

He holds a hand up, gesturing to the patio. Maybe to me.

"Tell me about him, your grandfather," I say gently.

Bishop's cheeks reach his eyes. His smile is something I could get used to quite quickly, I imagine.

85

"Well, he was spectacular, simply put. He was a Marine, a hardass, loved my grandmother to death, and loved life. He was funny when the situation called for all seriousness, and everyone loved him. I sure do miss him. He was a hard worker and a businessman. Anything he wanted in life, he made happen. And, he loved to read."

Bishop adds this last bit in like he's trying to convince me of something.

"Most people worth keeping around love to read. Am I right?"

I smile back at him across the table.

"How old is Piper? Tell me about her," he asks.

That makes me smile because it's like someone asking me about my actual human child. It's something every parent can't wait to gush about—their baby.

"You'll think I'm making this up, but I actually got her from a crackhead in a mall a few years back."

He spits his ginger ale out a little bit, choking back a laugh.

"I'm sorry, what?"

His smile shows all of his teeth.

"I'm dead serious. A long time ago, I was walking through the mall on my lunch break from work. A lady looking for a bit of drug money was walking around with this tiny little dog in her arms. I was standing in line waiting to order food from the cafeteria and I told her that baby was so adorable, thinking she would let me pet it. She then proceeded to tell me I could have her for fifty dollars. I literally walked to the ATM there in the lobby, gave her the money thinking *my goodness, I have to save this baby.* Hands down, the best fifty dollars I've ever spent in my entire life."

I nod my head, so sure of this statement. I think about that interaction a lot.

"Wow. That was not what I was expecting."

"Do you love dogs?" I ask.

"They are the only thing on the planet I do love."

Bishop giggles, asking one more question about Piper, "Have you ever counted how many times in a row she will kiss you without stopping her?"

I laugh, because, of course, I have.

"Two hundred and seventy-eight times."

"Impressive," he counters.

I think to myself what an odd thing to know a dog lover would do. He continues.

"What made you want to open up a bookshop?"

I knew this question was coming. It always comes up. Folks want to know what someone so young thinks she will accomplish by opening a bookstore in a small town. Some days, I still wonder the same thing. No one opens a bookstore to become a millionaire, that's for sure. A bookshop is opened for the love of reading, and for the love of sharing that with others.

"Well..."

I grab my margarita and take a generous sip—if you could call it that.

He looks across the table to me and says, "Rule number one of playing twenty questions with me. If you hesitate longer than five seconds to answer, that means you really don't want to answer the question, and we move on."

"I mean, I do want to answer. It's just that I don't want to spend the next two hours telling you all about my shitty past."

Needless to say, I'm grateful for the out. And with that, he lets it go, for now.

"Okay, my turn." I lean in a little, "What is your favorite part of your life so far?"

"Whoa, now that's a question," he says. And it takes him no time at all to say, "I think my time spent in the military has been the best part."

"Really? But, I thought you said…"

"The war wasn't just a war, Campbell. I think that's something few people understand. If you weren't directly tied to it somehow, it's hard to comprehend what took place there, you know? My favorite part has been the aid that I provided to the people of Afghanistan. A humanitarian effort, you could say."

"Hey, I never thought of it like that, I guess."

"And why would you? You only see what's on TV, or learn about it through things you read. But, what people fail to understand is I was there giving people a second chance at life. Women and children were able to listen to music for the first time, work in jobs other than cooking or cleaning or staying at home raising children. When I first landed there, I would see groups of men riding in carts to their destination with their wives twenty yards behind them. Walking. They weren't allowed to be in the cart with the men. It was very eye-opening, the inequality. Women's rights didn't exist. Now, with U.S. troops on the ground there, they do."

He continues, and talks about this with such quickness, it's like his life depends on it. Like he's been waiting a lifetime to get this off his chest.

"When I couldn't do that job anymore, it was like I couldn't breathe. And let me tell you another thing. When I hear groups of people who didn't serve say 'bring our troops home,' it aggravates the hell out of me. The men and women who serve *want* to be there. It's life-changing. For them and for the people they are saving. They are there making a difference. If people believe otherwise, they haven't a clue. If I could go back, I would in a heartbeat. I wish people would stay out of the business of someone else's service."

"Wow, okay then. I had no idea, Bishop. I can see how that is frustrating. Everyone is trying to make a decision for you about the service your heart wants to give someone. That must be so hard. All your life you want to be a part of something, and now you can't."

A thought crosses my mind— *Why do you no longer serve?*

"Enough about me. What's next for you?" he asks.

He smiles, and I relax.

"With what, life?"

He nods yes.

"Well, now that the shop seems to be taking off, of course, I need to figure out where I'm going to move next." This admission shocks him, and he's all ears now.

"When I signed the lease on the building I'm in, I did so with a twelve-month term. Meaning, I need to figure out, in like three months, if I can even stay in the building or not. You see, Benny, the landlord... super nice guy. He's out of the country traveling and living his best life. He let me rent the space, and I'm assuming that when he comes back, he may want

S. C. Gray

that space back."

He scoffs loudly, "Oh, I doubt that."

I wrinkle my forehead, eyebrows coming together.

"What makes you say that?"

I lean forward a bit over the table like I'm about to be let in on a secret.

"Benny wouldn't know what to do with that building if his life depended on it."

"All I know is I need to have that conversation with him, somehow. And fast."

The longer I put it off, the worse this anxiety of mine will get. Why do I do this to myself?

"What makes you think he will want the space back?" he asks. And I start to wonder what gave me the idea.

"Hmm, I'm not sure. I just figured with the amazing location and all the character, who wouldn't want it?"

Bishop looks off in the distance.

"Wait, do you know Benny?" Just then, our waitress pops back into view with our dinner, and she's moving so fast like she can't keep up with the number of tables she has. She asks if we need anything else, and she's gone as quickly as she appeared. We hardly say a word once our food has arrived until both of us devoured just about every crumb on our plates.

Once we finish with our dinner, we share a moment of complete fulfillment. We cannot get over how excellent the food and service is. The restaurant's atmosphere is unmatched here in town. At least from what I've experienced. The night could not have been more perfect.

90

"We have to come back here again. This was amazing."

I smile the biggest smile, not to Bishop, but to myself. For some reason, automatically, I have an overwhelming feeling this is too effortless. It feels so good, so right. Our eyes meet from across the table, our plates cleared off, and our glasses emptied, only ice remaining.

"Thank you for such a lovely night, Bishop."

He sighs across from me in agreement.

"I have had the best night with you. To be honest, I actually haven't had a *great* night like this in a very long time."

I reach out my freshly manicured hand, letting the Cajun-shrimp red nail polish float back and forth between us over the table. "I don't want this to end, our time together, but I really need to head home."

I lift my wrist to check my watch. It's getting late, and somehow, two and a half hours passed in the blink of an eye.

"I've got an early morning tomorrow at the shop."

I give a reluctant smile. Saturdays are easily the busiest and most fun day of the week for me at the shop, but for the first time since opening it, I wish I could sleep in so that I can stay here a little longer.

"Of course. Rules for dating a bookshop owner... Never get in the way of her beauty sleep."

I snap my eyes up, not missing this little slip from him.

"Dating, huh, so it's confirmed?"

My smile reaches my eyes.

"Speaking of which... I hear you told your crew at the station about our impromptu 'date' at Luca's this morning. That didn't take long."

I raise my eyebrows, waiting for him to confess.

He stands up from the table, smiling wide with a "let me walk you home" look in his eyes. I bite my lip to avoid letting a chuckle slip out, standing from the table as well. I let him get off without having to explain this one. He sighs with relief of getting off the hook this time around, but he won't be so lucky next time.

Rule Number Seven

Give her the space to G R O W in the uncomfortable.

Do you ever get that silent longing of "Lord, please send me a sign I am where I'm meant to be?" Like you need someone or something to reassure you things will be okay?

Life has a funny way about it, doesn't it? I mean, long story short, you're born to what are seemingly well-intentioned parents. Parents who are supposed to be *in love*. Sometimes they raise you in a loving and kind home, and by the end of it all, everyone involved hopes you turn out to be a somewhat adjusted adult that contributes to society. Or at least they hope that's how it goes.

But somewhere along the way, what if you got lost in it all? Maybe your parents aren't parents at all. Maybe they weren't ever in love, to begin with. Maybe they were and fell out of love. Maybe they *unintentionally* tore you apart by fighting all the time in the open, right there in the kitchen while cooking what was supposed to be a nice family meal. You know what they say... "A family that eats together stays together."

Maybe they didn't even try to hide it anymore. Maybe they expected you to be the middleman, to pick sides, even though you were just a child. Maybe they made it your job to help them through *their* emotions instead of the other way around. As parents, you would think it would be their job to... I don't know, *parent*? As a child, it's not supposed to be their job to help the adults work through their shit.

When I was younger, I saw too much. I saw the fighting. I saw the cheating. I saw the verbal and emotional abuse. Both sides were guilty. It had become too much to bear in the end. One day, I thought to myself—*if there is a God, where is he now, in the midst of this horrible struggle? Because surely, I'm not meant to sit in my room crying like this. Surely, there is more out there than this for me.*

Even as I got older, I needed more than they could ever possibly think to give. Each of them is at fault in their own way—with my mom's underlying angst to escape a situation she never should have put herself in, to begin with, and my father and his underlying hope to get her to stay. In the end, I packed up my old red Honda with the few things I could call my own and left.

All these years later, I know that my dysfunction and side dish of anxiety is something I take with me everywhere I go. For the most part, I know this stems from my childhood—this inability to handle emotion and stress in a semi-rational way.

Just the other day, I thought about calling my mother and asking her about the shortcomings in our dysfunctional relationship. I wonder what she would say.

I imagine it would be something like, "I did the best I could." And maybe she did. She would think that was enough of an explanation, and she'd want me to figure the rest out. Or so I imagine. Yeah, another conversation I'm dreading to have. I need to get to it, don't I?

————

The sun set hours ago, and the moon hangs above. The sky remains a stark black beside all the twinkling stars that shine—no clouds floating around tonight. We turn left, crossing the street after leaving the patio of The Bodega.

The wind is beginning to pick up again. As I shudder a chill away, Bishop reaches across the pavement and grabs my hand as if in reflex. I cup his hand in return, thinking to myself how gratifying this moment is, but how it will be over in about ten minutes.

Wishing the walk home from the restaurant was longer, I try walking a little slower. Our game of twenty questions continues here on the quiet street.

"What are you thinking?" Bishop asks, looking down at his feet.

Then he moves his eyes over to me. There remains a lot unsaid. So much of the time together at dinner was spent *not* talking about what we wanted to talk about but we didn't have the courage to.

"To be honest, I'm thinking about how and *why* you're so single."

I laugh about it, but I'm serious. What's a seemingly great guy like Bishop Graham doing in a small, random town like this? One could ask the same thing about me.

I'm here because I needed a fresh start, a fresh breath of air. I'm here because it's far from my parents. I'm here because I needed something for myself that isn't attached to anyone else that tries to take it away.

I have a feeling he's here running from something, just like I am. I can feel it in the way he spoke with me tonight at dinner.

"You first."

He gives my hand a reassuring squeeze, and all of a sudden, I'm thankful for the chill of the night because I can already feel heat making its way up my neck. This conversation needs to happen sooner rather than later, and what better time than now, out in the open, where my words can just float off into the breeze? Maybe he won't hear half of them.

Without any warning, I stop mid-stride. Turning to Bishop, all my focus is on him.

"These damn shoes will be the death of me."

He laughs, not expecting *that*. I bend down at the hip, and unstrap the first shoe, then the second one, and remove them both, holding them up in evidence.

"There, much better."

He laughs a belly laugh over my shoulder, palm on his stomach, and then pulls me in for a hug. I walk the rest of the way home barefoot and happy.

Thankful for some liquid courage, I let him have the thoughts that have consumed my mind for months:

"To answer your question, I needed something to save me. Back home before coming here, I was suffocating. Like, an unbearable feeling of needing to be more than I was, yet also holding onto more than one person should have to keep." I take a deep breath. Speaking that sentence alone gives me a feeling of release, not unlike a volcano waiting to erupt.

"My parents were going through a bad divorce. My sister, the only thing keeping me sane, was busy planning her wedding. When I reached the peak, my dead-end job was starting to feel like a scapegoat for all my anger toward everyone I came in contact with. Deep down, I was just unhappy. I was so unsatisfied, and I knew in my heart that something was missing. I desperately needed to get the hell out of there."

About to open Pandora's box, I can feel the margaritas taking over, my voice raising three octaves higher.

"On top of all that, I was dating this guy. We had been together for about two years. At first, everything was a dream. We did everything together. We had been living together. Things were *good*. Like an idiot, I thought he was '*the one*'." I inwardly roll my eyes at myself and my now-known stupidity. I realize I have slowed my pace beside Bishop, causing him to slow too. I look up to the sky for a second. I turn back to Bishop, facing him head-on.

"Toward the end, I knew something had changed. I started to pick up

97

on things he would do that were so out of character. I started to wonder if there was someone else. I'd hint to him my thoughts, trying to share my fears and voice my concerns, and he would make me feel insane for even considering that was a possibility." Gaslighting at its best, folks. Fucking charmer, let me tell you.

"In moments when I'm honest with myself, I knew deep down that things were heading south. Like, Antarctica, south."

By now, I've completely stopped walking, and I look down at my bare feet. I am finally feeling the full effects of those margaritas in my chest and the cold of the night on the bottom of my feet.

"A few months before I came here, I found out he slept with one of my closest friends, someone I trusted with everything." I take a deep breath. "It completely devastated me."

I feel subtle drops of moisture at the corners of my eyes, embarrassed now that I might have a full-on breakdown in front of the guy I've only just started dating. What is wrong with me?

Just when I think I'm about to lose all composure here on this empty street with no other soul in sight, under a lit lamp post, Bishop gently lifts my chin with a few rough fingers and looks at me as if he's seeing me for the first time.

I bear a weak smile and ask quietly, barely audible even to myself, as a tear flows down my cheek, "How could they do that to someone they both supposedly loved?" I look down at my bare feet, trying to move my toes a little to give them some warmth. I feel silly for not having shoes on, but also completely satisfied. "They deserve each other."

Letting it out, I have an overwhelming sense of sadness come over me. I no longer feel cold, just numb. The topic of this conversation is something I've racked over in my mind repeatedly for months. Wasted energy if you ask me. You don't have to be employed by NASA to realize that.

On days spent alone in the bookshop, the silence sometimes gets to me, I admit, and I find myself being eaten away by my sorrows, that some days seem to have followed me thousands of miles away. I put that thought at the back of my mind, trying to stay here, present with Bishop. I'm usually a pretty positive person, but when it comes to this...

As if on cue, he wraps his arms around me, tightly squeezes me to his chest, and if I pay attention closely enough, I can subtly feel the beat of his pounding heart. I can now feel him breathing in my hair, and he moves to my ear ever so lightly.

"Love isn't supposed to hurt, Campbell. You know that, right?" I feel his warmth engulf me. "And if it does, then you're doing it wrong."

The softness in his voice comforts me. Why does he always have to say the right thing? Here on this deserted street, just the two of us just feels so right and so *good*.

This is all too much. For a moment, I have to remind myself about where I am and who I'm with. Here, standing in front of this fascinating and intrinsically motivated guy. His eyes are kind, and his arms are around *me*. We just had a wonderful dinner together. It was *enjoyable*.

I'm not back home in a smothering environment with two adults pretending to be happy with each other. I'm not wrapped up in issues I try to mask by working too much in an office where I'm appreciated but not satisfied. I'm surely not surrounded by a bunch of life-sucking, selfish assholes going nowhere in life. The joke is on that old friend... she can have him.

Standing here with Bishop, I think to myself—*how lucky was I to wake up one day and realize I deserve more than this. I deserve to be happy?* And thinking on it too—*how lucky was I that Bishop turned out not to be a murderer that night?* One point for Campbell.

For months now, I've worked so hard at proving to myself that I never again need to depend on someone else to create my happiness for me. I am more than capable of doing that for myself. I'm capable of creating a life that is wonderful, beautiful, full of *goodness*. Life doesn't have to be hard. Life can be content with balance, self-care, a little vitamin-D, and if you are doing it right, you don't have to work your life away, if you're doing something you love. You surely don't have to keep people in your life if they bring you down, lowering your self-esteem with guilt and negativity.

Life can be lovely, enjoyable, fantastic. It can be stacked full to the brim with wonder, potential, and adventure as long as you're open to seeing this *yourself*. And I know it takes time.

I turn to Bishop. "You make this between us so easy, Bishop."

He thumbs a tear away from my cheek.

"Campbell, in all the time I've spent with you, the word easy came to mind for me too. You know, besides trying to get coffee at Luca's without being harassed... Oh, and that time you tried to make me walk 500 miles to buy a book that I actually still have yet to get from you."

"Who the hell you calling easy?"

He stills.

"I'm joking."

I look him in the eyes, a smile across my face.

"Don't be so nervous. Not with me," I say.

He laughs. That book he ordered is *way* too pretentious to let him purchase. Store credit, it is.

He offers a compassionate look. "Listen. I, for one, know life can be difficult. It's full of hardships and things that are so dark, and you can't help but think you have done something in a past life to deserve it."

He takes a deep breath, and when he exhales, I can see just how cold it really is. The wind whistles and he grips both my hands tightly. Over his shoulder, I can see my front porch steps from where we stood.

"I've been looking for ways this past year to move forward. I need relief from my stress. I'm tired of feeling trapped in my mind. Drinking clouded my judgment. Drinking was holding me in this horrible place, one I felt I would never have been able to escape had I kept doing it day after day. It was never-ending. It's not to say I can't enjoy a beer here or there. I just am still trying to navigate what that looks like for me, so you've caught me at the beginning of my downhill ride."

I listen with intention.

"I've been climbing a mountain for so long. I've been trying for years to overcome things in my past that have been so hard to let go of, and then you came along. You stumbled right in my lap," Bishop explains.

I let out a laugh because I'm super mature for my age.

"You know what I mean." He smiles. "Here you are—this beautiful, smart, independent woman. You challenge me to be a better version of who I was before I met you, back when I wasn't struggling. As you said, it's just easy."

He looks down now, and I feel like this little therapy session was something we both needed, and had we gone on any longer without it, we would have burst at the seams.

"People hurt us, and we hurt people too. We do things we regret, and we make mistakes we have to live with the rest of our lives. And yet, with someone beside us to get through, life can maybe turn out to be all right." His optimism makes me warm inside. He looks back behind him. "I think this is you?"

I nod, and we pivot toward my doorstep. I already hear Piper barking into the night out of her front window from the upstairs landing. If I squint hard enough, I can just make her out behind the linen curtain hanging there, a subtle light shining behind her.

I look up, pointing to Piper. "Ahh, there it is. Now, she barks at you."

For the first time tonight, we both let out a sigh of relief. We laugh, and he lets go of the hand I forgot he was holding this entire time.

"Hey, I thought we were going to talk about *your* thing tonight?" How did this get turned around on me?" I think to myself quickly.

He tricked me.

We are almost to my doorstep when I giggle, letting him know I'm joking. He then pulls me back to him, twisting me halfway around and holding me to his chest, hard as titanium.

"You've been a pleasant surprise, Campbell. How did I not know you existed here in this little town, let alone five steps away from the station I work at, until now?"

We both look to the lit bay at the corner across the street. He turns back to me, and his eyes drop to my lips, cold from the night's blistering wind. Ridiculously, I think about how I wish I could apply some Chapstick right about now. No one wants to fall face-first into a sandbox, am I right?

Thinking how absurd I'm being, I wonder how we somehow turned a ten-minute walk into a forty-five-minute stroll, not that I'm complaining about it. Adult conversation is hard to come by these days, especially with someone who has all of their teeth and doesn't eat poop in the yard. I look up at the window to where Piper was just standing.

"Thank you for tonight, for feeling safe enough to let me in." Bishop shifts a little with me firmly in his arms. "I like the way you make me feel, Campbell."

"Well, damn. I like the way you make me feel, too."

A rush comes over me.

I stumble over what to say next. I'm suddenly nervous about what's to come, and my lips won't move.

Just when I feel like it's all I can do to fill the silence, Bishop leans in slightly, asking with his eyes if he can kiss me. The last thing I need right now is another guy to fill my time, to take up what little space I have left in my brain. But I can't help it. Everything about tonight and every day leading up to this feels too good to resist. His strong arms around me seem to keep my feet planted to the sidewalk to stop me from floating away. I'm on cloud nine.

"I really like you, Bishop Graham."

Untold story and all. With that, he bends down and slowly kisses me, taking my bottom lip in between his. As soon as it begins, it's over, and I can't resist. I need more.

I stand on my tippy toes, realizing for the first time how short I am compared to him. Reaching up, I plant just one more slow kiss on his lips before reaching into my clutch. With a smile seemingly stuck permanently to my face, I search for my keys, thankful for once they are not challenging to find. I can't bear to stand out here with him any longer without wanting to indulge the urge to invite him in. Under my porch light, I give him one last look.

"When do I get to see you again?" he asks before I get the chance.

"You can see me anytime you want."

He reluctantly lets my hands go. His smile chips away at my anxiety, and I put my key into the door, listening for Piper running down the stairs. I'm impressed by her little legs and how fast they move.

I open my front door, taking a step inside, the light from the foyer table lamp glowing, although dim.

"Goodnight, Bishop Graham."

"Goodnight, Campbell."

I give him one last smile, trying to memorize his face before closing the door behind me. Inside now, I reach down to pet Piper, greeting me with a stretch on my legs, and I lean down to meet her the rest of the way to get my kisses from her. Is there anything better than love from a dog that adores you?

With that, I run upstairs to the front window. I push the linen curtain back ever so slightly, looking to see if I can find Bishop walking in the dark. He's nowhere to be seen. I take a deep breath, exhausted from the day. I head to my closet to change into something more comfortable before hopping into bed, Piper right behind me. I stare for a while at the ceiling, thinking about our conversation at dinner and on the walk home.

After what seems like an hour, I grab my book from the bedside table, some simpleton rom-com with barely any substance to it. My favorite kind. I'm half asleep by the time I crack open the spine.

I've told myself for the past few months, I deserve happy. I deserve to feel *alive*. And right now, I'm over the fucking moon. I fall into a peaceful lull in no time at all.

S. C. Gray

Rule Number Eight

Reading before bed may cause nightmares, but don't let that keep you from dreaming.

You know that feeling you get when you *know* someone is watching you? It's the most bizarre phenomenon, a sixth sense almost, and I'm not talking about one like that moment when Cole tells Dr. Malcolm Crowe that he sees dead people.

I mean, there's just this weird change in the air, like one extra person in your space moves the room just a smidgen, and that movement in the air then tsunamis into you.

I knew someone was in my room watching me the morning after my walk home with Bishop Graham. That walk was one of the best walks I've ever been on. And one of the most therapeutic at that.

107

Lying in bed, I feel a subtle kiss on my lips. Startling, soft, and cold at first, like Alaskan snow falling from a gray, cloudy sky. As quickly as it lands, it melts. I lick my lips as if I have just a few seconds to remember the taste. Oh, and it is heavenly.

My eyes are still heavy with sleep, and I am so out of it, unable to fully wake. I don't even ask myself how he got in here. The warmth of the bed from my feathered duvet makes it hard to stir and awaken. The weight of his chest on mine is heavy enough for me to know he is there, but not heavy enough to crush my windpipe. This feels so *good*. It's been so long since I've had someone kind to share a bed with.

He smells of cinnamon and, wait. Is that bacon?? Oh shit, it just gets better and better. He leans down to kiss me again and again, this time, harder. And this is just the way every girl *dreams* of being woken up, isn't it? Breakfast in bed, being woken up with wonderful...

What is that cold I feel with every kiss? I really like it.

I reach out to touch him and run my hands through his long, shaggy hair. It's rough to the touch, not at all like how I imagined it would be.

Let me tell you how I've longed to reach out and push the hair off your face.

It's a bit tangled this morning... not soft like I remember it looking like last night at dinner. But I'm sure in his hurry and angst to see me this morning, brushing his hair was the last thing on his mind.

I can feel his need for *us* as he drags his tongue from my chin? Then to my ear, moving to my neck, my eyebrows pull together, eyes still closed.

Well, this is different.

Nevertheless, Bishop Graham is in my bedroom. On my bed. Kissing me. And I *think* he brought breakfast. Now, I'm starting to second-guess my judgment. What is that I'm smelling?

Even so, it's a good thing because breakfast is my favorite, and I always wake up starving. The smell is making my stomach growl. Is there anything better than a guy with food? In bed, at that!

The kisses become *more* urgent, *messier.*

Okay, tongue is everywhere now, and suddenly, I am floored. Like, rock bottom has a creepy basement, floored. This is not what I expected our second makeout session to be like. I don't understand how a great kiss like the wonderful one we shared on the porch last night can segue into this disaster. I'm about to come up for air for fear of drowning. It's so... *wet.*

What. Is. The. Rush?

Starting to feel like I'm back in high school kissing bad-haircut Dylan Lancer for the first time by the lockers while everyone circles around, cheering us on (oh, the actual fucking horror). I'm beginning to think we need to slow this speeding train down. Tongue is swirling round and round, wet and slippery like it's getting its first use, similar to what I imagine a trip into the toilet bowl water slide at Busch Gardens would be akin to.

"Bishop, slow down..." I say, stirring a bit, reaching my hand up in protest, opening one eye and then the other, trying to give them time to adjust to the just barely-there morning light that's peeking through the linen curtain. The sun is just beginning to rise. What time is it? I try to sit up just a little bit. The weight is still holding me down.

My eyes blink quickly in succession as confusion sets in. I see two familiar dark black, beady eyes above a dark wet nose stare back at me. A wiry head full of haphazard blonde hair turns down to the left, then down to the right, like I've just said, "*snack*?" A wagging tail hits my knees on top of the duvet. Tap. Tap. Tap.

There sitting on my chest, is Piper.

P I P E R. *Not* Bishop Graham.

"Oh, for fuck's sake! What the hell, Piper?"

I sit up so suddenly, and she is all but thrown off the bed onto the floor, making her morning walk-of-shame all the more pitiful. I'm half tempted to scream, "put some damn clothes on!" I feel so *used*. How could she?

She rushes to her bed in the corner, looking up at me, and yet, gives me the world's biggest sigh like *I'm* the one who just violated *her*, before circling round and round and dropping down into a curled-up ball.

I look around the room quickly, making sure I'm actually alone and that no one else on the planet knows this monstrous event has taken place.

What has my life *actually* become? I did not get woken up this morning with breakfast in bed by a thoughtful and hot-for-me firefighter. Bishop Graham is not here, in my room, kissing me. My neck, face, and ears are wet with dog slobber. I'm still starving. And I just made out with my god damn dog.

————

In a rush to get to Luca's before heading to the shop for the day, I brush my teeth, if only to get the dog breath off mine. I'm still half-embarrassed that I had a wet dream about Bishop. And not the good kind.

I quickly get dressed, slipping on a pair of what Generation Z would call "mom jeans" and my favorite white wrap top, tying the bow at my hip. I throw my hair up in a very messy "no time to do anything else" low bun. Mascara and a little bit of eyeshadow are all that's in the cards for me this morning. I call it a success—word of the wise: beggars can't be choosers.

I slip on a pair of leopard print ballet flats, bend to roll up the cuff of my jeans, and grab my tote. Piper is waiting by her leash because she knows even though she assaulted me this morning with the tease of a lifetime, I would never spend a day without her at the shop.

I take a quick look in the mirror above the entryway console before heading out the front door, ready to face whatever comes our way. Together.

———

Desperate for coffee as soon as possible, I decide to bike to Luca's. We walk to the side yard where I keep my bike. I slip Piper comfortably into her woven basket on the front, secured above the tire. There's a little blanket at the bottom for her to lay on.

I picked up the basket at a farmer's market a few years back. It's still one of our favorite purchases we've ever made together. The breeze through our hair this morning is exquisite—another one of life's simple pleasures.

As soon as I pop into Luca's, I spot Anders behind the coffee bar, and he already has the biggest grin spread across his smug face. I think back to the coconut macaroons. Teller of all secrets, this one. I walk to the back of the coffee shop. I've got a bone to pick with him.

"Campbell, please tell me, 'what is a *horrific* looking girl like you doing in such a beautiful place as Salter's Ridge'?" he says loudly, so everyone and their mother can hear.

And great, he overheard the conversation between Bishop and me over coffee the other day.

"Anders, please tell me, why the hell are you so annoying?"

He laughs insatiably, and I can't help but feel the straining smile on my face. I give in to it, and it fills my cheeks.

I order my usual pumpkin spiced latte with a splash of caramel, to go. Those extra few minutes this morning in bed have put me behind schedule. I'm in serious need of some caffeine. Waking up to what I thought was breakfast, but actually turned out to be Piper's day old *Beggin' Strips* breath, was really hard.

"Okay, so how was it?" he asks, beginning to make my coffee. The crushed beans and caramel filling the air along with the sound of the espresso machine stirring to life.

"How was what?"

And immediately, my thoughts guiltily flashback to an hour ago when I thought I was having the time of my life making out with Bishop but was actually rendezvousing with Piper. My life is in actual shambles. He breaks me from my thoughts.

"Oh, stop! Don't make me have to drag it from you! How was your date with Bishop?!"

He's jumping up and down, living vicariously through me, obviously. Because my life is just *so* much cooler than his is. He's having way too much fun with this.

"Well, let's see. Bishop showed up late to dinner, ate with his mouth open while he talked about himself all night long, and then, in the end, he asked me to pick up the tab…"

I roll my eyes and wait in anticipation, hoping he takes the bait and doesn't see right through my bullshit.

"You're shitting me. No, he did *not*."

He stops and tries to gauge if I'm kidding or actually telling the truth.

"Make my coffee. I'm joking."

I smile back at him. I think I almost had him.

He holds a hand to his chest dramatically.

"Oh, for the love of all that is holy. Don't scare me like that!"

We laugh, and as he puts a lid on top of my cup, he reaches under the register to pull an envelope out and hands it to me.

"Here, I was told to give this to you if I saw you this morning."

He leans over just a little, seemingly expecting me to read it right then and there. I roll my eyes again, telepathically telling him to mind his own business, and he moves to clean up the machine. I slide my finger in the envelope, opening it with enthusiasm, and pull out a folded piece of paper. My heart is racing because I have a feeling I know who it's from. I begin to read the messy handwriting:

"Like a good book, last night shouldn't be the end. It can't be the end. I need more. And in the heat of the moment, I forgot to get your number, so I had to resort to this, an old-fashioned letter. So, please, forgive me.

Ready for our next adventure?"

I unfolded the letter the rest of the way, and two tickets fall away and almost drop to the floor, but I catch them just in time. I struggle to understand what I'm looking at in my hands, but upon closer inspection, barcodes to be scanned and all, I begin to comprehend what Bishop has done.

For the first time in my life, I get to hear *Sunrise* playing in the moment. I get to see the beautiful snare drums beating to the strum of the guitar, all while she plays the piano in the middle, while everyone looks on. I get to see my childhood on a calm stage, me sitting in the calm crowd.

Someone told him I adore Norah. And of all the people in the world, all the subpar relationships before leading up to this moment, I'm going to listen to that soulful voice *live* with Bishop Graham.

Rule Number Nine

Bring her snacks.

"Okay, but how is it that you can get a date, like, three days in a row, and I can't secure a measly *one*. Ever?" Anders asks, disappointed and excited at the same time. He gives me the evil eye as he finishes wiping down the counter. Secretly, he's as over the moon as I am.

"Anders, what is happening? What did you do?!" I squeal as I tuck the tickets and the letter into my tote, adjusting it on my shoulder. Anders is one of the only people on the planet that knows about my obsession with Norah Jones. In my disbelief, I almost forgot I needed to get to the shop, like now.

Serious now, I point to my bag. "Anders, did you do this? You know how much Norah means to me."

I look down at my feet, suddenly feeling like I have a place in this world for the first time in a very, very long time. I have my bookshop. I have a cozy home with Piper. I have good friends. Ones that won't try and steal my boyfriend, if I dare call him that... Well, I won't speak too quickly because I'm starting to wonder about Anders.

It's been just a few weeks, and already, this entire thing seems too perplexing to be true. Is this just a case of things being *super good* while we get to know each other? Is he just trying to impress me to hook me, and then once he has me... I've been through *that* a time or two.

And yet, Anders somewhat arranged this. Again, he voiced to Bishop something compelling about me, about my addiction to Norah. Bishop took the hint and acted on it. Quick, too. Who does that? I almost feel like I'm on the verge of crying the best kind of tears, but I don't want to mess up my "just rolled out of bed look."

"Listen, I've got to head out, but holy shit, can we get together soon, go for drinks next weekend maybe? I owe you one."

My soul is *so* ecstatic right now, and I need to sit and talk this through with Anders.

How is it that after everything I've been up against this past year, this random guy walks into my life, quite literally to the stoop of *my* bookshop, and has made the impression of a lifetime? I look to Anders, now standing in front of the register.

"This one is on me," he says as he pushes my coffee across the counter.

"Thank you, Anders. Thank you for being a good friend. For being someone who gives Bishop all the hints."

Some of the wisest people would call that "planting the seed." And it worked. Look at that.

All along, I've told myself that I am deserving when good things happen. I've waited years for my life to pan out just right, to have simple pleasures just noticeable enough that I feel fortunate even when the slightest happiness comes my way. Why should this be any different?

Anders winks at me as I grab my coffee and turn to go. He calls out, "Have the *best* day!" And as I move to open the door, I wave over my shoulder in a goodbye, Piper follows closely behind me, leash dragging behind her.

We walk out into the sunshine and hop onto|into our bike. I push the kickstand back with my foot, and we're off. The temperature is raw this morning, but I can tell it's going to be an "open the Dutch door" kind of day—my favorite kind of day. The breeze gives way as a reminder that the weather is about to get ugly tonight. The weatherman calls for rain. Although he is usually wrong about sixty percent of the time.

I arrive at the shop in no time at all, and when I do, I cannot help but think this has just become one of the best days of my life—sans my makeout sesh with Piper.

———

I lean my bike up against the side of the brick building covered in vines as Piper takes it upon herself to hop out of her basket. She grunts as she lands onto the stone gravel and shakes it off.

"Are you ready for another beautiful day, Pip?"

I pet her on the side of her sweet face, and we walk around the corner to unlock the front door to the shop. I glance to my left and notice that some of the books in the front window are fading a bit, which reminds me. I need to replace some of the holiday reads in the window that have sold.

I pull open the heavy door, again with the squeaking, and walk into a space of books from floor to ceiling. I sigh, breathing in the scent of thousands of books. This is where I am meant to be.

————

As soon as I flip on the open sign, ready to start the day, I hear a couple walk through the bottom of the Dutch door, the top half already opened and secured to the wall beside it by a golden latch. Hot coffee in hand, I raise my cup.

"Good morning! Is there anything I can help you find?"

With a smile, they lift a hand.

"Good morning! We are just looking."

One of my favorite things in the entire world is when customers say they are just looking. They end up making a pile of treasures at the front counter, and in the end, I get to see what kind of treats they find for themselves.

While looking around, the couple's wife bends down to pet Piper, several books already in the crook of her elbow, while her husband ganders at the psychological thriller table.

"She is such a doll. A Dachshund?" she asks.

"Yes, she is! Hard to mistake a Weiner, am I right?"

I wink, and we both laugh out loud. It's always hard to gauge if that joke is going to offend someone. I haven't come across anyone yet, but my days are numbered. Piper doesn't seem to get it. I reach my hands out.

"May I place those books up front for you while you continue to shop? Clear up those hands for you?" I ask after placing my coffee on a shelf that I need to organize today.

So much has sold the last few weeks because everyone is gifting books for the holidays. I just love pushing books all the way to the left or the right on a shelf to make room for more. My back stock is getting low. It's a great problem to have, but I make a mental note to place an order for some new books today if it's slow.

It's been a nice thing to see—folks gifting their favorite reads to friends and family. I just love wrapping stacks of books up.

After taking her stack from her, I look down to see a few of my favorites.

"Wow, you guys found some great reads. You've got good taste in books."

I put the stack onto the counter and palm through her finds, checking out the covers.

Lily and the Octopus.

The Girl He Used to Know.

The Light We Lost.

All listed in a blog post as some of my top reads last year.

"If I didn't know any better, I'd think you were reading my mind. Or stalking me. These books are some of my favorites," I say with a sincere smile, covered in excitement.

She looks up. "Oh, I've been stalking you!" she says with a laugh, and I look up.

"My name is Ainley! And, yes, guilty! I am in love with your Instagram feed. What are the cool kids calling it these days? Bookstagram?"

She looks back to her husband, and he holds his hands up to say *who knows?*

"Anyway, we're visiting some family this weekend. We were told, as book lovers, we had to come and visit the only bookshop within a hundred miles from here. They said it was worth the walk." She gives the most genuine of smiles. "I can't say they were wrong. You have the loveliest shop. Maybe you know our cousin, Sienna?"

"Oh, of course! She brings my post. She's so sweet. Thank you. I didn't know people even looked at my Instagram page. It's really just a hobby."

I try to think back to the last time I even posted anything there. Maybe I need to start keeping up with it again.

"Well, I'm glad you guys came by! Is there anything else I can help you find?"

She turns around. "I'll take one of those." I look to see her pointing down to Piper. I smile big.

"Sorry, she's not for sale. Except on the days she eats something she shouldn't."

The other day, I walked into my bathroom to find that Piper had dug through the trash and had shredded every piece of toilet paper in the bin.

She somehow turned ten pieces into 1,000. All because I hadn't given her some of my popcorn while reading in bed...

"You know, there is something you can help me with."

I turn to find her husband has joined our conversation. He's charming, years older than Ainley, and taller than the average human, and dresses like he is from Italy. I love a man in a wool cardigan. And that messy, yet perfected, hair swipe.

"I would love a book for the flight home. Something full of twists and turns. Something *thrilling*. I need a quick read."

"Come, follow me." I walk him back over to the psychological thriller table he was just standing in front of. "This one." I hold up *The Silent Patient*. "It's a couple of years old, but my goodness, what a book. Alex can really write a page-turner. Have you read this one yet?" He takes it from my hands and places it on the counter near his wife's pile. "Nope. I'll take it!"

I have a moment of gratitude. How is this my life? Months ago, I was standing in the middle of a graceless city, full of angst and sorrow, feeling so sorry for myself and the life I was all but consumed in. Now, I'm working in a bookshop, *my* bookshop, giving advice on what books people should spend their hard-earned money on. All I can think is, *wow, I'm so fortunate*. I also know I've worked my ass off. I feel myself getting emotional for a serendipitous moment.

Ainley snaps me from my daydreaming and points to her husband.

"Bill here thinks any book is worth a read, if only just once."

She winks his way, and I think for a split second, I want *that*. I want to have a partner who loves reading just as much as I do—someone who will take half the space on my bookshelves.

"I love that, Bill. Yes, that might be true. That's a great philosophy. Although I'm not sure I have the courage or persistence to pick up *Gone with the Wind*.

I move around to the back of the cash wrap to start an invoice for them. I look up, and Ainley has a look of complete distraught on her face.

"You have never read *Gone with the Wind*?" she asks, in utter shock.

"I know, I know. What bookshop owner hasn't read the most famous book in the world besides *The Bible*? But, it's true. That and *The Great Gatsby*."

"Okay, Bill. Let's go. I can't be associated with this lady," Ainley jokes as she pulls out her wallet to pay for their books.

All three of us share a moment as laughter fills the shop, while I move the computer mouse slightly, bringing the screen to life. Piper's ears perk up from her bed. The twinkling Christmas tree lights behind me catch my attention, reminding me of the season, and I feel a sense of calm wash over me.

"Do you need anything here wrapped?"

"They are all for Bill and me."

My kind of lady. We are all guilty of shopping during the holidays for friends and family and somehow buy things for ourselves. In the end, whatever makes you happy. Buy the books.

When we finish the transaction, I walk their full bag of books around the counter to them.

"It was so nice to meet you both. I hope you enjoy the holiday with your family. I'm so glad you stopped in."

Bill looks me in the eye.

"You've done such a great job with the space, young lady. A year ago, this place was obviously a dump, as I'm sure you saw, and look what you have done with it. It's beautiful. Keep up the good work. People need a bookshop to come to, to walk into, to be able to take something *home.*"

I have an overwhelming love for whoever this couple is. Do they know how badly I need to hear this right now?

"Thank you so much, Bill. This is a dream come true for me. And I can't imagine being anywhere else right now."

I take a quick look around, Piper at my feet now like she knows I'm about to start bawling. There is so much truth in our conversation, it's validating. Securing, even.

Yes. People do need bookshops wherever they go. Yes. I have done a great deal of work on this space and have turned it into somewhat of a destination spot for folks living in Salter's Ridge. Yes. I have made connections and built relationships here in this sleepy town. Life is so *good.* My hard work is paying off, and my heart is so full right now.

"You never know you've said the right thing to someone unless they tell you, and by God, Bill, you have made my day," I say with a laugh.

I'm on the edge of what feels like a moment one could compare to opening up your one choice of all the presents under the tree on Christmas Eve, when that choice was the *right* one.

I quickly begin to realize just how grateful I am at this moment to have met this sweet pair—Ainley with her brilliant smile and Bill in that ridiculous yet spectacular male cardigan.

"I'll be sure to tell Sienna thank you. I hope you guys have safe travels..."

And with that, they are gone.

I take a deep breath, alone again. I find myself near the door, looking in. And I feel for the first time in my entire life that I do deserve all of *this.*

———

Hours after Bill and Ainley leave, I switch my music to something more upbeat for the season as I clean and straighten up the shop before closing. Putting on some Christmas music, I make a hot cup of cocoa, adding in extra marshmallows and a lick of caramel. I had to shut the vintage Dutch door earlier. The wind became a bit too cold for Piper's little chicken legs to handle. My legs weren't that far off, either.

I walk cheerfully to the back of the shop after a great rest of the day, filling a vintage rattan bar cart-turned-book cart I found at a yard sale a few years ago, with books that have sold recently and need to be replenished on the floor. I grab a few extra to spruce up the front window. These days, the cart needs a little more effort with my push, but everything that's lucky ages.

I grab a few signed copies of *Christmas Socks*, a new book just released this past October. I've got a stack of them by the cash wrap and one copy propped up on a bookstand. It's flying out the door, particularly because of the time of the season.

The author and I met by complete happenstance several years back and hit it off. Since then, I immediately place an order and fill that section of shelves in the shop with every single one of her releases. I adore signed books, hence, their designated spot. It grows every year, and I just love it.

Most of the cart is full now, not much room for more. Much of what is here is holiday. With Michael Bublé crooning in the background, Christmas books at Christmas time are what I live for.

I grab a copy of each of the books that I just sold to Ainley and Bill and a few more books for my ever-growing self-help section that folks love, and push the cart back through the shop, careful not to get stuck on the old rugs spread throughout.

Startled, I look up to see Bishop, and my heart stops. Once I realize it's him, my beating heart slows. *Breathe*. He's got to be the one thing my day has been missing.

"I come bearing gifts."

Okay, maybe my day has been missing a few things. He holds up what looks to me to be a fresh sack of salted tortilla chips (evident by the grease stains on the bottom of the paper bag) and a larger-than-life container of salsa.

"Okay, I love you," I say subconsciously, and I'd be lying if I said I missed the beat of pure happiness in Bishop's face as I say this. "How did you know I need chips and salsa at all times of the day?"

"This one, I picked up on my own."

It's true. I could eat chips and salsa for every single meal, especially if it's fresh pico from The Bodega. And I am not ashamed to say this. I cannot be the only one.

"What a nice surprise. A guy that brings me snacks in the middle of my workday is a guy I need to keep around."

I give him a subtle wink and walk over, reach out my hand to take the bag from him, and there is a moment that I question what I should do next. I can see the gears turning in his eyes. Will I pick up where he left off on my porch? I find that I can't second guess any decisions, especially in this season of my life. Otherwise, I miss out on opportunities.

It's at this moment before I can change my mind that I reach up on my tippy toes and kiss Bishop every so slightly on his soft lips, not thinking twice about it. Our eyelashes touch and the tickle of it wakes me.

"If I can get a kiss from you every day like this, I'll bring you all. the. snacks."

"Okay, it's done. That settles that..."

We share a moment of ease, and his eyes crinkle at the corners. I could get used to this. Simple and calm.

"How are you? What are you up to today?" I ask, walking past Piper to take our snack to the counter.

She hasn't missed a beat and is already waiting for me to toss her a chip. I open the bag and throw her a few.

"I just finished a shift and thought, what excuse could I use to go see Campbell? Don't think I didn't notice how you chowed down at dinner the other night. I felt like I was watching a lion in the wild. Their chips and salsa don't stand a chance in hell against you." I walk back over and playfully knock him on the shoulder.

"Never get in between a girl and her chips and salsa," I say, dead serious.

"How was work last night? Anything good happen?"

"Well, if you count running over to Mr. Magnolia's house a few times to assist with making bags of popcorn, only for him to burn each one, set off his touchy fire alarm, and then make another, I would say my night was super busy and *very* eventful."

His face holds a look of annoyance.

"I'm sure you're glad to have gotten a good night's sleep then."

Urging him to look at the bright side of things, I reach out and touch his cheek. He presses his palm against my hand.

His eyes fall to the ground just then. "What's wrong, Bishop?"

"It's nothing."

"There's something. What did I say? You can always tell me anything."

"I don't know. It's just that some days, I wonder what I'm doing here. What is it all for?"

He is troubled, and I don't like this look for him. It's the complete opposite of what I'm used to. Him being happy. Free.

"I thought you loved your job. Everyone says you're amazing at it."

I try to encourage him, but I realize at this moment I don't know everything there is to know about his job. I'm sure it's not all rescuing cats from trees and carrying old ladies down a flight of stairs or saving them from raging fires. The fact that there are no fires here in Salter's Ridge is like salt to a wound.

"Some days, I really don't know how I feel about this job, to be honest. Don't get me wrong, every once in a while I'll have a great day where I feel good about it like I'm actually putting my need to save someone to the test, *when* I'm putting my skills to the test. When there's an accident or a small kitchen fire, or when we get a call of a child choking—that's when I feel like I'm meant to be here. I guess, sometimes I just miss feeling like I'm part of something bigger than me," he continues.

"The adrenaline that runs through me when I'm saving someone, that's all unmatched. That's when it's good. But putting that all aside, how often in a small town does something like that actually happen? Chances are slim to none, and most days, I'm stuck in the engine bay bullshitting with a bunch of guys, half of whom are out of shape, haven't experienced anything in life, and are just there to collect a paycheck."

Hearing him say this surprises me. He takes a breath, willing the words out. Frustration is written all over his face. How long has he been holding all that in? What else does he have left to say but doesn't want to?

"When I moved here from New York, it was to get away from people that reminded me of my past. People from high school would stop me in the grocery store checkout and ask me about Foster." He stills like he's already said too much, but then he continues.

"I also wanted to go somewhere slow, where life wasn't moving a million miles a minute. I needed to get away from people who were holding me back from moving forward. But I know now there is hardly anything I can do to run away from what I've already been through and what already occurred. The past follows me like my shadow, Campbell. I'll never be able to separate from it, and I need to learn to cope with that."

He's fallen silent, lost in a memory.

Gently, I ask, "Bishop, who is Foster?"

He stares at me, blank-faced and ashen.

I'm overwhelmed with the emotion that's just been laid on the table.

I'm at a loss for words now just as much as Bishop is. I notice suddenly that he has moisture in his eyes. The moment stills us.

We went from sharing a lovely kiss to him divulging all of his frustrations in a manner of a few short moments. What has this beautiful man seen? What has he done that makes him so *haunted*? Before I can even begin to wonder how to ask, he interrupts my thoughts.

"Listen, I didn't come here to ruin your day. It seems Michael Bublé is doing a fine job of that."

I laugh because, of course, he doesn't understand the obsession that I and every other woman has with Michael, especially during the holidays. He reaches his hand up and gently runs the pad of his thumb over my cheek.

"I just wanted to see you and bring you something to eat. What are you doing later?" he asks, trying to skirt past every single bit of urgency in the words he just released. This conversation isn't over. I decide to let it go for now.

"I have zero plans for the evening... I think it's going to rain into tomorrow." I look down to see Piper's ears perk up at the mention of rain. She hates the rain, unlike her mother. It's one of the most calming parts of my life. And I hold onto this kind of luxe with a tight grip.

Bishop looks at his watch. "Well, you're off in half an hour. I have an idea. Let's make a pot of coffee, lie in bed, and read the rest of the day."

"Oh my God, are we a couple that reads while listening to the rain?"

He smiles at the mention that we are a couple.

"I think we are. Isn't that the goal?"

He bites his lip, and I agree that this entire scenario is very much indeed *the* goal. I've waited forever for this. And now that it's finally here, I am not going to let it go.

My feet pull me closer to where he is standing, and I look into his eyes, sparked this afternoon with a glimmer of sand and sea.

"I cannot wait to lie in bed with you and read… and listen to the rain. Promise me this won't be the only time we do this either."

"I never make a promise I can't keep, Campbell. You should know that about me."

He pulls away, grinning. He moves to walk out into the rain. He smiles broadly, looks back before he turns to head off, and says, "I promise always to be someone who will read with you, listen to the rain, and share a bed with Piper because we all know how much room that little ass dog needs."

Piper's head lifts at the sounds of her name, and I agree. She does take up a lot of space for someone so small. And just like that, I'm alone again with Piper, but his presence is still so very much here.

Rule Number Ten

Rain is meant for cozy nights in. Take advantage of it.

Long ago, my mom taught me the importance of taking and keeping photos. It's one of the things I'm most thankful for when it comes to her. The oldest photo I have in my home is still in its original frame of my mother and father celebrating her 22nd birthday. She was holding me in her arms when I was just a few months old. Everyone surrounded her, singing happy birthday.

It's grainy and a bit wrinkled. The frame is old, and the metal has lost its shine. But, it's my favorite photo in the world. It's quite possible this frame holds the only moment in their entire marriage where my parents weren't fighting.

Walking through the small foyer, I switch on the entryway table lamp, toss my keys into the wooden bowl, and take my shoes off. Another habit my mom instilled in me. *Less to sweep up later*, I always think to myself.

I look at the photo of my parents on the table, willing myself to understand why she stayed with him for so long. I think of how unhappy they were and I'm filled with angst I can't describe all over again. This picture brings back a good memory but a lasting hurt because that memory lasted all but three hours. How *real* could that happy moment have been if it ended as soon as it had begun?

Taking a deep breath, I unhook Piper from her leash, dropping my heavy tote to the ground. It's filled with books I took from the shop. I need to catch up on this season's reading so I know what to suggest to people who ask for recommendations. It's one of the best parts of working in a bookshop—all the reading.

I walk deeper into the house, and when I reach the white and gray kitchen, I turn on the basket light pendants above the island. They illuminate the room, and I am filled with a fondness for the small but cozy space I've built. Piper gets a running start and jumps onto my slipcovered couch, one I paid way too much money for a few years back. After all this time, I still don't regret it.

She jumps to the top of the couch's back cushion and turns around twice before plopping down on top of the gray throw that drapes across. No matter where she is, you can bet your top dollar Piper will find the coziest spot to lay. You'll never catch her lying on the bare floor. She's too good for it.

I reach for my coffee tin, fill the coffee maker with filtered water from the fridge, and start to brew a pot for the evening. I know they say you shouldn't drink coffee late in the day, good sleeping habits and all that... but it's one of life's little luxuries, and I don't believe in limiting that luxury to just a few hours a day.

I pull two white mugs from the glass cabinet above and reach for a spoon. I grab the cream and sugar cubes and set them on the counter in front of the coffee maker. The rich smell of beans and contentment fills the air.

While the coffee brews, I head to my bedroom, change into some joggers and an old, oversized sweatshirt, and slip on a pair of my favorite thick socks. If Bishop can handle me in sweats, he can handle me every other which way. I throw my hair up into a messy bun, made frizzy by the bike ride home in the misty afternoon.

Thankfully, the heaviest rain held off until I pulled up to the house. Before jumping from her basket, Piper gave me the evil eye and jumped to the soggy ground before I leaned the bike up against the side of the house. We ran inside like our lives depended on it.

I walk into the living room, grab a candle to light, and a couple of throws from the wicker basket beside the couch. I take all the rainy day essentials into the bedroom, strike a match and place the sizzling candle on my bedside table.

What a day it's been. The past few nights are starting to catch up to me, and I suddenly realize I'm more exhausted than I have been in a long while. Piper hops onto the bed and makes herself comfortable on one of the blankets I set there. Like one is always meant to be hers.

"I love you, girl," I say.

And I mean it. She looks at me too, like there's no place she would rather be than here with me. There are very few things in life I would save from a fire. The photo of my parents, my prized tote with what seems to contain my entire life these days, and Piper, of course.

Just as the coffee finishes, there is a knock at the door. Piper goes wild, running toward the door acting as if she's a German Shepard and not a ten-pound Dachshund. For more reasons than I can count, butterflies bounce around. I give the living room a once-over, thankful I usually keep it somewhat clean and decent.

Wait, what am I doing? Isn't this all happening rather quickly? I've known this guy for a few weeks now, we just started dating, and it seems the major parts of what tell me who he is he won't talk about. And now he's about to spend the evening with me in my bed. Reading. Who do I think I am? Who do *we* think we are?

Before I have another second to call it quits for the night and text him to cancel, I find myself unlocking the door. I take a deep breath, and as I pull it open, I'm filled with an automatic relief and immediately forget where my deviant mind was heading. My shoulders fall to the floor. I think I'm falling in love with someone I've known for three weeks. And I'm okay with it.

"I come bearing *more* gifts."

His eyes share love, warmth, and happiness. And I'm *so* overjoyed I could actually die here in my foyer.

"Bishop, you have a dog?!"

"Of course, I have a dog. Would you honestly date or even trust to date someone who didn't have a dog? This is Ghost."

He nonchalantly points down to what looks to be a Border Collie mixed with... Labrador? Piper greets her new friend. Her tail is sticking straight up in the air on high alert. Ghost licks Piper's nose, and they start to do a dog dance of sorts.

Just when I started to think something was wrong, the universe has its way of pulling me back to reality. And this reality, somehow very different from my past in the best way possible, seems to be just what it's supposed to be. With not one dog, but two.

"How could you have never mentioned that you have a dog?"

It seems like this is something you would want to tell everyone you come in contact with, no? I mean, I talk about Piper like she is an actual human child. She kind of is, depending on who you ask.

"I hope it's okay I brought him. I mean, I know you love Piper so much. I didn't think you would totally hate the idea of having a bed full of books and dogs... and us."

He scratches a hand through his hair, pushing it back. His eyes are trying to gauge whether what he thought was a brilliant idea was actually a bad one.

"Are you kidding? I am so in love with him."

My voice is out of this world, my pitch so high I could make Mariah wish she was never born. I fall weakly to my knees, and Ghost rushes to greet me with the biggest of slobbery kisses. I fall backward right there on the entryway rug, laughing. Piper is all but amused. Although once again, I'm stilled by the fact she isn't barking at either one of these two boys.

135

"Oh, hi baby! He's amazing, Bishop."

I look up from the floor, giddy with glee, and suddenly, I realize Bishop may use this very moment in time to run as far away as he can from the psychopath making out with his dog on the floor. I wouldn't be completely surprised. And what is with me making out with dogs lately? Jesus Christ. I'm well aware I'm very much so in need of this human interaction I'm about to get tonight.

With a laugh, he says, "You're amazing, Campbell. But yeah, he's pretty cool. I brought him home with me when I came back from my last tour in Afghanistan. I rescued him while I was out on patrol, securing an area, doing a sweep of IEDs. When I found him, it was about 120 degrees outside, and he was chained to a tree with no food or water and only weighed about twenty pounds. He was so close to death. We brought him back to base, nourished him back to life, and he's been with me ever since."

He reaches down and rubs Ghost's head, and I am actually dying to get in bed with this man. I may have lost my actual mind. And yet, I'm still very okay with it if it means all the dogs and all the reading and all this goodness. This man has my heart racing.

"Wow, that is incredible, Bishop." It's quiet for a moment. "You're full of surprises. And you, mister, are the cutest boy ever. I'd get in bed with you any day."

I give Ghost one last rub under his chin, kiss his nose, and move to get up, Bishop reaching down to stabilize me.

"Come in, guys! Coffee just finished brewing."

Piper and I make way to let them in, and I close the door behind me, locking it.

"It sure does smell amazing in here," he says, taking in the foyer and making his way past my living room, and settling in the kitchen. "Your place is wonderful. It's so... *lived* in. I love it."

"Thank you. It does the job. It's not much, but it doesn't take much to make a space lovely when you've got books and dogs to fill it."

I catch him looking around, stacks of books in every corner that can be seen, and even in those that can't. It's a wonder I have space to walk around in here. Watching him admiring the place makes me smile with pride.

"Holy shit, you have a lot of books," he observes, smiling.

That makes me laugh.

"Yeah, I do own a bookshop, you know." I smile. "Every time I stock a new book, or find a new author, I have what one might call 'buyer's contentment'."

"Oh, really? What is that?" he asks, chuckling.

"It's the opposite of buyer's remorse."
He laughs out loud. It's true. Every book added to my collection is one more happy checkmark off my list of things that will satisfy my soul.

"Wow, that is too perfect. It makes sense. Does one ever feel regret when purchasing a book? I would think *not*."

I'm liking this guy more and more. He gets me.

"Have you read them all?" he asks.

"God, no! I'm saving them for when the end of the world comes. I'll use them for bartering. Maybe for a fire or two."

He looks at me in horror.

"I'm kidding. About the fire..." I smile. "What book did you bring with you?" I ask, curious what a tough, mysterious man like him reads in today's age.

I try to look over to see which book he toted here, noticing he brought two. I'm impressed.

"I'm currently finishing up the last few chapters of Ken Follett's *The Pillars of the Earth*. And then it's onto *The Silent Patient*. An oldie, but a goodie." He holds both books up in evidence.

"We were meant for each other. You know that, right?" I say, excited that he's into psychological thrillers, especially one that happens to be one of my absolute favorites.

"I do know that. But, you said it first."

My body goes still, and for a second, I picture what we could look like fifteen years from now. "I was thinking, what better way to spend a quiet, rainy evening than curled up next to you? Here we are. I'm so thankful. I miss this."

I pour some coffee into each of our cups.

"Black?" And he confirms what I know already—that he's simple, reserved. And yet, he all but exposes a complexity that I know is hidden deep down somewhere behind this facade of "okay." I hand him his cup, put some cream and sugar in mine, and we look into each other's eyes as we each take our first sips.

"And you miss what, exactly?"

I raise my eyebrows, smiling into my cup.

He laughs and says, "Relax. I just mean, I miss being with people, friends. I miss spending time in a calm environment. It's been a while since I had something like this, someone to talk to and be with."

"Has it been a while since you dated someone?"

I'm scared to hear the answer for some reason, jealousy already rearing its ugly head at the thought of someone else making Bishop coffee. Bishop reading beside someone else. In bed.

"It's been a few years, yes. Nothing too serious. She didn't make me coffee in her kitchen with the sound of rain pouring in the background if that's what you're asking."

He thinks he's funny, and he eases over to me. I laugh, not embarrassed by my prodding.

The rain is starting to come down hard now. The lamp in the living room is lit but not too bright, giving the space a warm feeling. It's easy to breathe here. It's moments like these I'm actually thankful for the rain. It's so peaceful. The sound of the heavy drops landing on the roof relaxes even the heaviest of apprehension in my chest. I take a deep breath, begging my mind to slow down.

I look past Bishop out the back window and notice the rain steadily falling down the glass in a trickle. It's lovely any way you look at it. He stands in front of me now, suggestive.

"So…"

"So…?"

He's hesitant, yet confident.

"When I asked if I could come over and listen to the rain and lie in bed with you, I didn't actually think you would say yes." We laugh. "I have no

139

idea what I'm doing here."

"Well, dang, should I have said no?"

I chuckle again, his eyelashes looking up as he ponders on what to say next. He towers over me, and I've never felt safer in my life. I stare into his hazel eyes.

"I'm glad you said yes."

"I need you to let me get to know you, Bishop." He kisses the top of my forehead. "That's what you're doing here." I look up, reminding him.

"In due time, my lady. In due time."

A sense of minor frustration moves through me, and I roll my eyes, but this lasts just a moment. He reaches his hand up and passes his thumb over my lips, and they part slightly. I want to kiss him and hold him and tell him everything is okay.

"I promise you I'm trying to be vulnerable with you. You deserve that. Hell, I deserve that. It just takes a lot out of me. There is still so much I'm trying to work through, and I'm just trying to figure it out. But I am trying. I am trying for *you*."

I sigh, and all I know is I couldn't ask to be standing here with anyone else but him.

"I know. And I'm here, Bishop. Trust me. I'm listening to every word you say without any judgment."

I can only imagine what he has been through. I've heard the stories in the news. I've read the articles online. I have lain in bed, still for hours looking up at the ceiling, thinking of the worst possible scenarios, and even the best ones don't begin to touch the tip of the iceberg—everything else below the surface and underneath is impassable and hard.

Every which way I look at it, this man has been through hell. I'm scared to death of what's to come. I know that by the simple fact his eyes change whenever this subject is brought up, so I tread lightly. I don't want to push him.

"Want to go lay down?" I ask in barely a whisper.

The invitation garners a visible pleasure that overcomes him. He releases a breath of relief I didn't know he was holding on to.

"I thought you would never ask."

And with that, he throws me over his shoulder, lifting me with no effort at all.

"Wait, our coffee, Bishop!" I squeal.

I don't know what tonight will bring. I don't know what the next week will bring either. But I know what the rain will bring. It brings life. It spreads a kind of wealth not many other things on this Earth can. It brings fortune. And tonight, I feel like we both hold the winning ticket. He just doesn't know it yet.

S. C. Gray

Rule Number Eleven

Stacks of books are not for decoration.

As we walk into my room, shadows dance on the walls as the rain falls down the window just behind my headboard. The candle has done a nice job of erasing the smell of dog and week-old laundry that has yet to be put into the wash. My life appears to be neat and in order, but it's very deceiving. It's at this very moment I realize how much housework I've let go down the drain these past few weeks.

I'm hyper-aware that I could practice more tidy behaviors to ease my sense of anxiety, but I'm a busy woman. If I have thirty extra minutes in my day after checking emails, working in the bookshop, ordering books, walking Piper, or talking shit with Anders over a cup of coffee, I'm sorry. I'm just not one to spend it cleaning. I'd rather be reading. As long as I pick up here and there as I go, I'm okay with that. And so Bishop has to be too.

I look over as I move a stack of recently-read books and set my cup of coffee on the bedside table. Thankfully, he doesn't seem to notice the things I'm self-consciously raging over in my mind as we settle in.

In fact, after he sets his cup down, he makes a running start for it, and cannonballs into an abyss of white linens, and makes a moan that gets my insides stirring.

"I'm a sucker for a nice, comfortable bed."

I eye him with suspicion. "How many beds have you jumped into lately?"

He turns his head over to me and says, "None, but my own. I *did* try to envision what yours would be like. This pretty much surpasses all expectations."

He turns his head back to face the ceiling and closes his eyes. He looks so peaceful, and it makes me happy.

"I'm glad you like it." I take another gander around. Lord, could I not have even attempted to hide the underwear I changed out of before he came over? You know what they say, "Always wear your best underwear because if you're ever in an accident and they have to remove your clothing, you don't want the fireman to see your granny panties." I can't remember where I heard that from, but it has always stuck. If Bishop notices them, he doesn't let on. First impressions of a person's bedroom are everlasting.

Just ask sixteen-year-old me when I walked into Patrick Stacey's room after a track meet one Saturday and saw stiff tube socks. EVERYWHERE.

It was very traumatic and confusing to my virgin eyes. I never went into a boy's room again for many years, for fear of being in an awkward position of having to excuse myself to go home five seconds after I had been dropped off by my mother.

Most Asians, my mother included, seem to have an adjustment affliction. When I asked my mom to come back to get me with no explanation, she was so upset, she irrationally grounded me for two weeks. It was devastating, to say the least because I missed two episodes of WWE Raw, and I never want to put myself into that position again. Today, it's a different sense of loss. But, you know what I mean. I don't want to expose someone else to that horror. That following Monday back at school, walking through the halls was super fun. For both of us.

Never mind my mess. It's not every day I have a guy invite himself into my bed. It's not every day I have a guy invite himself over to my house at all, period.

"Oh please, I love your home. You should, too. It's definitely a change of scenery compared to my place. I've been there for two years, and I finally got a couch a few months ago."

He winks, joking. Or at least I think he is.

"I really do love this place. When I saw the listing for it, I jumped right on it just like I did for the shop's space. When you know, you know, I guess."

It's true. I knew exactly what I was looking for when I moved here. I'm just happy I've seemed to have found it.

"The best part is the courtyard in the back. The pebble stone, the bistro table out there, the hanging lights. It's a dream." I hop into bed right beside him, fluffing my pillow before I lay down too, making sure it's just right before settling in. Somehow, being with Bishop here like this, it doesn't feel uncomfortable at all. It feels... *right*.

"If it's not raining in the morning, let's make breakfast and eat out there," he suggests—and it's a lovely idea.

"How are you this wonderful?" I ask, propping up on my elbow to rest my chin on the palm of my hand. I face him. "I'm serious. How is it that you walk into my life after all this time, and this, whatever is happening between us? It's just so straightforward and simple. It's starting to worry me."

He laughs and flips over to face me.

"You are spectacular in your own way too, Campbell. Maybe you attract a certain kind of energy now that you're in a place of happiness."

Hmm, there's a thought. Is he right? Do you attract a different kind of light when you're in a better place in life? I guess this makes sense. Look at all the good that has come my way so far this year. I'm the happiest I've ever been.

"Have you always been this wise?" I ask.

"Absolutely not."

And with that, we fall into a place of comfort. We both grab our books. The dogs are settled at the end of the bed next to each other on top of the duvet.

"Seems Ghost has made himself right at home."

I look over at Bishop.

"Where he comes from, any place is better."

And I'm reminded that both of these guys come from a place I know nothing about.

———

We spend the next two hours in silence, save for the turning of pages and the few laughs I let out while reading what happens to be one of the funniest books I've read in a really long time. These days, light and cheesy are my jam. I live for books that are quick and full of bickering characters. Give me all the frenemy vibes. People who are bound to fall in love.

My brain has been in a fog because the shop has been so incredibly busy, and in my spare time, I can't spend it thinking any more than I already do. I need *uncomplicated*. Now is not the time to pick up *Moby Dick*.

After what seems like a lifetime of quiet, I look over, and notice Bishop has fallen into a peaceful lull. Both dogs have been lightly snoring for hours now but that is something I'm used to with Piper. She basically is six years past due for a pulmonology appointment. She very well could need a CPAP machine, and I've neglected to get her looked at. I imagine if she were in a partnership with someone, they would ask her to sleep in another room at night.

"Bishop," I whisper gently.

I tap on his shoulder. He's out cold, book cracked open still, face-down on his chest. His head is slightly turned toward me. God, he is so striking. I resist the urge to kiss his full lips.

One of Ghost's ears perk up at the sound of my voice, and I reach out to pet his back gently. He's softer than he looks.

"Hey, sweet boy," I say.

He looks over to me and then lays his head back down. He lets out a heavy sigh. In the silence, there's no reason to wake Bishop. I should just let him rest. Knowing he just worked a twenty-four-hour shift, I'm sure he's exhausted.

I reluctantly move to turn the bedside lamp off. As I lean over, I'm startled by a sudden break in the silence by a laugh. Or what starts as a laugh. I'm still lying down, but I turn back around suddenly to face Bishop, who is surprisingly still asleep. Hmm... he must be dreaming. His breathing intensifies.

I sit up, and suddenly, as if he's done this a hundred times, Ghost moves up the bed to lay in between Bishop and me, almost as if he anticipates what is to come. As soon as Ghost settles in, Bishop stirs, his head turning back and forth, side to side, and I'm an innocent bystander.

"Stop! Don't move!" he yells.

I'm confident now he is not dreaming of something pleasant.

"Foster, no! Stay low."

I lean over Ghost to grab Bishop's shoulder.

"Bishop, wake up!" I'm breathless as he sits up and looks around the room, unsure of where he is for the first few moments. He looks absolutely haunted. And embarrassed.

"Campbell."

"It's okay. It's all right. I'm here. You're okay."

With concern written all over his face, he wraps an arm around Ghost. He lays back down, and Ghost is all but on top of him.

"I'm so sorry." All of a sudden, he sits up, like he's deciding whether or not he should stay. "I should go. It's late."

I tap my phone on the nightstand, and the time illuminates. "It's almost midnight, Bishop. It's okay to stay," I offer knowing his best bet right now is to be with someone who cares for him. I hate the thought of him going back to his apartment alone.

"No, I'll go. I didn't mean to fall asleep. Come on, boy."

He gathers his books, slips on his shoes, and comes to my side of the bed to kiss me goodbye. There's something in his eyes. Something I've never seen before in him, in anyone. And when I pull the blanket off to walk him to the door, he puts his hands up in protest.

"No, stay in bed. I'm fine, Campbell. Really. I'll lock up behind me."

He presses hard for a smile, albeit one that is devastated.

As quickly as the dream is over, he and Ghost are headed out the front door. I'm rattled, left behind alone with Piper, the lamp still on. Piper is still cuddled into a ball, fighting sleep again.

And for the first time since meeting Bishop on the stoop of my bookshop, I realize that as charming and as lovely as he has been, there is something very horrible and plaguing that he is keeping from me. All is quiet, aside from the unrelenting rain beating down outside. I lie there for hours, holding Piper tight until the sun rises through the curtain.

S. C. Gray

Rule Number Twelve

Nothing is as it seems.

Horrible things happen to good people. All the time. More often than we tend to think. Sometimes, it's something they are born into. Life happens, quite literally. And then life is just a downhill roller coaster from there on out for one reason or another.

Sometimes, people are given every opportunity to live a wonderful life. They are born into a loving family. They are educated, healthy, and motivated. And maybe they make a very bad decision, and from that day on, they have to live with that decision for the rest of their lives.

But then, sometimes, someone tries their best to live the most honest, brave, and subtle kind of life. Maybe up until then, life was wonderful. It was full of meaning and expectations of good things to come. Maybe life was full of opportunity, and every single one was seized, grasped like life depended on it. And then, one day, a split decision is made in the blink of an unexpecting eye, a moment suspended in time hanging there like a single feather blowing in the wind. It changes everything.

As I walk to Luca's the following morning, wearing old jeans, my favorite knitted sweater, and a ball cap over my swollen eyes, I wonder: In which category does Bishop fall? Because I know horrible things happen to good people—all the time. And something horrible has happened to him. He just doesn't trust enough that I'll be able to handle it.

———

"Hey, Campbell!" I look from side to side as I step in and walk quickly across the coffee shop to Anders, sitting at the coffee bar chit-chatting with someone I don't know but I recognize from before.

"Hi."

I offer a quick wave to Anders' friend. Or is he more than a friend? I can't tell.

I look over at Anders.

"Can you spare two minutes?"

The urgency with which he jumps up from his stool and steers me toward a table around the corner tells me he knows it's important.

As soon as we sit, I look Anders in the eyes.

"Listen, I need you to tell me what you know about Bishop," I say with a quickness he's not used to.

"Um, I know he's hot. He's a firefighter. His ass in those jeans..." He laughs like he is being helpful. Which he is not.

"Look, now is not the time for daydreaming, Anders. Something happened last night. Bishop was asleep in my bed and..."

"Wait, shut the front DOOR, Campbell. Bishop spent the night at your house? Where the *hell* have I been?" he asks, and I immediately cut him off.

"No. Focus. Nothing happened. We were reading in my bed and he fell asleep. And while he was sleeping, he had a nightmare."

"Okay, what the fuck are you talking about? Why do I care if he had a nightmare? I need you to skip that part and hop right to what I need to know... how he ended up in your bed in the first place, and what happened after..."

He wiggles his eyebrows up and down suggestively, and I'm beginning to lose my patience at this point. I take a deep breath, trying to remember this is the first time I've seen Anders since Bishop and I became "official."

"Nothing happened. We didn't get that far because as I watched Bishop sleeping," (repeating that out loud makes it sound like some *Silence of the Lambs* shit was about to go down, and it was not. I promise) "he started screaming these horrible things. Like, actually screaming. His cries were so... troubled. And then I woke him up, somewhat violently. His dog calmed him down, and he all but dashed out of my room and out the front door like it was all a big mistake."

I let it all out in one fluid, run-on sentence, not breathing in the process.

"He has a dog?"

I roll my eyes, and he laughs. Now is also not the time for ADHD and jokes. I'm frustrated, to say the least, and I think now he sees the desperation in my eyes. Tears threaten to drop at any moment.

"Whoa, hang on. Slow down, Campbell." He puts his hand on top of mine, tears just barely on the ledge of goodbye from my eyes, and says, "Let's take a second to compose ourselves because we are classy, sassy, and a little smart-assy..." He tries to make me feel better for a second, and I'm appreciative.

"I know what will make you feel better."

Anders rises from the table, rushes to the back counter, pours me a quick cup of coffee, adding some caramel, and walks over to place it in front of me calmly.

"Start from the beginning. What in the world has you so concerned about one nightmare?" he asks.

Suddenly, I'm so overwhelmed by the possibility that something is going on that I am not equipped to handle. I feel a horrible pressure in my chest that will not subside as quickly as it has shown itself.

"Anders, I am in over my head. Bishop, he was in my bed. And he had this... this nightmare. One that was... *tragic*... it's the only way I can describe it."

I am at a standstill. My hands are under the table, and I find them rubbing my knees as if trying to calm myself down, and I hardly even realize it.

What was I thinking coming here this morning? Anders probably knows as much as I do, which is nothing. I just didn't know who else to turn to.

Who else in town can I actually talk to about this? I am suddenly caught off guard by how worried I am that I didn't go to anyone else *but* Anders. My coffee guy. For all I know, Anders and Bishop talk all the time, and maybe they are much closer than I think he and I are.

"Anders, are we good friends?"

I can feel my facial expression go from hopeful to concerned. He brushes my paranoia away as if I'm crazy for even thinking to ask such a thing. He rolls his eyes at me.

"What do you mean by tragic, Campbell? You're starting to scare me."

"I... I just don't know. I know he said he was in the military, that he said he had been deployed to Afghanistan on a few tours, and I just thought maybe he had brought it up to you in passing, is all. Maybe while he was ordering coffee or something."

I know I'm reaching because Bishop has jumped ship anytime this subject even comes close to coming up as far as I'm concerned. And why would he want to talk about war with a flamboyant feminist like Anders? But Anders has told him some of our secrets. Maybe Bishop told him some of his.

"He did bring it up slightly, almost. One time."

And to that, he goes quiet.

"Well, what did he say?"

Throw me a freaking bone here.

"I was kind of sworn to secrecy," he says.

And now I'm annoyed...

"Anders. I need to know who I'm dating. I need to know what is going on. What I saw last night was concerning, and that is putting it lightly."

I need an explanation for the sadness in his voice as he screamed next to me last night. I need to understand how I can help if something like this ever were to happen again.

"Well, here's your chance. Ask him yourself."

He points over my shoulder to the door, and I quickly turn around to see Bishop walking in. He pauses for a split second, something only I seem to notice, and we lock eyes.

"Good morning. How are you guys?" Bishop asks as he walks over to our table.

"Hey, bud! We were just talking about..." I give Anders a look of death.

I pick up where he left off, interrupting quickly, "We were just talking about how they need to spruce up the menu and add a few more holiday options. I hear folks really love a gingerbread latte."

Just then, I realize Bublé is playing overhead, and when I look at Bishop, we know we both have escaped an awkward conversation that I'm afraid we both are too terrified to face.

"Michael is following me everywhere I go," Bishop says.

I release a breath, but I see the sadness in his eyes.

"I was just finishing up here. I've got to head to the shop to clean up a bit."

The shop is closed on Mondays. My day to catch up. I grab my bag before anyone at the table can protest. Piper is beside me, and I grab my coffee from the table.

"I'll let you guys catch up. I'm sure there's lots Anders has missed out on in the last few days."

Bishop can explain our current "dating" situation, I think to myself.

I move toward the door, my heart aching. I feel a gentle hand on my elbow. I thought he would have used any opportunity to sweep last night under the rug. I ache to think of what it could have been with the rain throughout the night. Waking up next to each other. Breakfast in the courtyard.

"Want to meet for lunch?"

"What?"

"Well, we didn't get to have breakfast together this morning."

As if I needed a reminder.

"I'll be at the shop for a few hours. I can meet you somewhere when I'm finished up?"

I reach up to thumb his cheek and he leans into it like it's something he's been missing his entire life instead of just a few hours. I know then that I need to find a way to get down to what happened in my bed last night before we can even begin to move forward in what I thought was beginning to be the best thing that has ever happened to me. And to Piper.

S. C. Gray

Rule Number Thirteen

Courage in the face of pain merits honor, not weakness.

If you had told me a year ago that I would have my own bookshop, a cozy place to call home, and a sweet and charismatic dog lover pining over me, I would have told you to find a hobby. Happiness from pain takes *courage*. A year ago, did I have that? Did I realize what I had then? Of course, we always find out what you had looking back.

I think moving away from home took all the courage I had left in me. Leaving my ex, well, that took every bit of courage I had deep down in my bones. That was the rug that was pulled out from under me. Having to go through the process of having to replace it with all the money I had left to my name.

Leaving everything I knew to find myself in a place I knew absolutely no one, well, that was risky. But, what better place to do it than in Salter's

Ridge? A small enough place to swallow you whole, but still not big enough that you choke if you didn't land just right.

Hell, Salter's Ridge is a place hardly large enough to make it on a map. The odds of my finger landing here... slim to none. But this is where soul searching begins. Is it any wonder why two lost souls ended up here? Is it just a coincidence we found each other in the most unlikely way—in the most unlikely place of all places?

A year ago, I left behind everything I knew. Here in Salter's Ridge, I found hope. I found safety in the form of a few shelves. And here, maybe I'll find I'm not the only one running from a past that seems to follow me no matter how hard I try to turn the corner. Because after all, it's memories that follow us, no matter the physical things you tend to leave behind.

————

I left Anders and Bishop in a hurry while they were still standing there. There was something in Bishop's gaze that warned me, told me that if I stayed any longer, I wouldn't be able to endure being at Luca's without the urge to ask him more about what happened last night. But, I know he has to tell me in his own time, right?

That's just it, isn't it? It's never our story to tell—the secrets people around us have. In my case, is it my place to even ask about it? I can't keep prodding. Every time I've given him a safe place to explain, he shuts down. He runs away.

Everyone has at least *one* secret they hold onto just for themselves. The secret could be big. It could be small. It could eat them alive. Change their being. It may not even be an actual secret. Maybe it's just a fact about them that they don't want anyone else knowing. Like how much money you have in your savings account. It's all relative, isn't it? Like a harmless weed growing in the cracks of a sidewalk that is stepped over each day.

Why do we do it? Hold onto it for so long? I've asked myself that a lot recently, thinking back to that chilly night Bishop walked me home from The Bodega, and I told him about leaving home.

The expectations I used to hold relationships to in my past held me back from a lifetime of full potential. However late it may be, I realize now that doing so only enabled people around me to mistreat me. And if I had just convinced myself sooner that I deserved more than just subpar relationships and friendships that were truly one-sided, what would I have become? How much happier would I have been had I spoken up sooner?

I stand in the sunshine looking up at the striped awning above the door to Turning Pages, and I feel a sense of defeat pressing down hard on my shoulders. I look down to see Piper panting from her walk, wondering if I'll open the door.

"I love you, Piper. You know that?"

She seems to pull her smile back even further, totally exhausted, her eyes looking back and forth from the door. She always seems to know when I need her. She's always there, waiting to listen. I reach down and pet her on top of her blonde head, her hair a tangled mess, in dire need of a good brushing.

"Let's get inside, baby."

She wags her tail as I slip the key into the lock and open the door. I notice the familiar creak is missing from a normally harder pull. It's enough that I notice the absence of that sound immediately; it has been part of my day for nine months.

I shut the door behind us and lock it back up. I drop my bag onto the front counter and reach inside for my list of things I need to do today.

First on my list before I can make any excuses: email my landlord. Something I should have done days ago. I pull my computer from my bag and move to sit in the chair by the old fireplace. I think a few weeks back to when I told myself to stop procrastinating. I can't keep doing it.

I open a blank screen and log into my Gmail account and click the "compose" button. I type out a short message to Benny, asking for a quick phone call, should his vacation allow for a break. You know, in between hiking through plush forests halfway across the world and stopping for a whole seared fish, freshly topped with mango and lemon. Oh, what a dream. I picture it now.

Trying to stay on task and not getting sidetracked by thinking of the amazing food he must be indulging in, I finish my email. I let him know I have something pretty important I need to discuss, something I'd rather not get into through exchanging email. I know it's a cop-out, but honestly, it probably should be discussed in person, as important as it is. Right?

I need this bookshop. The past few months have been proof. This is where I belong. Where Piper and I both belong, together. It's our happy place. It completes us. Before I met Bishop, I thought my life was complete and didn't need anything else. Well, maybe need is the wrong word. Maybe I don't need anything else, but perhaps want is more like it. Anyhow, if it's not here in the leased building, as beautiful and as comfortable as it is, where else would I go? Surely, there are other spaces to rent in town. I'm sure of it. But, that's not something I'm interested in.

I hit send, hoping he calls me sooner rather than later if only to get it over with. I need to know once and for all. Am I going to be able to lease the space in this building for just a little while longer? Although if I had it my way, let's face it. I'd stay here forever.

I look over to the full shelves, to the many tables in the middle of the store. I look over to Piper's bed with Bunny in it. We finally found a place to be. And it's not even permanent. The unsettling pit in my stomach lands with a thud.

With the email sent to Benny, I look down at my list to see what else I need to do today. Thinking I need to lighten my mood because dwelling on the unknown is one of the worst things I can do for my mental health, I turn on my favorite music station, *I Miss the '90s,* light a candle that reminds me Christmas is just around the corner, and pull up the list from *Penguin Random House* to have a look at what is going to be available soon for order.

Hey, Jealousy by Gin Blossoms comes on, and my mood is instantly transformed. The only thing missing right now is a nice, hot coffee.

Just then, a knock startles me at the door. With the open sign turned off, it's hard to believe it's a customer. I move to unlock the door, and upon opening it, Bishop pushes his way in, and I'm pleasantly surprised. With an urgent kiss, my hand finds its way around his neck. In his hair.

"I couldn't have possibly waited three more hours to see you."

His urgency grows, pushing me into the shop, and I almost trip over a stack of books on the floor that I plan on shelving today. As they fall over with a subtle thud, I gather my footing, raising my hands.

"Although I'm thrilled to see you, I'm confused. Actually, I'm more than confused." I move back a few steps, touching my fingertips to my lips.

"Listen, I know this is all a lot. We meet up, we banter, we kiss. We enjoy each other's company over and over. The time with you is never enough. And then last night... I'm sorry if something changed all of that," he says breathlessly.

"And I can't wait until lunch to see you. I can't wait until then or a week, a month from now, to explain, even if it's just a little bit. I can't wait any longer to explain to you what it is that you saw."

Bishop is talking so fast and his hands are flying everywhere. He's pacing, back and forth, moving around, almost as if he's talking to himself and not to me.

He looks up then, and I smile. "I just need to know that you're okay—that we're okay. The rest will figure itself out. Right?" I'm telling him and asking him at the same time.

"I don't know if I'm all right, Campbell. That's what I'm trying to get at." He shuffles back, moves the hair from his face, and stands there. He looks up at me.

"Sometimes, selfishly, I think to myself I shouldn't care if I drag you into this, into my life. But these past few weeks... this past month even. It's been a comfort that I feel I can't live without. I leave you, and I find myself lying awake at night thinking of you. I come back to you, and I can't keep my hands off you. I want my fingers laced in yours. I want my lips on you."

He sighs, looking at me.

"If I'm honest with myself, I should have never asked to sit with you for coffee at Luca's that day. But I did. I should have never asked you to dinner. But, of course, I'm greedy. I needed *more* time with you. I always do. I've been thinking of myself when I should have been thinking of you."

Stunned, I offer my hand.

"You're not selfish, Bishop. I cannot stand here and say I'm not concerned. But, the suspense kills me. After last night, the *things* you were saying in your sleep... I know something has happened. I know there's a lot you've not told me. But how can I help you, and how can we move forward if you won't tell me what happened?"

"There are things I've seen, things I've done. It's hard to imagine a world that exists where I tell you those things, and you still want to be with me."

He's close to tears. And now, I'm mad.

"You've said that already, Bishop. I'm here. I'm still here." I step closer and reach up to touch his face. "Why won't you just let me help you?" I reach out again, but he steps back like I've slapped him across the face.

In a split second, something like anger is in his eyes. "I don't need you to help me." In nothing but a whisper, his face falls. "You can't help me, Campbell. No one can."

I want to be with him, and I'm finding it hard to come up with words he seems to want to believe. "What do I have to do to show you what you mean to me? I need you to know that I will be here for you, whatever is waiting on the other side of that conversation."

"I want to believe that to be true, Campbell, I really do."

I want to scream. I've never been so frustrated with anything or anyone in my life. I want to tell him to stop dragging this on. But I know it will only push him away, and I don't want to put more space between us than I already feel there is. There is something unpleasant growing between us, and I don't like it one bit.

He takes a breath, a breath someone takes before diving into deep waters. I step back over one of the rugs, turning around and looking at all I have created for myself.

"Look, I'm so happy here, Bishop. I've made a life for myself here. You make me happy. I have everything I could ask for. You're enough for me at this moment. No matter your past. No matter mine. I know it's hard to talk about right now, whatever it is. I'm sure you're uncomfortable, but for you to move past it, whatever *it* is, and for us to continue to get to know each other and grow in this relationship, you're going to have to grow in that discomfort and talk to me." I sit back down in a chair I was sitting in just a few moments ago.

He stands, silent, and I beg him with my eyes to say something, to say anything, to make this a little easier on both of us. I look out across the room, thinking back.

"You know, a few years ago, in my last relationship, I was always the one to press. The one to urge a conversation. Each time, when it went nowhere with silence, it became easier and easier to just let it go. And the longer I allowed myself to just *let it go*, the easier it was to just let *him* go. It was like my mind was telling me it was coming to an end, the relationship, and the longer I allowed myself to be hurt in it, the further away we got from each other. That distance became a canyon."

The room reeks with disappointment.

"I don't want that with us, Bishop. I really don't, and so I'll only beg you once. I *need* to know what I saw last night."

I look into his eyes and he still says nothing. Even though it pains me to say it, I know it must be done.

"Bishop, I need to know we can communicate and have open conversations because, in every other relationship I've ever had, a lack of those two things is what ended them."

Maybe we are over as quickly as we began. I think back to old friendships—my ex, my parents.

With that, he says nothing. He looks like he doesn't know what to say.

With tears in my eyes, I rise from the chair, a million things running through my mind, and I move to open the front door. As much as I've tried to be understanding, I can't begin to pretend to understand things he won't be open about. And I can't pretend it doesn't hurt to know he doesn't trust me enough to talk to me about the one thing that stands between us and having a solid relationship. I'm not crazy. I know there is something here.

I know in my heart he doesn't want to hurt me. But people hurt us, and we hurt people. And right now, at this moment, Bishop Graham has no idea he's the only reason in the world I'm hurting. For the first time in over a year since moving to Salter's Ridge, my escape just isn't enough. Problems are still following me everywhere I go.

167

S. C. Gray

PART TWO

Forever is Made from a Bunch of *Nows*.

S. C. Gray

Rule Number Fourteen

Keep Christ in Christmas. Or, at least, on the plate...

Coming back home always stirs up raw emotions in me. Going to my mom's for our annual holiday get-together. Well, just sign me up for weekly therapy sessions once I leave.

The drive to the beach is about twelve hours, and every time I get in the car to make it, I put on a playlist with a mix of gangster rap, country hits, and '90s throwbacks. It's all I can do to take my mind off what's to come. I'm already in a particular mindset when I pull into her driveway.

I sigh, taking a deep breath. Piper is in my lap, panting in anticipation. She's been asleep there for hours, but now, she's ready to party. She asks me with her eyes, "Are you going to let me out, mom?" If there's one thing

Piper loves, it's coming to my mom's house, and I'm conflicted. If it were a two-hour drive back to Salter's Ridge and not twelve, I might be half-tempted to pull away right now and leave. I could make something up. "Hey, mom, I got stuck with work stuff." Or "Piper ate something she shouldn't have, and now, she is sick... I'll catch the next one."

But, I know I'm supposed to go. We are all supposed to go. So, here I am. I can hear the seagulls above through the cracked car window, smell the salt, and feel the moisture in the air. My mom lives about a mile from the sand. I used to dream big here. But, that was years ago.

You see, right next door... that's where my ex used to live. The ex I'm all but completely over—the one we all hate. Looking back now, I have no idea what I was thinking. I should have heeded the warnings and seen the red flags. But, of course, no one could tell me anything because I wouldn't let them.

Next door, it's how we met. Years ago, our parents had a little neighborly get-together, a barbeque with the inlet in the background. It was beautiful, with fifty guests in attendance. We instantly locked eyes, talked the entire night, just the two of us, like no one else existed. We hit it off immediately, talking about our aspirations, about our dreams, and the rest is history. After the hell that came after, it's one I won't let repeat itself.

I'm not naive to think I'll be over the things I've been through so quickly. All the emotional abuse, even the physical. That might take years, decades perhaps. But being as far away from here as possible is the closest thing I've found to finding that forgetfulness I'm searching for with the least amount of reminders. I hate reminders.

I honestly have no idea where he is now. I heard he moved somewhere north. Three hundred sixty-five days later, give or take, and it's like he's vanished into thin air. If only...

One of the reasons I despise coming back is because every time I get here, I see that stupid colored house next door I try to avoid looking at. It sets off a million alarms in my mind, reminding me of one of the worst times of my life. It all falls back to that barbecue. Most recently, though, I've tried to flip that mindset to "there are better things to come."

I take a deep breath and close my eyes, inhaling the coast. When I open them, I recognize a few other cars in the drive parked next to mine.

My sister is here, with her new husband, Jett, we call him. He talks a mile a minute and is the life of every party. A catch if you ask me. He's kind to her, treats her well, and she's better off because of him.

My favorite uncle is here too with his wife, the second one he's hooked. We like her well enough. She keeps to herself, which is probably a good thing. She's wise to stay out of the way of all the family drama. Leah is sweet, smart, smiles when she's supposed to, and frowns when you're telling a sad story. She's all ears. Makes for a great listener.

There are also a few close friends of the family, some of whom have been attending mom's Christmas dinners since before I was born. The dinner is usually held the week before Christmas. That way, everyone can be in the peace of their own homes on Christmas Day. I prefer it that way. This year, I'd like to be able to spend it in Salter's Ridge. A first.

I want to start my own traditions. I want to wake up to my own Christmas tree, decorated with things I love. I want to collect special memories of my own.

I twist to reach in the back seat, maneuvering around Piper, and pull my weekender bag to the front, taking a final deep breath.

"No matter what happens, don't look her in the eye. Not even for food, Piper."

She scoffs, and I know in my heart that this warning is useless. And she will, indeed, take all the snacks offered by my mother. My mom, the woman who keeps giving my dog snacks, but then, ten minutes later, calls her fat. I get aggravated just thinking about it.

I open the car door, and as I do, I notice the neighbor's house has been painted a different color. This acknowledgment does something to the synapses in my brain—nerve to message. I feel a weird sense of relief come over me—a reminder erased like chalk on a school board.

One point for Campbell.

"Hi, Anak!" I hear my mother shout from the balcony overlooking her driveway ("Anak" means "daughter" in her native language, Tagalog) and if I didn't know any better, I think I see her squint her eyes a little to see if I've left Piper behind this trip around. For someone who's had dogs her entire life, she sure has gotten finicky in her "old" age about pets and the cleanup that comes along with them. She's gotten finicky about a lot of things. Money, social settings, pets, me...

"Hi, mom, and yes. I brought Piper with me. I always do."

And I always will... I think to myself. She quickly gives me a look of denial, like she didn't think I would notice her annoyed concern at my traveling with a dirty dog (or so she thinks).

Piper isn't dirty. I just don't give her unnecessary baths until she rolls in shit. I imagine I'd do the same thing once I have human children as well. But that's beside the point.

"Come on up, Campbell! We were just about to break open a bottle of red your dad gave me for our anniversary in 1995!"

She laughs, but the joke's on her. In her mind, she's killing his very existence by popping the cork and drinking it. In reality, it only provides the table with a nice glass of vintage wine we otherwise would not be able to afford. She does this every Christmas dinner. Last year, it was the *Moet Chandon*. Now *that* was a treat. I laugh a little internally at the pettiness that divorce has brought out in my mother.

As I walk up the steps to her duplex, I once again cringe at the thought of being back here.

"Why do you do this to yourself, Campbell?" I ask audibly as I grab my things with a tight grip, my mother already back inside and the door to the balcony closed.

For multiple reasons, it's just never a good idea, nor is it pleasant. But, with the newfound glory and happiness I've found in Salter's Ridge, it's funny how it all seems to disappear the moment I step foot into my mother's home.

I open the front door to the sounds of laughter and immediately spot a fake Christmas tree in the corner of the living room, decorated with every ornament she's ever owned. The tree leans a little to the left because of all the weight it holds. There's no theme to it. Just *Christmas*. I think to myself, *I bet it's been up since October 1st.*

175

Music is playing and I'm immediately thrown back to every time Bublé played while Bishop was near. I wonder what he's doing right now.

It's been several weeks since I opened the door for him to leave my bookshop. I'm still reeling from that conversation. I've not so much as heard from him—no texts, not even an old-fashioned letter. I've told myself not to look toward the fire station every time I leave my house. I can't say I'm surprised. He seems like a level-headed guy, and the way I excused him from the shop, I can't say I expected him to come running back begging for forgiveness. I took the hint of reluctance from him all the times we spent together. There was nothing left to be said.

Since that day, I've done coffee at Luca's without him. I've gone to The Bodega for drinks with Sienna and Anders without him. I'm still just *without* him. Anders says he hasn't seen him at Luca's, either. Even if I'd like to say I'm dealing with it perfectly well, I know I'm not fooling anyone. Especially Piper.

She's been acting funny these last few weeks. I can't help but think it has everything to do with Bishop not coming around. I'm starting to think she likes him more than she likes me. Piper spends hours looking out the window toward the station, past the linen curtain at the top landing. Every time the sirens go off, she's down the stairs and stares at the front door, expecting someone to come through, although no one ever does.

At mom's duplex, there is a super-long staircase that works its way up to a second-story landing, which holds the living room, kitchen, and dining area. All these rooms lead to another set of steps, which leads to all of the bedrooms on a third floor with views of the water.

Nothing about this place has changed since my mom and dad split. The couch is still the same. The decorations are still the same as they were in 1990. She hasn't parted with anything except for the photos of my father. When my father departed and went his separate way, I guess he didn't want any reminders either.

I walk up. Piper is eight steps ahead of me, her nails tap, tap, tapping on the distressed wooden steps. We land in the living room together, and my sister immediately gets up from her seat at the bar, bringing her glass of red wine with her.

"Oh, thank God someone with some normalcy is here," she whispers into my ear. I laugh nervously because the last time I saw her, I was far from "normal," and I don't like that word to begin with.

Who is "normal" these days? Normal sounds boring and overrated, and I think that word should just be erased from all languages.

I drop my bag along with Piper's leash. She's off to the kitchen, and my sister moves in to give me a genuine hug.

"Well, hello, Lou. Nice to see someone got a head start on taking the edge off. Lucky you. Give me some of that." I grab the wine glass from her and take a generous gulp.

"There's plenty more where that came from," Lou tells me, "although, mom seems to be winding down on the number of bottles she has left. She's probably got just a few more dinners' worth before she drinks him completely away."

We laugh, and I'm so relieved to have her here with me—someone who truly understands the expanse of craziness that is *the* Christmas dinner.

I look around and wave to my uncle. He is sitting on the couch with his wife, and I already feel bad for the amount of distress he subjects her to. *What an idiot,* I think to myself. *Everyone knows you don't bring anyone that sweet around on this day.*

"Hey, Uncle Cecil. How are you?"

I offer a smile, hoping he knows I miss him. I haven't seen him since last year.

He rises from his seat to come over. "Hey, dear. How is my darling, Campbell?" His embrace calms me more than he could possibly know.

Uncle Cecil is my mom's brother. He came here to the U.S. shortly after my mother did. He's tall, striking, and successful. He has been running his own charter boat company here in town since he first learned he loved being out on the ocean. I personally don't have the stomach for it.

But also, he's the one who should take the crown for most "normal" in the family. He wouldn't hurt a fly and does and says all the right things. He is wonderful in every way, and I just love him. Everyone in town does. He never had any kids with Aunt Clara, God rest her soul. She always said, "It wasn't in the cards." She never elaborated. I know he misses her.

"Your Campbell is doing great, actually," I answer.

Minus my situation back home with Bishop. One might call it the "annoying miscommunication" trope in literary terms. There's also the dilemma with my lease on the shop's building space. And the fact that I haven't heard from Benny yet...

"How is that bookshop of yours doing? Selling any books?" he asks with a wide-casted smile laced with sincere interest. At this very moment, mom chimes in with, "Making any money, dear?"

I turn to look at my sister, who makes a face that only I can see. One that says, "*Why is it always about money with her?*" I feel my neck get warm.

Here's the thing that upsets me about my mother: Has she ever once, just *once*, said she was proud of me? Does she understand that I created a life and a business for myself from nothing, with *no one's* help? Does she realize she should be lucky I am not asking *her* for money left and right? I'm stable on my own two feet, just like she always wanted. Just like any *normal* parent would. What more could she want from me? I've always had a weird sense of fear in the back of my mind that I'll never be good enough for her. Whatever the reasoning may be.

She's never even made the trip to Salter's Ridge to see the damn place. Not once. She's never been to my new house. She's never offered to come to check out the shop. I feel my sense of resentment boiling inside, and I try to remind myself I'm here for just one day. And then it's back to the peaceful sanctuary that is my new life, away from here.

"The bookshop is doing amazing," I say to everyone, including my mom, who has moved on to cutting up some vegetables for the Sinigang (the main reason I came today). It seems when she says these things, she doesn't even realize she's doing it. So, I let it go. Again.

"I'm finally settled in, finally turning a profit. Gearing up for the holidays. It has been amazing."

It truly is the best time of the year. For me, at least. I won't let my issues with my mother take that away. She's the one who instilled that in me anyway—the love of Christmas. All the decorations, the lights, the shopping, the gift-giving. The time spent with family making and collecting memories. All the reading cozied up on the couch with Piper.

"Well, good. I'm glad. You deserve that success. It seems I'm not the only one in the family that has a business mindset. Gotta make a life for yourself, Campbell." Uncle Cecil winks and adds, "No one else will."

He gives my shoulder a reassuring squeeze. And there it is. Him saying the right thing. Like always.

"Don't mind your mom, Campbell. You know her... always in everyone's business, pretending not to be."

We laugh. I move into the kitchen to grab a wine glass from the cabinet. I give myself an unhealthy pour and gulp down half of it in the first sip. It's lovely, sweet even, and goes down a little too easily.

I grab my weekender bag, taking it into my old bedroom. Lou follows behind me. "So... how's life out in Salter's Ridge? It's been what, almost a year?"

She sits on my bed, and I follow suit, careful not to disturb the carefully placed pillows my mom has arranged. Always putting on a show.

"It's been amazing, Lou. I'm not going to lie."

My sister smiles approvingly.

"I knew it would be. It was good for you to leave this place."

I have a flashback to the night I called my sister from the hospital. At the time, she was the only person I could have possibly called. I pictured my mom so many times saying, "I told you so..." and my father getting the courage for the first time in his life to do one manly thing and kill my ex. But that night, all I had was Lou. She's been in my corner ever since.

You know, over the years, I knew what I was doing was wrong. I knew staying in that situation was wrong. I have no one to blame but myself. Of course, my ex was to blame for the black eyes and the hospital stays. But in the end, my hiding them with makeup and long-sleeve sweaters in the summer was my doing. All the times I said life was good when really it was a shit bag. Those times, those I hate myself for.

What a sad disservice to my heart, to my potential. All that time I chiseled off my life, times that held zero meaning. But then again, I learned so much, didn't I? Anyhow, I'm still coping with that time in my life.

Here I am, all about "love yourself" this and "you deserve it all, that." Where do I find the nerve? Who do I think I'm fooling? Everyone in this house has heard the stories. They all know what I've been through, why I left.

Being in this room, the one I came back to after that night I called Lou. The room where my mom silently told me sincerely for what seemed like the first time that she loved me. This room just drags it all out again.

"I seriously hate coming here," I admit.

"Then, why do you do it?"

"I asked myself that, and I don't have an answer, Lou."

I am not sure why I subject myself to this uncomfortable mess. Maybe, it's because I feel I have to, even though I should know by now that I don't.

"You know, I understand mom is hard on us, but it's just because she is who she is. She's never going to change."

I sigh because Lou knows firsthand how mom makes me feel, and I wonder if I'll ever understand that concept. My mom, her culture, where she came from, the life she created for herself. It somehow doesn't mesh with how I would picture myself becoming as a woman, as a mom. I know eventually, I need to come to terms with that too. Lou is right. She is never going to change. I need to stop taking it so personally.

I feel a sense of guilt and selfishness come over me. Because after all, some people don't understand my life either. How I could just pick up everything, leave, and start over? I guess as I get older, I'm learning that I don't have to live a life everyone understands, and neither does she.

"I just feel like sometimes she doesn't understand that I'm not against her. I'm more like her than I care to admit."

I think back to all the times I felt guilty about my successes in life. Especially after leaving and opening the bookshop. *Why* do I feel that?

"Have you ever thought that sometimes mom may think the more successful you get, the more distant you will become?"

Lou shocks me by saying this.

"What are you talking about?" I lean forward a bit, wobbly for a moment, the wine going straight to my head. Have I eaten today?

"I just mean that maybe she wanted all the things you have now. A nice home, a job to take pride in. When dad was here, did she get to do all the things she had the potential to do? Maybe she wanted more out of her life than she could achieve, and now, here she is, in this beach house. Fifty years have gone by, and is she happy?"

I need more wine for this conversation. Just then, mom pops her head in, and we both go still, each hoping that she didn't hear anything.

"Dinner's ready," she says as she eyes us with suspicion. "What are you two doing?"

"Nothing," we both say at the same time and quickly jump up to move into the dining room before she can ask any more questions.

The dining table is set beautifully with the usual Waterford crystal wine glasses, different from the ones my mom lets Lou and I use if it's not Christmas. There are endless bowls and platters of food. So much food, we will have leftovers for at least a week. I suddenly notice that there are also unfamiliar plates set out. I lean in for a closer look, squinting my eyes.

"Is that Jesus' face?" I ask, unsure of how I can possibly enjoy dinner with Him staring at me. I imagine scraping up a spoonful of potatoes, only to reveal an eye smeared over with gravy or a partial nostril covered by a piece of turkey. I think the only thing worse than this would be a *baby* Jesus.

"Yeah, so? Do you have a problem with that?" my mom asks in her naturally offended tone of voice when anyone asks her *any* question.

I cannot imagine the idea of spending hard-earned money on these plates. But clearly, that's just something I need to work through. They aren't my plates.

Everyone is now looking back and forth between my mom and me. My mother, looking down at her plates, ones she clearly was excited to share with everyone today, and then me, ruining her moment of sharing The Word on classic china bone memorabilia.

"Let's eat," Lou says, breaking through the awkwardness. And so, it begins.

S. C. Gray

Rule Number Fifteen

Always bring a book. Just in case.

My mom and I have misunderstood each other since the dawn of time. There have been times when, at its worst, our relationship hung on by a thread. As I've gotten older, I have understood why that was and notice now I try to avoid it happening going forward. I tip-toe around her, and I think she feels she has to tip-toe around me. We coexist, at best.

We are both short-fused. You can say one wrong thing, and the other screams and gets upset. The one who said the "wrong" thing gets upset that the other just doesn't "get it." It's always been a thing. And today I know will be no different.

It's not very frequently that my mom and I can be in the same room without something coming up in conversation that offends the other, whether it is in the form of words or action. Let me give you an example that frequently comes to mind.

When I was thirteen years old, I had ten of my closest friends over at our family home, in the middle of one of the most crime-ridden neighborhoods in California, for my birthday. That last bit about crime is just for effect. We were pretty safe in that peach and mint-colored home my parents were leasing. Minus the bullet holes in the front door.

My mom made all the crowd favorites—her famous lumpia, her veggie and fruit platters, pancit, and three different types of punches. She always goes above and beyond when she has a group of guests to feed.

When it came time to open presents, we all moved into the living room, and I stood in front of all of those in attendance.

Before presents, my parents were excited and insisted I show everyone the dance I spent many nights rehearsing in my bedroom for a solid month straight. *Genie in a Bottle* by Christina Aguilera was the song. On-trend.

Over and over, I flopped my hands across my exposed belly. Have you ever seen that music video? YouTube it. It's a national treasure.

By the time my concert was over, looking back now, I'm sure this is when parents would have insisted their children be picked up, so as not to further insult their minds with the filth that was my family's insanity. Somehow though, the party continued.

My mom handed me a bag with recycled tissue paper from the last three birthdays she had saved up.

"Open mine first!" she said excitedly.

And I was all but excited to have this big, beautiful bag to open.

Growing up, we didn't have much. We had just enough that my sister and I didn't ever feel like we were without. We never noticed anything different about our family from another, and I think that's one of the most interesting qualities my parents had. Security in hiding things from us. Sometimes, it was a bad thing. In this instance, though, I think they did what any parent would—give all you could to your kids.

Here I was, sitting in front of all my eighth-grade friends, including Lord, help him, Tube Socks Patrick Stacey. I vigorously ripped the tissue paper from the top of the bag and pulled out the contents without thinking twice about it.

Two boxes of Barbies.

Nervously, I looked out to the crowd of concertgoers, then to my mom, who had the biggest smile on her face. Confusion was on everyone else's. Here I was, this scantily clad thirteen-year-old, dancing around her parent's living room in a tube top, being given dolls for her birthday!

I immediately felt a sense of overwhelming embarrassment. Something I often feel when I'm around my mom, even today. In the moment, I thought to myself— *Why in the hell would you get me a Barbie doll, mom?!?! I'm THIRTEEN, for Christ's sake!*

That day, she had no clue how embarrassing that was. In her mind, she was giving me all the things she never even dreamed of receiving as a child. Having grown up in the Philippines, she used to tell us stories of how she would get in trouble for the most menial of things, and her father would put her in a flour sack and beat her with a sugar cane stalk. And here I was, embarrassed to death of a gift.

Day in and day out, all I heard from my friends was how they were out kissing boys behind their houses while their parents were at work, keeping diaries hidden under their beds filled with secrets, solo MASH games, and lying about their pretend occupations in online Instant Messaging chat rooms. And then, there was me. Still getting dolls from my Asian mother.

That day, after all my friends had left, I freaked out on my mom like the immature child I was.

"Mom, what the hell are these?" I asked.

I pointed to the dolls on the dining room table she had just cleaned off of all of the food she had slaved over all morning. That night, when I came out of my room from locking myself in like I was somehow punishing her, and not myself, the dolls were gone from the table, and I never saw them again.

I think to myself years later— *When exactly was the moment I started caring what people thought of me?* In hindsight, do I realize I create some sort of image I've put pressure on myself to keep? Thinking back, I truly think that moment, the doll moment, that was it for me. That moment when my mother completely betrayed my trust in front of all my friends by getting me a Barbie for my thirteenth birthday. Who to this day, I'm sure, doesn't remember or even realize the significance of this tragedy I created for myself in my mind.

But for twelve years, that has stayed with me. It's never left. That damn Barbie, pushing her baby in a pink carriage from just behind the clear plastic of the packaging. The Christmas bag my mom had recycled and gave to me on my birthday. It all has stayed with me, and for what? And why?

In more recent years, I've noticed this about myself. My getting irritated and embarrassed when my mother does or says something I think she shouldn't. Things that, to her, are helpful. Things that, to her, may even be compliments. I realize that sometimes, I tend to care too much about what people think of me. And I need to work on it.

But to work on it, I need to get down to why I care too much about what people think of me, to begin with. Is it because I feel I have something to prove to those around me? Growing up, my mom and dad would ground me if I came home with a "B" on a report card. I grew up terrified that I would disappoint my parents. This, in turn, created the workaholic I see in myself today—that constant need to be "perfect" or to always be right. I'm always working. Always thinking about the next step, the next thing to do. The next project to undertake. I can never just *relax*. It's non-stop. I'm always thinking of ways I can be better and do better. All these thoughts, stemming back to a Barbie.

———

I pick a seat at the dinner table, the one farthest away from my mom, and choose an empty one next to my uncle, my sister sitting across from me. I can make out my mom eyeing me down at the opposite end of the table.

"Okay, let's eat," my mom says to everyone, cheerfully and condescendingly all at once.

We dig in. I move to reach for the beautifully roasted turkey my mom has had in the oven since 4:30 am, and it smells absolutely divine.

If there is one thing my mom can do right in this world, it's cooking a nice meal for a large group of people. By herself. She never wants any help when it comes to cooking, and she will shoo you away from the kitchen if you offer to do anything. She will make you go and enjoy the company and laugh and play games until the food is ready.

With two glasses of wine down and another full one in my hand, I say, "Wow, mom. You've outdone yourself. This all looks delicious, as always."

I genuinely mean it, and she looks across the table with a thank you and smiles broadly, proud of her accomplishment. It's Asian culture, after all—Feed everyone until they burst at the seams, then offer dessert.

Sounds of clicking spoons on the Jesus plates and sips of wine can be heard over the Christmas music playing softly in the background, easy conversations happening all around the table. A rerun of some past football game is playing on the TV, and I spot Piper just under my mom's feet, hoping for food to fall. Voluntary or involuntary. It's all the same to her.

Everyone seems to be enjoying themselves, and all seems to be going well until I hear my sister say a little too loud, "Are you serious?" And I look over to her husband with the expression, "What did I miss?"

This is the moment I dread every time I come to my mother's home. Anxiety plagues me like flour on a celebrity walking a red carpet. The moment of panic, knowing a blowout is tiptoeing in from the east, and I'd be lying if I said I wasn't a little disappointed because I haven't even gotten to the desserts yet—the best part.

Just then, my sister raises her glass, sloshing just a little bit of red wine onto my mom's tablecloth spread underneath all the food. Accident, or one glass too many, who knows?

"Mom here seems to think that she cooks the best Sinigang in the family." My sister proclaims.

I breathed out the air I was holding in. I notice my brother-in-law does the same. I avoid eye contact because this is just playful banter between my mom and my sister. As we all know, this is the truth. Mom does make the best Sinigang in the family. No secret there. There is no competition.

But I'm not naive to think I've narrowly missed a disaster. It's here, somewhere, lingering. I can feel it—a whisper in the wind that blows away, only to boomerang back into my face. I rise from the table, hoping others will do the same, clearing our plates so that we can move to the key lime pies and the cheesecakes. I didn't drive twelve hours just for turkey.

"Campbell, when are you going to find a nice boy?" I hear my mom say to my back, in front of everyone at the table.

Because she wouldn't dare to ask this question to my face, alone. She knows it's a touchy subject, especially with that damn house right next door. After everything I've been through. She was there. She knows. So, then, why mom? Why ask about it here, before dessert? In front of my happily married, younger sister.

I turn to face her, more upset that I'm risking pie versus being asked this silly question.

"Mom, not that you would know, because you've yet to come out to Salter's Ridge to see me. Or the bookshop I've created. Or the place I call home. But I have found a nice boy."

Albeit one I'm not necessarily talking to right now. But she doesn't need to know that.

My mother mocks surprise, and of course, underneath, radiates offense that I've now exposed her "perfect mother" facade at Christmas dinner. I see my uncle and brother-in-law squirm in their seats, the other dinner guests feeling uncomfortable too, I'm sure.

"Why is that, mom? Why haven't you come to Salter's Ridge to see me?" I ask, my liquid courage building up resentment in its ugliest form.

"Well, I was waiting for you to get settled in. You haven't even invited me, yet. So..."

And there it is, the diversion. I've been there almost a year! I haven't *invited* her yet? My mother does this. She is always using reverse psychology to place blame on the person sitting next to her, even if she's on a subway and the person next to her is a complete stranger. This is what she does. She cannot take responsibility for anything, even when it comes to her own children. And I just can't take it anymore.

"Mom, why do you do that?"

"Do what, Campbell?"

And she looks around, pretending to act like she doesn't know that she's actually doing the thing, begging someone to come to her defense because she doesn't do good with confrontation. Mainly, because no one ever confronts her, for fear of her lashing out. And missing on dessert, in my case.

"Why do you act like you're the innocent? Every time, mom. Why is it you think you need an 'invitation' to come to Salter's Ridge? For once, it would be nice not to have to ask for my mother to pick up the phone and say, 'Hey, Campbell! I'm thinking of coming to see you. And you know, the LIFE you've built for yourself'."

All eyes are on me now, and instead of having a private conversation about something that is, you know, very much so private and personal, here I am, having this discussion at Christmas dinner.

"Well, there you go, Campbell. It's always about you, isn't it? It all leads back to Campbell, the girl who escaped her hometown and never looked back. Campbell, the girl who doesn't need anyone or anything because she can do it all on her own."

My mom never argues with me in front of anyone. She always shuts down. But here, at this dinner, she's ready to fight.

"Oh, have you been stewing here, in this beach house that used to be dad's, for the ten months since I've left? You could have picked up the phone, you know, mom? But go ahead. Tell everyone how you really feel about me."

I move to get up from my seat, but her response stops me.

"Campbell, first of all. Your father left me with maxed-out credit cards and a steaming pile of shit to clean up that you know nothing about. Second…" And she pauses to look down at Piper, there begging at her feet for just one more bite of potato. "There isn't a single mother on this planet that is prouder of her daughter than I am." And she breaks from the table to go to her bedroom, leaving her plate where she sat. Everyone else is sitting still, backs straight. On edge.

I blink away tears as she says this, and I look around the table. Shock covers everyone's face. Sadness is etched on mine, surely. I pick up my cloth napkin from the table, wearing my emotions on my sleeve, as always. Nothing is new about this dinner. It's the same dinner every year. Just a different argument, a few tears, too much wine. As always, never anything new.

Why is it that my mother can tell ten people at a family dinner that she's proud of me, but she can't admit this to me in private? Ever.

I pick up my plate, toss my napkin on top, and move to the fridge to grab the pie. Closing the door, I spin around. I feel drained from this day already, and the sun hasn't even gone down yet.

"So, you met a guy?!" my sister exclaims behind me, the nosy little shit she is.

Rule Number Sixteen

Remember, the nut doesn't fall far from the tree.

One of the hardest things in life is apologizing when we do something wrong. And I mean, of course, it's easy to say you're sorry when you've bumped into someone at the grocery store by accident. It's easy to say you're sorry when you've called the wrong number. But when it comes to family issues, why do we wait?

Looking back on every other family dinner, it's easy to see why an argument at that table always occurs. We have this dinner once a year, and when we congregate again, we sit down with a year's worth of pent-up aggression. And yet, we've failed to realize this when we walk up those steps to my mom's. Every year, until now.

I've learned over the years that communication is key in everything I do, especially in the relationships I keep. As for the ones lost? Well, those fell victim to the lack of it, I guess.

So much miscommunication.

In many circumstances, when something goes awry, it falls to us, the communicator. And yet, we fail to correct something we continue to do when we already know the repercussions.

The definition of insanity: Thinking we will get a different outcome when we keep doing the same thing over and over. It's like voting. You can't keep voting for the same kind of book at a book club, expecting there to be a different kind of conversation at the next meeting. It just doesn't make sense. We know this, subconsciously, I think. And yet...

After my mom is summoned from her bedroom by my sister, dinner at my mom's doesn't last past dessert. Folks pack up their to-go plates she makes for them, placing tinfoil on top. Hugs are given, and car lights fade away as everyone but Piper and I remain.

"Mom, can we talk?"

My mom moves to start to load the dishwasher, exhaustion written all over her face and in her eyes.

"What do you want to talk about, Campbell?" she asks, making it even harder for this conversation to begin.

"Why does it have to be like this, mom?"

"Like what?"

"Um, I don't know. Us never talking... about anything?"

"We talk."

"You know what I mean, mom. We talk, of course. But we never *really* talk. About emotions, about things that are bothering us. Nothing. We continuously sweep things under the rug, mom. I don't want to do it anymore."

And here, I know I should be more understanding about her culture and her upbringing—but I just can't. Not when I feel like I've missed out on so much. I feel like I've been cheated. I know how selfish that sounds, but I just cannot help it.

"Campbell, you can talk to me about anything. And just because I don't say I'm proud of you doesn't mean that I'm not. You should know I'm proud of you."

"Yes, but I want to hear it from you. I want to see it, mom. Why is that so hard to understand?"

"Campbell, you *must* know how proud I am of you. I tell all of my friends about you. About your bookshop, about all the money you're making."

"Mom! Why would you be talking to your friends about the money I'm making? Some of them don't even know me. That's so inappropriate!"

"What do you mean?"

"Mom, I don't sell books because I want to make a ton of money. That's not what it's about. That's not why I left home. I opened that shop so I could have something that's *my own*. I moved to Salter's Ridge to have something to make me feel like I *belong*. Don't you get that?"

I start to get frustrated because, of course, what I want to say is not coming out correctly. Nothing in these conversations ever does. Either that or my mom just truly doesn't understand. She just cannot comprehend it.

I continue, "Look, mom, I get it. You grew up without much and in a different time. You've been through so much here. But, I have too. You know I opened my bookshop, and you are proud that I'm financially aligned with how you think things should be. I get that. However, I need you to be proud of me for different reasons, not because I have a little bit of money, mom."

And it's like it clicks in her mind.

"Oh, well. I'm sorry, Campbell. I didn't know all of that bothered you. You should have said something. I never want you to feel that way. I never want to hurt you, Campbell," she says across the counter to me.

I'm shocked. My mom *genuinely* apologizing. I am at a loss for words. She and I remain silent.

"So. Who is this guy you mentioned at dinner?"

And she's onto the next subject like she cannot wait to escape the awkward tension. I'm almost thankful for it, but I'm not ready to be done.

"Mom, I need to hear from you that you're proud of me. And not just in front of a room full of people. I need to hear it from you on your own, and not when some dumb argument prompts it."

If there is anything I've learned this year, it's to say exactly what's on my mind and not hold back when telling people what it is I need. Only good has come from it. And it can't be much different with my mom, right?

"You know, when your dad and I were married, I did the best I could with what I had. I was young, and so was he. And I won't blame him for our shortcomings because we were both in those decisions together. But I never got to live out a life where I discovered a sense of who I truly was meant to be. That is until I had you."

She's looking down into the sink now, into all the muck and mess from dinner.

"You are who I was meant to become—as you are now, Campbell. You're self-sufficient, and you have a good head on your shoulders. You're driven. You don't take no for an answer, you don't take shit from anyone, and you make things happen. You are who I dreamed of becoming when I came here with your father."

My mom takes a breath.

"You know, I think marrying him and staying with him long after I should have left... tainted everything in me. It made me feel small and made me weak. And I wholeheartedly regret that. I regret a lot of that part of my life. I just didn't want that to be you. I saw you here with that ex of yours. I saw the bruises on your arms. I saw the heavy makeup under your eyes, and I felt like I saw the last fifteen, twenty years of my own life flash in front of me. Every time I saw you, I saw a little bit of me. And that scared me. I'm sorry if I'm not entirely the mom you deserve. Then, or now. Coming to me is something you can always do, even if it doesn't feel comfortable."

"Mom..."

"No, let me finish," she says. She closes the dishwasher and starts it up.

"I look at you now, all grown up. And I honestly couldn't be prouder of you. I think back to when you were here, suffering after everything that happened with you and Nate..."

Mom says his name, something we always said we would never do again as if saying it would give it all life again.

"You got the chance to leave. You knew in your heart you needed to leave. No one else needed to tell you that. If I had tried, I don't think you would have listened. I think I wish I had had that type of strength." Her voice gets lower. "Nate is long gone. He's in your past. You've moved on beautifully from that. Look at you now. *That* is what I'm proud of."

My heart has gone still, and my lungs expand with air. I don't even notice the tears in my eyes until she finally says, "Baby, don't cry."

And it's at this very moment I run to my mom's shoulder and cry on it as I've never cried before, Piper right under both of us.

Rule Number Seventeen

Sorrow and celebration can coexist.

- a wise friend of mine

Why is it we give grace so easily to everyone but ourselves?

Over the past year, life has tugged and pulled at every aspect of my being. Emotionally, it's wrecked my world. Some of it has been good, some of it not so good. And if not for that one shitty year before, where would I be now?

The next morning, I pull out of my mom's driveway, beginning the trek back to Salter's Ridge, back to the happiness I keep telling everyone about. The happiness I keep telling myself I deserve. The hours alone in the car with Piper leaves plenty of time for me to sing botched lyrics with her cuddled on my lap. It took me a whole year to realize Imagine Dragons was singing "Radioactive" instead of "Ready to rock you..."

Windows down, the wind blowing through our messy hair, we are *ready* to go home. Mom and I chatted for a while in front of the refrigerator light, eating ice cream on the floor, sharing a spoon, talking about life.

After we figured the drama of the night was over, and we moved on from our conversation about my daughterly need for affirmation in my successes, my mother gave me thirty years worth of love and acceptance in thirty minutes. I told her about the guy I'd met. The guy named Bishop Graham.

A charmer. A guy who holds the door open for me and for Piper too. I told her about the night we met on the stoop of my bookshop, under the strands of lights hanging above us, light snow falling from the gray sky. I told her about our dinner at The Bodega and how we laughed so hard during our half-completed game of twenty questions. I told her about the nightmare he had. But he's also a guy that reads in bed with me and tells me how beautiful I am in sweats, with my hair all in a mess. I let her know that I think there is something worth telling that he's hiding.

On the floor, I asked her if it was possible, crazy even, to be able to feel love for someone, even if you hardly know them.

"Mom, did you ever feel that way when you were with dad?" I asked as our shadows danced on the walls like sparkling lights on a Christmas tree.

"Honey, don't ever compare a relationship you're in with mine and your father's. That relationship, that was a shit-show. We're done with shit-shows, remember?"

We laughed harder than we'd ever laughed before.

"What is it that you think he's hiding from you?" she asks.

"I think it has something to do with his time in the military. He's alluded to something terrible happening. I just don't know what that something is. I know that whatever it is, it's going to affect him for the rest of his life." I take a breath. "I just don't know how we can continue to move forward in whatever the future holds if he can't even tell me what it is."

My mom is quiet for a moment.

"I think we all have something we keep hidden from others. Sometimes, you have to realize, Campbell, that it may not be such a bad thing. Maybe he's trying to protect you from something or trying to shield you from something that would only hurt you by knowing the truth."

Wow, I never thought of it like that. What if what Bishop doesn't want to talk about is just so tragic that it doesn't help either of us by being out in the world? Maybe he's not ready to share what has happened because it's already hurt too many people. This thought changes things for me.

"Thank you, mom."

Her wisdom is another thing I didn't know I was missing out on.

Hours later, I stop for gas and let Piper out for a walk to stretch our legs.

"I love you, sweet girl," I say to Piper.

She looks up at me, wagging her tail, her eyes cloudy with the sunlight shining into them.

Just then, my phone buzzes in my back pocket. I look at the screen, smile, and touch the button to accept the call.

"So, how did visiting with your favorite dictator go?" Anders asks. I wish I were already back at Luca's having a cup of hot coffee, sitting with my best friend.

"Well, where do I begin?"

I think back to the moment my mother told me she was proud of me, when she told me there wasn't anyone in the world prouder than she.

"Anders, would you believe me if I told you it actually wasn't so bad?"

Silence on the other end of the line.

"Really? Well, shit, where's the fun in that?"

"No, honestly. I mean, we had a nice family meal, for the most part. Granted, Nate and dating, or my lack thereof, came up, which led to some pretty awkward conversations in front of everyone.

Other than that, I literally told my mom what I needed from our relationship. We talked, and deep too. And now, hopefully, things will improve."

Not that I want to have to tell her every time I need her to say motherly things, but we have to start somewhere.

"You know, moms are funny. They're tricky. Some are easy, and some are difficult. Your mom, though, grew up entirely different from what we are accustomed to. Being understanding of that can only help you both, right?"

"Okay, who are you? And what did you do with my dramatic best friend? Why are you so wise all of a sudden?"

"One of us needs to be mature sometimes. All I'm saying is you can't go the rest of your life being angry or upset at your mom for something she has no idea she's even doing. Ask yourself, are you each doing your best?"

I think about that for a moment. I think back to all the times my mom and I misunderstood each other, thinking we were always on the defensive, always against each other. It's hard to imagine a world where that isn't the case, but I can see now how it's possible. I got a glimpse of it last night.

A cow *moos* in the background as I walk back to my car to finish our drive home. It's twenty degrees cooler here as we make our way back up north, and my thin cardigan offers little help against the chill. It's freezing.

"Were those *actual* cattle, Campbell? Where the hell are you?" Anders asks. "If you're gone any longer, I'm sending out the renegade."

It's just about dark when we arrive home after what seemed like the longest drive ever. The car inched forward. The drive home is never as quick as I'd like it to be coming home, especially after an exhausting night.

I open my door and lug my bags and Piper out of the car, and as I walk up the sidewalk and open the gate to my walk-up, I notice someone in a dark hoodie, jeans, and ball cap pulled down over his eyes, sitting on the steps.

"Holy *shit*, what the hell is up with you and scaring the life out of me?" I take a step back, exasperated. "How long have you been sitting here, Bishop?"

He smiles.

"Since Anders told me you were on your way home. So, a few hours."

"You could have called," I say.

"I hate phones," he says.

I believe him. Since meeting him, he's never texted or called me. He's only come by the shop, met me for coffee, or written letters.

"A bit old-fashioned, don't you think?"

I move to open my door.

"So, what's up?" Bishop asks.

"What's up? I just got home from an exhausting trip to my mother's. If it's okay with you, I'm going to take my things upstairs, run a bath, and drown myself in my sorrows."

"That bad, huh?"

I think on that for a moment, save for being *too* dramatic.

"Well, no, actually. I think I'm just used to feeling that way when coming back from being there. She actually wasn't too bad this time around. We had a long conversation about life and relationships. And about you."

I wait for his reaction. He's quiet, and his eyebrows raise ever so slightly.

"Listen, Campbell. It's been weeks of us avoiding each other. I hate that. Can't we talk about what happened?"

"Oh, now you want to talk, Bishop?"

I hear the hypocrisy in my question. Stubbornness is one of my strongest and weakest characteristics. I can play this card all day. Should I? No. But, here we are. It seems I want to keep this stupid argument dragging, only wanting it to end on my terms.

"Campbell. I know you're upset with me. I hope that I can sit with you one day and be as open with you as you could possibly want. Even *more* than you want." He's begging again like he did the night we first met. "I cannot stop thinking about you. I miss you. I see your house from the station every shift. It's absolute torture."

I've missed him too—more than he could possibly imagine. I don't tell him that, of course. I, too, see the station from the house every flipping day. Torture doesn't even begin to describe it. Does he know what it took for me not to walk Piper *toward* the station every morning instead of the opposite way?

I don't tell him how handsome he looks here on my doorstep, and how I wish I could kiss him, and how I've missed his soft lips on mine after all these weeks of silence.

I put my key into my door and push it open.

"Yes, I'm glad you realize I'm mad at you. I'm glad you want to talk. But, that 'someday' is not tonight, Bishop. I'm tired. Look, I'll see you around, okay?"

I can't pretend I'm fine with waiting around anymore. Silence is dangerous. It plagues a person. But tonight, it's all I want. And with that, I close the door, leaving Bishop outside with the millions of sorrows he, and now I, can't seem to let go of.

————

The following morning, I slowly wake to Piper cuddled at my side, buried under the blankets like coffee under whipped cream. After my bath last night, I hopped in bed and fell asleep reading one of my favorite genres this time of year calls for—Hallmark romance. It's trash reading, and it's so lovely. The drama, the unrealistic love, the games played. It's what I live for.

I want to take one more day off from the shop to catch up on sleep, but I can't keep it closed any longer. Two days is plenty enough. I called Sophie last week and asked if she could meet me there this morning to start working some hours, preparing for Christmas and the weeks that come after that. It'll be here before we know it. These next few days will be insane and very busy with customers coming in to do any last-minute shopping. Afterward, things will slow down, but until then, it's go-time.

I get dressed, leash up Piper, and move as quickly as our legs will carry us to Luca's. Even two days away from here is too long.

I pull open the door, and I'm immediately back to a few weeks ago when all was semi-okay in the world, when life was peachy, when Bishop and I were falling for each other.

I walk to the front and notice something in the air.

"Leave again, and I'll kill you."

I turn around and almost slip on the geometric tile Anders picked out years ago before catching myself.

"Oh shit, I'm so sorry!"

Anders laughs, and I punch him in the arm.

"Hi. Can I get a couple of coffees to go? I'm meeting Sophie at the shop this morning."

"Oh, wow. She decided to come back?" he asks this like it's a bad thing.

When I was her age, I would have killed to work in a bookshop.

"Anders, I need the help. Desperately. I need to go through all of the back stock and rearrange a few things on the floor to put up a giant Christmas tree."

Hell, I might need two people if it keeps up the way it's going. I think forward to a time when I'll be able to take a weekend off.

"I'm so excited. You know how much I love Christmas."

"Who knew people still read these days? Weird."

I glare at him.

"No tip for you today, asshole."

We share a laugh as I put a $5 bill in the jar by the register.

Before I move to turn around to head out the door, I do a double-take at the menu.

"Hey, nice to see someone added a Gingerbread Latte to the menu. About damn time."

In the year I've been in Salter's Ridge, I've learned many things. One is that I can build a life for myself relative to the dreams I had years ago. Those dreams don't have to be put on hold any longer than I want them to be. They can sit on the shelf, or they can fly off the shelf. They can lie stagnant. They can also accept risk and reap a reward. When I ask myself what holds me back from achieving anything in life, I realize it's me. I'm what holds me back.

I came here, opened this bookshop, and found I'm free if I want to be. I can leave, I can stay, I can *be*. To ask someone why they leave, why they stay, why they *are*: It's all relative. Our perception of circumstance changes depending on its context. It depends on the stages or seasons of life. Wisdom, things we have gone through, and age, it all changes relativity. Don't you agree?

When I arrive at Turning Pages, I see her there, waiting for me. Sophie. My savior.

"Well, hello stranger! Long time, no see." I move in to give her a solid hug, holding on to her for a few moments. "I'm so thankful you could help out this week. Lord knows I need it!"

When I think of all the books about to be given as gifts, I almost hyperventilate. Is there anything better than books gifted for *any* holiday?

"Thank you for having me back. Being here in this shop, it's just amazing. Lots of work, don't get me wrong. But, still fun."

I smile at her, thankful for such a loyal employee, even now after all this time. I don't deserve her, to be honest.

"You're not mad at me for having to let you go for a little bit?" I ask.

"I understand, lady! Don't worry. I actually left for school for a little while and took a few classes in the city. I'm glad to be back home, though. That city life is not for me."

I can resonate with that.

"Well, I really missed the company, that's for sure. Anyway, are you ready? I've got a few things already on my list that we need to tackle before we get bombarded with online orders this week. I'm sure everyone and their grandmother is going to be out looking for last-minute stocking stuffers. What better way to shop late than with the small guy, right?"

Or so I think in my head.

"Number one on the list: Clean out the back room and pull everything onto the floor that we can sell. We have to do it strategically because I really want to fit a Christmas tree in here. I want to decorate it and put a tree skirt and some books under it."

I put on a Christmas playlist, strike a match, and light my favorite Fraser Fir candle from Birch Hill Candle Co.—absolute heaven. I put the candle safely in the middle of the counter at the cash wrap, and we both move to the back storage area. It's dark back here, so we turn on a few lights.

"Whoa, you sure have built up your inventory since I've last been in,"

Sophie says.

I'm thrilled that she has noticed.

"Yeah. I have had such a great time in the shop lately. You should see it: People are coming in from all over to shop. It's been a great last few months."

Suddenly, I'm anchored here, in this moment, lost in what I've created. So much can be said for someone who shares their pain with others in the hopes of a better sunrise and a better sunset. Here, I've found a *home*. I've found peace in these four walls. This bookshop is everything to me. And then, I think about Benny. About how he has yet to call me or respond to my email for that matter—I think of that letter to Benny marked in red ink: URGENT.

I'm pulled from my daydreaming when Sophie accidentally knocks over a stack of books. I need to focus on getting all of these on the floor.

"We should probably take all the Christmas books that we have left out there first and make piles out front. There's room in the front window too—no sense in making it look too fancy. I'm sure they will go fast. And besides, there aren't too many of those remaining."

I grab a ton of my favorites and pile them onto the book cart. We take what we have to the front, disperse them all, and head back to do it all again. We do this for a few hours, helping customers in between trips.

"Thank you for coming in! Have a Merry Christmas, Mrs. Harrison."

I smile as I finish checking out one of my favorite regulars, my sweet neighbor.

"You sure did find some amazing books. I hope your grandchildren love them."

Once again, I envy Mrs. Harrison and her seemingly simple life—Shopping for books bundled up, strolling the streets in such a pretty town on a chilly night, not a care in the world. Suddenly, she breaks into my thoughts.

"I hear you've been cozying up with my good friend Eleanor's grandson. Bishop Graham?"

She winks, and I'm slightly caught off guard.

"What? No, I don't cozy up with anyone but my dog, Mrs. Harrison. You know that."

Jesus, news travels around here faster than I thought. I wink at her and nod over to Piper for proof.

"All I know is you better be careful around that one. He's a catch. Don't get yourself too caught up unless you want to end up with a ring on your finger."

I choke a bit on the saliva in my mouth. "Excuse me?" I laugh because hearing her say that is a bit ridiculous.

"All I'm saying is that boy was a hell-raiser back in the day, but I'll be damned if I didn't think you two would make the prettiest babies!"

I roll my eyes. We've only just met. What is up with older generations pressuring the younger to start families? When did this become a thing? Also, when will it end?

"Okay, Mrs. Harrison, I think you've forgotten to take your medicine or something. That or you have too much vodka in your cup... We are hardly dating these days. Actually, I don't even know if you would call it that anymore."

She grabs her bags on the counter, hands now full. I follow behind her to the door, opening it up for her.

"It's never too early, or too late, for a sip of happy liquid. Or at least, that's what I say." She winks. "I hope you have the merriest of Christmases also, Campbell. Take care. And just remember, love comes in all different shapes. And sizes."

She laughs so hard I think she might have a stroke in my bookshop, so I shoo her ass out. I'm still smiling as I close the door behind her, shivering a bit at the cold draft that just flew in when I hear Sophie say something from the back room.

"Campbell, come in here," Sophie calls from the back.

I rush back, Piper hopping out of her bed too.

"What? What is it? Are you okay?"

I all but trip into the back room.

"You're going to want to see this."

She hands me a large decorative box with a lid on top that lifts off a smidgeon as she hands it to me.

"What the hell is this?" I ask.

I take the box. I've never seen it before until now.

"Where did you find this?" I ask her, looking down at the box. "It's not mine. It must be Benny's."

I set the box down on the floor because heavy doesn't even begin to describe it. My heart is racing. For what? I'm not sure.

"Where did you find this?" I ask her again, looking at her now with wide eyes.

"It was hidden behind a few stacks of books. I didn't even realize what it was until I moved all of the thrillers to that shelf over there, and there it was." Her eyes are full of excitement. "It must have been left here when Benny moved all of his stuff out after letting you lease the place."

I stare down at the box, lifting the lid out of curiosity, and I look inside.

"Well! What's in it?" She leans over, trying to see what's inside.

It takes me a moment to catch my breath, to realize what I'm holding in my hands.

"Sophie, thanks for all of your help today. I think I've got it from here, okay? I'll see you tomorrow?"

She must know from the look in my eyes that right now, I just need space. She locks up behind her, leaving Piper and me alone, Christmas music playing in the background.

Rule Number Eighteen

Be brave in everything you do. In the end, it's bravery that saves you.

Woodland News
November 2, 2009

Local Hero Returns Home After Tour in Helmand Province, Afghanistan

Last week, Combat Marine Bishop Graham, 20, returned to Woodland from a seven-month tour, in support of Operation Enduring Freedom. This was his first deployment to Afghanistan. Although he declined to give an interview, with permission, his grandparents, Thomas and Eleanor Graham, agreed to have a few words with us. "We could not be prouder of the man Bishop has become. He always said he wanted to be a Marine. He joined right out of high school and followed Thomas's footsteps. We can't thank him enough for his bravery and service. We are just heartbroken at the news of the death of his friend, Foster. I cannot even imagine what he must be going through. Our thoughts and sympathy are with his family," Mrs. Graham shares.

Foster Jackson, Graham's best friend, was gravely injured when their unit came under fire in the Helmand Province just days after their arrival. Because Graham was not injured in that incident, he administered first aid to Jackson before medics arrived. Jackson did not regain consciousness and had been pronounced deceased shortly after. His body was later returned to his family in the United States for proper burial at Arlington Cemetery. Thereafter, it had been discovered that Graham and his unit would endure several more dangerous firefights after the transport of Jackson's body, lasting several weeks in length. There were many efforts to gain control of the Taliban, leading to an expansive loss of life for their unit. Their deployment is said to have been the largest helicopter invasion since Vietnam.

"We are thankful for his return. We know many families didn't get that comfort. There are many days of healing ahead, but we are sure glad to have him home," Graham's grandmother told us.

After this interview, the family wished for continued privacy for Bishop as he grieves the loss of his friend.

———

Salter's Ridge Tribune
September 14, 2011

Local Marine Returns Home After Second Tour to Afghanistan

Bishop Graham, 22, returns to Salter's Ridge from his second deployment to Afghanistan.

Eleanor Graham, Bishop's grandmother, sat down with us once again, as she did two years ago on behalf of Bishop Graham and the rest of her family. She is the wife of the late Thomas Graham, local businessman and former owner of Chapters, the bookshop and printing company on Main Street. Mr. Graham sadly passed away just days ago, before Bishop could make it home.

"My grandson, he's an angel, coming back here to take care of me. I don't know what I would do without him now that Thomas is gone. I cannot thank Bishop enough for his bravery and his service after all this time. Thomas would have been so proud of him." Just after graduating high school, Bishop enlisted in the United States Marine Corps in the hopes of following in his grandfather's footsteps. Thomas, a mortarman in the Korean War, served honorably and earned the National Defense Service Medal. He was very proud to be a United States Marine Corps veteran. After being honorably discharged from the service, and being the lover of reading that he was, Thomas opened Chapters, a

S. C. Gray

local bookshop and printing company, which served his community for twenty years before closing its doors a year ago when Thomas was diagnosed with a terminal illness.

―――――

MAINE HARBOR CHRONICLES

Space for Rent

Vacant: available immediately. The space is 1,500 sq. ft. Prime location. Original wood floors and functional fireplace. Beautiful floor-to-ceiling built-ins. Curb-side parking. Perfect space for a bookshop.

―――――

Something like unadulterated sadness, confusion, and shock overcomes me as I position myself here on the floor in the back room of the bookshop.

Splayed out in front of me are some of the contents from a large dusty box. Inside, there are dozens of newspaper clippings, letters, and military uniform metals. Everything inside seems to be part of a puzzle, the mystery that is Bishop—a war veteran, a Marine. And apparently, the grandson of a former bookshop owner? I'm just now learning of Bishop's past life for the first time. I sit for hours sifting through everything. There is so much here to process.

I reach inside the box, finding many black and white photos, grainy

218

from years of wear from someone holding and touching them time and time again, memorizing them.

I flip one over and it reads "*T. Graham, Christmas Day, 1953.*" In perfectly pressed Dress Blues, Bishop's grandfather's enlisted dress cap is tilted just slightly to his right. His wide smile of white, straight teeth that match Bishop's smile to a T. They look so much alike.

Here I sit, in Turning Pages, which was once called Chapters. Bishop's grandfather owned a bookshop in this very space. How could he not have told me? My mind flashes back to when Bishop first came into the shop. "My grandfather would have loved this place," I heard him whisper. And now I know why.

I think back to my email to Benny, the one that is still unanswered. Had Benny possibly inherited this building? It's sat empty since Chapters closed ten years ago. Bishop must know Benny. They must be related somehow. An uncle, maybe?

Stunned from all that is here to unravel, I look at everything in front of me. Years' worth of memories, collected by someone, kept here for safekeeping? Maybe forgotten altogether?

Before even thinking twice, I grab the box, gather everything on the floor and gently place the items back inside. I move to put the lid back on the box, but not before realizing one of the photos sticking out keeps it from closing completely.

I pull it out gently and quickly realize it's a younger version of Bishop. His arm is thrown around someone that looks to be about the same age. Both men are laughing into the sky at some unknown thing. I flip it over and it says *"Bishop & Foster. Boys of Summer, 2008. Parris Island|Boot Camp."*

In a few short months, everything has changed. Nothing would be the same. I place the photo on top of the rest of the items in the box and head to the only place I know to go right now.

Rule Number Nineteen

Never trust anyone who has a TV bigger than their book collection.

Everything is within walking distance from the bookshop. It's one of the things I adore about Salter's Ridge. After dropping Piper off at the house, I grab my thickest coat and decide some fresh air is much needed.

After texting Mrs. Harrison with what was undoubtedly a very ominous (and creepy) message asking for information about her best friend, I arrive by foot at the front of what is presumably Bishop's grandmother's home.

After Sophie's discovery in the back room of the bookshop, I figured by reasonable logic that this box must belong to the Grahams. Years of dust and grime covered the box, and who else would have had access to that back room besides Thomas, Bishop's grandfather, and his wife, Eleanor? After the shop closed for good, I assumed it was just left behind. Forgotten.

I stand at the street now, waiting on the sidewalk, holding the damn thing like something out of a movie. What am I even doing here? I'm unsure of what I will even say. I take a deep breath and make my way toward the door. It's now or never.

The front porch is beautiful, expansive, painted white, and has large pillars that hold up the front of the house. Plus, it has fresh wreaths hanging from the outside of every window visible from the street. Christmas is just a few days away. As I walk up the steps, I notice there is a bronze sign hanging to the left of the door:

THOMAS L. GRAHAM HOUSE

1882

BUILT BY THE FISCHER ARCHITECT FIRM

HISTORIC SALTER'S RIDGE FOUNDATION, INC.

I knock firmly twice, aware of the missing doorbell. Historic homes can't be changed too much from the exterior, or so I've heard. When my knocking goes unanswered, I bang a little bit harder. The house is so large, and I imagine it must be hard for her to hear anything if she were on the opposite end of it. Just before I give up and turn back toward the street, I hear the latch unlock, and the door pulls open to a beautifully decorated foyer. The ceiling must reach at least twenty feet. An enormous crystal chandelier hangs above, throwing mirrored shadows on the walls.

"Hello... Mrs. Graham?" I ask, unsure if she's who I'm looking for.

She's younger-looking than I imagined. Her hair is up in a classic chignon bun, and even though it's getting late, she's still dressed in lovely, pressed slacks and a cashmere sweater with a silk scarf thrown over her shoulders. The backdrop of a winding staircase to a wide landing is charming.

"Hello, dear. Can I help you?"

Her eyes pan down to the box in my hands.

"Hi, yes. I'm looking for Mrs. Graham?"

"That's me. How can I help you, dear?"

She has a wide and welcoming smile on her face.

"My name is Campbell. Campbell Harrison. I was wondering, you see. I found this box, and I, um. I own Turning Pages..."

I'm nervous for a variety of reasons. She smiles.

"Ah. You're THE Campbell. So, you're the one who's swept my sweet grandson off his feet."

She steps back to allow room for me to step inside.

"Come in, come in, dear," she says.

I wouldn't dare tell her no. She seems like someone who commands a room and doesn't take no for an answer, no matter how welcoming her smile is.

Before I know it, she's leading me into a very large office space off the main entryway, just behind a set of huge iron and glass double doors. Once inside, I take in my surroundings.

223

My eyes are immediately drawn to the massive library that surrounds us along all four walls of the room. The shelves go from the floor to the ceiling. Hundreds, maybe thousands of spines are leather with gold etchings visible. Collectibles. And, there is a ladder. There is a very tall ladder.

She gestures for me to sit on one of the worn-in unmatching brown sofas that face one another. An immense neutral rug is under them, and they are placed next to a wide fireplace painted a cerulean blue. Above it, a modern painting signed by the artist leans on the original mantel. Bronze sconces light each side. She sits across from me, a large wooden coffee table topped with dozens of coffee table books separating us.

"Wow, Mrs. Graham. This place is spectacular," I say in awe.

"Call me Eleanor. You know, I tried to tell the designer the balance between modern and historical better be kosher. I think she did an all right job of it." She gives me a familiar wink. "But, thank you. It's been in the family for generations. This room is, of course, our favorite," she says with a spark of pride.

I have a feeling she's referencing her late husband.

"Of course, it is. I could live in here. It's lovely."

"Would you like something to drink? Tea, perhaps?"

"No, no, thank you. That's so kind of you to offer. I actually can't stay long. I've got to get back to my dog." I'm aware I'm looking for any excuse not to overstay my welcome. "I wanted to bring this by." I place a hand on top of the box. "I found it in the back room of the bookshop. I think it belongs to your family."

She looks at the box.

"Hmm... I see. That old box—it belonged to my husband, Thomas." She speaks just like it was yesterday that she had last seen it. "I know he used to find articles on Bishop, some from all over the country, the world, sometimes. He would clip them or print them off. He collected them. Yes, he was so proud." She smiles, her eyes filled with what I sense is a little bit of sadness mixed with pride. "I sure do miss him. I appreciate you bringing it by. There are a lot of memories there in that old thing, I'm sure." Eleanor moves around the table, glancing over at it.

"May I?" she asks like it's mine to give.

"Of course. Please do."

I push the box toward her.

She opens the lid, puts a hand to her chest, and lifts the photo of Bishop and Foster from the box, the same one I had placed back in right before leaving the shop.

"Eleanor, the reason I'm here, and I apologize if I'm a bother. You can tell me to leave, and I would understand. But, not knowing very much about Bishop, you are the closest thing I know to any chance of clarity."

I'm desperate. Bishop has had so many chances to explain. It's hard for me to fully understand what he's been through. And maybe I never will. But I'm willing to try anything at this point. Maybe his grandmother can give me some insight. And not the watered-down version. Hoping she is willing to shed some light on him, I take a deep breath.

"I think I'm starting to fall for your grandson, Eleanor. And I'll be honest, I know it's all happening so fast, and things are starting to blend, and time isn't stopping for anybody. Before things between us go any further, I need to know if there is anything concerning about Bishop that I should know about. I hope I don't sound like I'm reaching and going into territories I don't belong. But, if this is what I think it is, if the feelings I'm having for Bishop are mutual, I want to understand who he was before he met me."

It all pours out so quickly, and I don't even take a breath in between any of the words. When I look up to meet her eyes, she's grinning at me. She reaches over and gently places her hand on mine.

"Campbell, dear. My grandson hasn't been the same since the night he met you. Before you, everything was black. Dark. This light you bring to Bishop shines on his face. You can see right through him. You can see the change in everything he does. I know, in my heart, he cares so deeply for you. And I know you care for him too. I can tell because you came here. You want answers. Answers, though, I'm afraid that must come from him. I know you say time... it's flying by, but time is all we have. Time to make amends, time to gather thoughts, and then time to share them. I urge you, dear, to give him time. Patience is something I live without as well. I'm a stubborn old woman. I know patience is hard to come by. But time. You must give it to him. Let him rest. Let him be. He's been through a lot. You saw what was in the box. It's been a hard time for all of us over the years. He will come to you. In his own time."

"But..." I begin, but she gently cuts me off.

"You know, he called us that night. After Foster had been killed. He said he couldn't talk long, but he told us he loved us. Assured us that he was okay. I could tell from his shaking voice that he was far from okay. Thomas got on the phone with him, told him to be brave. Told him to trust in the decisions he was making, not to second guess anything, not even for a moment. For me, it was hard, because, on one hand, I'm thankful Foster wasn't alone and that he had Bishop there with him. On the other, Bishop changed that day, forever. He will never be the same, and my heart hurts at that. I hurt for him. Even after all this time, it's like it'll never cease. That hurt. It's stayed with all of us. Foster was family, and the day he was killed out there, I think we all died a little too."

Tears threaten to spill over as we are sitting on the sofa together, facing one another.

"I'm so sorry, Eleanor. And of course, I knew something terrible had happened. Bishop let on that much. I can imagine it all being so hard to talk about. I want him to have someone to talk to, and I don't understand why he feels like it can't be me. I won't judge him."

"Darling, that man has seen and done so much. He made decisions there with his friends that we cannot begin to comprehend. He has seen and done things no man should have to do. We know you won't judge him. But, maybe it's a matter of how he thinks you may see him after that frightens him. He must feel guilt, right? I take it you should know that much. That guilt will eat at him forever. He thinks he should have been able to save Foster. In his mind, he had Foster's life in his hands that day. Bishop got to come home to his family, but he didn't bring everyone back. That deployment was recognized by leaders in our country—our President, even. Movies and documentaries have been made about it. It was horrific what they went through."

I listen intently as she continues.

"Bishop and his friends went there to fight for our country, naive to what that really, truly meant. Those men deserve everything—all of our respect. You should know, he was in charge of the entire unit for that deployment. He was their section leader, but it was every man for himself when they came under attack. Still, in Bishop's mind, he was supposed to protect them. And even though we see him as brave, courageous, admirable... I think all he sees and feels now is the guilt. That's it. For a long while, he was here trying to take care of me, when he should have been taking care of himself. He could only go to the grocery store if it was before 8 a.m. He couldn't be in crowds. He could hardly be around people. He would sit here, go to work, come back and go nowhere in between.

The time right after he came home was the hardest, I think. All of his friends that made it home had a hard time adjusting to this life again. Bishop had a few dear friends that just couldn't take the guilt. They couldn't handle it. Of course, who could? Living in a constant nightmare they could never wake from. And when they're alone with their thoughts, it's damning.

The struggles one must try to overcome don't end overseas. They follow servicemembers home like a plague they cannot be rid of. They deal with one struggle, and then another arises, right? Bishop had to block everything out because to feel so much weight is crushing. It built until there was nothing left of him."

She seems to understand it all so well and I'm left reeling.

"But then, Campbell, he met you. And it was like that dark cloud was lifted. You changed it all for him. He talks about you... I've never heard him chatter about anyone so fondly. He's brighter, and he smiles more. You help him see the beauty in things that aren't that shiny. You help him realize there is more to life than your past. Hell, he's even reading again. He used to love reading. I haven't seen him read in a long time."

This admission electrifies me.

"You think he's reading again because of me?"

Could that be true?

"Oh, I know he's reading again because of you. He wants to do things that you love, and he wants to open up and talk to you about things. Maybe, just not about this."

A sudden melancholy comes over me.

"I know I will never be able to fully understand this part of his life. It's all so new to me. But I am willing to do what it takes to help him along the way, whatever that may look like."

I sit back. I've never had to deal with anything like this before. I used to think my issues with my mom and my stupid ex were bad, but really? What could be worse than losing your best friend in such a tragic and life-altering way? And then, to have it happen so quickly, shortly upon arrival, only to have to fight for seven more months with a clear mind? Impossible. I cannot imagine it. And not to mention all of the life-or-death decision-making moments that led up to their departure. They had firefights for weeks on end sometimes. How exhausting.

"Listen, dear, I can tell something in Bishop has changed recently, and it's because of his time spent with you. My friend, Mrs. Harrison, told me you two have been dating, and when I heard that, I just thought to myself, well, that explains a whole lot," she says as she laughs through her tears.

"I'm happy he's found someone like you, dear. Someone who actually cares. But, as I had to figure out with my dear Thomas before he died, let Bishop express his love for you in his own way. With kisses, his gift-giving. Let him hold you. Let him read the books you like to read. He will show you he's all in, in his own way. He will love you right and take care of you in his own way. Just because he doesn't talk to you about this, doesn't mean he doesn't love you. It just means you're not someone who was on that deployment with him. Because let's face it, only they truly know how to comfort one another in these instances. Only they can truly understand.

There is a fragile line between saving lives and trying to save your own. All we can do for them is be here for them when they fall. And help pick them back up."

Rule Number Twenty

Don't hold a grudge.

"I really hope that you'll join us for our annual Christmas tree lighting. It's on Christmas Eve."

Eleanor stands up from her side of the couch and smooths her pants with her hands.

"It's right here in front of the house. The Historical Association always brings in a freshly cut tree. There is normally a great turnout."

"I would really love that. It sounds like a wonderful tradition," I say.

"It's a whole ordeal. Everyone comes, there are carolers, food is catered. It's very Gatsby-ish, actually. But without the shootings and people being run over, of course. And Bishop will be there too…"

She grins.

"Oh, then I have to come, don't I?"

We laugh, and she walks me to the door. The thought of starting new traditions here in Salter's Ridge, especially ones that involve Bishop and his family, gets me excited. I just need to straighten things out with him first.

"I really appreciate you sitting down with me tonight. I feel much better about everything going on. Bishop and I have known each other for just a short time, but I know there is something between us," I say.

I sound like I'm trying to convince even myself.

"I think there is too, dear. I'll see you at the tree lighting, Campbell."

And once again, I don't think she will take no for an answer.

We wave goodbye, and as she closes the door, I let out a deep breath. Having left the box with Mrs. Graham, I feel a sense of relief wash over me. Like I'm suddenly washed clean of all the information it contained. It would be a lot to hold on to.

I start my trek home into the night as quickly as my out-of-shape legs will carry me. The wind is blustering off the harbor, and I pull my coat tighter to my body. I wonder how long it takes to get acclimated to winter weather in Maine. It's absolutely freezing, and I hurt all over, down into my bones. Piper would have surely died out here had I not left her at home tonight.

I walk swiftly, huffing and puffing. I turn onto my street, lit by classic black and iron streetlights. I see a familiar face walking toward me. His shift has probably just turned over at the fire station.

"Hey, you," I say with a smile on my face.

"Oh, hi."

It's like Bishop sees me for the first time in years, surprised I'm still hanging around.

I point behind him. "Did you just get off from work? I actually just came from your grandmother's house," I offer cheerfully.

"Yikes. Hopefully, she was nice to you. She's a bit much to handle sometimes."

"Well, she loved me... so, there's that."

I grin and he offers me a slight smile.

"Of course she did. Who wouldn't?"

There's a tangible silence.

"Wait, why were you visiting with my grandmother anyway?" he asks.

"Do you have a few minutes? I'm just heading back to my house. I could make us a pot of coffee?" I ask, hopeful he will agree to come inside, out of the cold, so we can finally talk.

Surprisingly, he accepts.

We walk side by side to my porch, and as I unlock the front door, Piper is there to greet us as we walk in with me in front. Piper full-on bypasses me, runs straight for Bishop, and hops on her hind legs, begging to be pet. She's barking and panting and hopping around. I look on, amazed that she can show so much love and affection toward him after all this time.

"Hey, girl. You miss me?" he says to her, then looks up at me.

"I think it's safe to say we both missed you, Bishop."

He stands up and moves over to me. He stares into my eyes for just a moment, and it's all I can do not to kiss him right then and there. He caresses his thumb over my cheek, wraps his arms around me, then pulls me into his chest. I can hear his heart beating faster than the speed of light. Mine does the same. Piper looks up expectantly at both of us.

We break apart and move from the entryway to the kitchen. It's hard to believe that he and I were in this same space just a few weeks ago. Together. Coffee had been made. Books were read. And then, the unexpected took over.

"Well, the place hasn't changed much," he observes.

"Considering it's been just a few weeks, I don't think it should have changed at all."

"I would have thought that since having me in your bed, lots would have changed. For you, at least. Earth-shattering, am I right?"

He wiggles his eyebrows up and down and smiles off in the other direction.

"If you call me getting more action from your dog that night than from you, then yes, one hundred percent. Ground-breaking."

A belly laugh comes from each of us.

There are a few moments of silence.

"Bishop, I should have never walked away from you when I saw you on the porch the night I came back from my mom's. I realize now, at that moment, how hypocritical it was to continue asking for you to be open with me about your past, and there I was, closing the door quite literally on you as you tried with me, for once. I want to apologize for that. I shouldn't have been that way."

"I appreciate the apology, but I understand. That's not to say I enjoyed it. The things I've been through don't take away from the things you've been through, Campbell. You have every right to be angry with me."

"But do I, though? Why should I force you to talk with me about things you don't want to? If you have to keep it in, then so be it. I don't want it to have to be that way, but if that is what it takes for us to be together, for us to move forward somehow, then that's what I'll do."

"No, I get it. Trust me. I need to try better. I *will* do better. I never want to make you feel like I'm keeping things from you. It's not like that."

"Look, I found something at the bookshop when I was cleaning out the back room last night. Well actually, Sophie found it. But, that's beside the point."

He looks at me with good intentions but breaks my thoughts.

"Can we please make coffee first? This conversation sounds like I'll need coffee." I laugh a little.

"Yes, of course." I move to the cabinet, make a pot of coffee, and get out the cream and sugar and two white mugs. With the pot brewing away, I stand a few feet away from him. The way the kitchen light hits his face casts a shadow, giving him a somewhat perplexing look. Once enough coffee is ready to fill a cup for each of us, I fill both, handing one cup to him.

"Mmm... much better. As you were..."

"Oh, yeah. I found something in the bookshop. Something that belonged to your grandfather, Thomas. You never told me he owned a bookshop, Bishop. You know, in the building where mine currently is."

I eyeball him, giving him a chance to explain why he never mentioned it.

"Ah. Yes, grandad did own a bookshop there. That's correct."

He says this nonchalantly like it's no big deal at all.

"And... you didn't think that would be information worth sharing?"

"Why? What would the fun in that be? I loved seeing you in the shop with no connection to me. Seeing you in your element with no expectations was like breathing. I needed it. I loved having that to myself. Like I said, I'm selfish. I guess that does seem like something of importance when you say it like that. I would have told you eventually."

He smiles, then takes a large gulp of his coffee.

"Anything else you're hiding from me?" I ask him.

"I told my grandmother about you."

He smiles, and I smile too, but yes, I do know he told his grandmother about me. Everything she admitted to me on the couch was fuel to the fire that burns between us. And we are reigniting once again.

"So she told me," I say as my face is hot with heat. I look down into my cup.

"I haven't told my grandmother about anyone, ever."

He moves closer to me. Very close.

"And what did you say to her about me?" I whisper.

"That you're insatiable and very hard to please. And that you have a dog that is just like you."

I push him away, making him almost spill his coffee, laughing.

"Be nice. Leave Piper out of this! She's just a baby."

He sets his cup down and comes back to me, pulling me in, wrapping his large arms around my waist. He lifts me up unexpectedly onto the countertop I'm backed up against and settles his way in between my knees comfortably.

I shake my head. "What am I going to do with you, Bishop Graham?" I push his hair back with both hands and look into his eyes, waiting for him to answer.

"Whatever you want, Campbell Harrison."

I smile. Wide.

"You're a tease in the best way. I told you! The first chance you would get, you would attempt to swoon and seduce me."

"No, I said that!"

His calming laughter fills my kitchen, and I have a strange thought that I could get used to this. After a moment, though, he goes quiet. The sexual tension in the air can be cut with the sharpest of knives. Easy. Quick.

"Yeah, yeah... I'm not sure I'm the one trying to seduce the other, but who's to say?"

I shrug my shoulders.

"So, this box you found. What was in it?" he asks.

"Um, there was a lot in there. Mostly, it was stuff that had to do with... you, actually."

I say this slowly and wait for him to process what I just said. He stands back.

"Bishop, before your grandfather died, he collected things. Things like articles, pictures... things that were about you."

"What? Why would he do that?" he asks, puzzled.

"Well, he was proud of you, of course. He loved you. He clipped so many articles, Bishop. Hundreds of them, maybe. The ones I saw were about your deployments, articles about you saving women and children in

Afghanistan from horrible circumstances. Helping the men of households regain their footing, giving them resources to provide for their families. I read about your unit setting up pathways and safety nets for families. There were stories about you and your Afghan interpreter working alongside their military to train them and do things I never even knew would be part of a deployment there. I actually don't know what I expected." I pause. "Then, there were articles about you coming back here and starting over."

So much of what I saw is proof that this man standing in front of me is a living hero trying to survive after the unimaginable happened. Everything I know now, it makes sense. Why he is the way he is. Why he avoids talking about his time there. I can imagine him being hesitant in sharing any part of his life there with me.

"Campbell..."

"Bishop, I know it wasn't all good things there. I heard about the firefights. About Foster. About your time there for months after all of that happened. I know there were incidents that you'd rather not bring up, that you would rather I not bring up. I know this makes you uncomfortable. I just want you to know that I understand. I know now why that is. And I'm okay with it being left at that. I can't push you anymore. And I won't.

"Really? he asks, skeptical. "Where is the box now? Did you leave it with my grandmother?"

"Yeah, I did. I thought she would want it."

"My grandmother and grandfather were inseparable, you know. I'm sure she's just as shocked to have it as I am to hear it exists. Thank you for getting it to her. Wow."

He moves his hand down his chin.

"There was this one photo in there, Bishop. One of you with Foster," I say gently.

He's quiet again for a moment. He steps back a foot or so.

"I see."

He waits to see if I have anything to add to that.

"It was taken while you guys were in boot camp together."

He nods as he knows exactly the moment I'm referring to.

"That summer, and every summer before, were the best times of our lives."

"You guys looked so happy in the photo. Both of you were laughing, goofing off."

"I'm assuming my grandmother spoke with you about him?" he asks.

"Yes, she did, but only briefly. Listen, Bishop. I need to tell you something. I want to always be completely transparent with you."

Nervous and upside down doesn't even begin to describe the emotional roller coaster I am on. I've been on it since the moment he walked into my life.

"You can tell me anything."

He moves into me again and looks closely into my eyes with intention.

"I think I'm falling for you. Since the moment I met you, I knew there was something about you. Something I needed to grasp. Something I need to hold onto. And as time goes on, it's only growing with urgency. All my life, I've been running. I've been angry and sad. I'm complex. But, with you, I'm just none of those things. And I don't know what it is, I know we haven't been together that long, but I need to know if you feel anything close to what I'm feeling. Being apart has me realizing how much my life is missing when I'm not with you."

It's all so urgent-sounding, and I'm sure he's halfway out the door by now, but instead...

"Campbell, I told my grandmother about you."

He laughs like I'm supposed to understand the significance of that.

"I have been searching for meaning and purpose for too long. When I'm not with you, I'm thinking about you. I, too, know it hasn't been that long. We haven't experienced enough together yet. But I want that with you. I want to know that I have that to look forward to. You're interesting. You're on your own feet. You're here for me. Trust me. I want to know where we stand as well."

"Really?" I am so relieved. "I want to look forward to more time with you too."

Knowing that I could have that, no matter what happens, it's all I can ask for. I want time to figure us out, to figure him out. We hold each other's gaze before he moves his forehead to rest on mine.

"Bishop, if I could take away half of your pain, I would. I would carry it for you every single day. But I don't think I can, can I?"

"I just need you by my side, Campbell. That, right now, is enough. It's more than enough."

Knowing what I know now—about his time in the military, the struggles he faces now, and the struggles he'll face going forward... I know I just have to be here for him. Just as his grandmother suggested. I need to give him time. However long that may be.

He grabs his cup of coffee from the counter, taking another quick sip. This moment of clarity and affirmation between the two of us is exactly what both of us need. I'm here for him, and he's here for me. That's all we need to know. We don't have to have it all figured out in this very instance. We have, what are hopefully, years ahead to gain an understanding of what we each need after all is said and done.

"Who do we think we are drinking coffee so late in the evening?" he asks.

"Well, we've got all night to figure it out, don't we?"

S. C. Gray

Rule Number Twenty-One

Books and Christmas trees are all we need to stay lit.

Standing in the middle of the town's one and only Christmas tree lot, I rub my hands together and blow warm air into them.

"Piper, how the hell do people survive here in the winter?"

Piper looks up at me like, "How the hell should I know? You're asking the wrong dog, mom."

I reach down to pick her up, and she snuggles into my jacket.

"So, how big do you want it?" Bishop asks, winking my way.

"Not too big, not too small. There's not much space in there."

Bishop laughs. He's ridiculous, and I now get that he's trying to be dirty in the middle of the church parking lot.

"You know, God sees and hears all the things. You better be careful, mister," I say as I point up to the sky, then back to my ears.

"I think if there is a hell, you and I both already have a bench with our names on it after last night... I'm not worried about a dirty pun or two."

He's right. A joke is not what I should be worried about.

"Oh, look at this guy! This one looks perfect for the shop, right? It's full, with no bald spots. Let's grab this one."

"Looks good to me."

Without hesitation and with seemingly no effort at all, he grabs ahold of the bottom and middle parts of the tree, lifts it over his shoulder, and carries it to the front. He pulls out his wallet, attempting to pay, it seems.

"Whoa, no. What are you doing?" I move in quickly, one hand up in protest. I look up to the guy at the register, then back to Bishop.

"I'm getting the tree you asked for. Is this not the one you wanted?" he asks, looking back, making sure he grabbed the right one.

"No, it is. I'm just wondering why you're pulling out your wallet."

I laugh nervously.

"Because. I want to buy you a tree. Christmas is your favorite holiday," Bishop says, smiling.

"Bishop."

"Campbell."

He's not going to take no for an answer, like his grandmother. The truth is, I've never had anyone buy anything for me. I've never had anyone who wanted to treat me to something nice. And, let's face it. With Christmas as one of the most important things in my life, I'd say this is a grand gesture.

"Fine, but I get to decorate it and pick the wrapping paper."

The fun part.

"Oh, hell no!"

He holds a hand to his chest and mocks disappointment. I roll my eyes. We load up the tree and drive it over to the bookshop, just a few blocks away. As we pull up and park right in front, I notice someone standing at the front door. It's Monday. We're closed, and I really don't want to have to entertain a customer while I do one of my favorite holiday things.

Prettying up the tree is one of my long-standing traditions with Piper. We do this with as many trees as we can each season. There are already a couple at the house—one in the living room and one in the bedroom. The fresh scent of a tree is what *makes* the holiday. I make hot cocoa, toss Piper some marshmallows, and turn on some music. I pull out more decorations. The only part I hate is untangling the lights.

"Hmm... someone is here," I say as Bishop parks his truck. Upon closer inspection and with my signature hard squint (God knows where my glasses are), I realize I know exactly who it is.

"Oh, wow. It's my landlord, Benny! What the hell."

As we all hop out of the truck, I move toward the front door, unaware he was even in town. So much for returning my email or giving me that call I've been asking for.

Before I know it, Bishop is rounding the corner behind the truck, and as he lifts down the truck gate to take the tree into the shop, he looks up at the man. A sense of displeasure is written so plainly on his face.

"Hey, dad, so nice to see you around."

S. C. Gray

Rule Number Twenty-Two

Sometimes, parents are wrong.

"Dad?!" I exclaim, completely confused. "Wait." I turn to Bishop. "Benny is your *dad*? Then, I turn to Benny. "Bishop is your *son*?! What in the world is going *on*?"

All three of us are standing outside the bookshop. Two of us are very out of the loop.

"Hello, Campbell. Nice to see what you've done with the place." Benny points a thumb over his shoulder toward the building. "It really looks amazing."

Bishop looks over at me. "I don't want you to freeze out here. Let's get inside."

He hustles the tree over to the door, and I open it up. I notice the light above is lit, working again. Peculiar.

I look over to Bishop. "Let me guess, your doing?"

I grin, and he's not amused or in the mood, I gather. Now that I know his grandfather had the bookshop here, I have a feeling he was also the one that fixed the squeak in the door. I should have known.

The three of us move inside, and Bishop leans the tree up against the wall. I give him and Benny both the space and time to explain. When no one speaks, I break the silence.

"Okay, someone owes me an explanation," I look over to Bishop. "Again."

I cross my arms over my chest. Piper sits next to me. She's just as confused as I am.

"Let's be clear: Benny is your father?" I ask Bishop.

This town just gets smaller and smaller. I let out a frustrated sigh.

"Yes, if you could call him that," Bishop spits.

"Whoa, shots fired," Benny chuckles.

He jokes, but I feel a certain kind of tension here, although I'm not sure why it's lingering. If there are any more surprises this week, I might just need another vacation. And not the kind I take to my mother's house.

"Benny inherited this building from my grandfather when he died. You saw the condition it was in when you took over the space. It sat empty for years. No one kept up with it. Benny likes to travel the world. Benny doesn't like things tying him down. Benny gets restless," Bishop says like Benny isn't standing three feet from us in the same space. Like he can't hear us at all.

"Look, I'm sorry I haven't been around much lately," Benny says.

"Or ever…" Bishop adds in bitterly.

Benny clears his throat.

"When the opportunity came up, I couldn't pass up Asia. You understand?"

He explains, turning to me like he expects me to offer him some sort of ticket out of the mess he seems to currently find himself in.

Then, he asks Bishop, "What are you doing hanging around here? Working for the bookshop?"

I chime in at this very moment because curiosity is killing the book lady, "When did you get back? I've emailed you several times, but I never heard anything from you. I've needed to talk to you about something pretty important, actually."

Now that he's here, Benny and I need to chat before he disappears again.

"I got back a few days ago. Needed to get my bearings in place." Whatever that is supposed to mean. "What is it you need? What's so important?"

Is he serious?

"Respectfully, Benny, for starters, the lease is up soon."

I really didn't want to have to get into it here with Bishop standing within earshot, but I may not get another chance. This has to happen. Now.

"Oh, about that..."

"I was wondering... you see. I have really come to love this place. Me and Piper both." I look down at her, still sitting at my feet, protecting me. "I've wanted to ask if there is any possibility I could extend the lease..." I ask nervously.

I have no idea what he will say to this sudden proposition.

"Oh, THANK GOD!" Benny all but screams.

I am reeling with shock when he reaches over and gives me the tightest hug. At that, Bishop moves over and breaks us apart.

"Why am I not shocked in the slightest that you are so excited to be rid of this place?" Bishop asks, pulling me back from his father like he's saving me from something.

Yet, another thing I need to begin to understand about Bishop: his relationship with Benny, his father. I can't keep up.

"I recently got an opportunity to go down to Machu Picchu, get in on some tours down there, and eat some fantastic food. Did you know they built that entire city using no wheels and no mortar? It's so fascinating. We leave in a few weeks. I've got to get down there. Have you been? It's a once-in-a-lifetime offer. I clearly can't pass it up."

My first thought is, *how in the hell does he afford all of this?* Then again, none of my business...

"Look, I need someone to take this place off my hands. To be honest, what better way to let my father's legacy live on than by keeping his place as he would have always wanted it? A bookshop."

These words floor me completely. Did I just hear him right? He wants to sell the store to me? I could keep my bookshop here, forever?

"Are you serious? It's mine?"

I'm tearing up. Bishop looks over at me.

"Can I talk to you for a second," he points at Benny, "outside?"

He takes Benny to the sidewalk. When Bishop closes the door, of course, as anyone else in their right mind would, I eavesdrop. I press my ear up to the crack in the doorway.

"What the hell do you think you're doing?" I hear Bishop ask Benny.

"What do you mean? I'm going to sell the shop to that girl. She loves it!" he says with so much excitement. "Have you seen what she's done with the place?"

"Of course, she loves it. This is her dream. Which is exactly why I don't want you fucking around with it. Or with her, period."

"Wait, why do you care so much? Don't you just work here?"

"You literally have no clue what goes on around here, do you? No, I don't work here. Jesus Christ. I'm a firefighter in town. Not that you would know or clearly care. She's my girlfriend. We're dating."

"Oh, shit! Well, good for you. She's beautiful. And smart too, from what I gather."

"Watch it, Benny," Bishop warns.

I feel a twinge of thrill at the way he says this.

"I know things between us have been dicey. Since your grandfather died, things have been rough on us all."

"Are you kidding? Rough on you, how? You have been peacefully traveling the world for a decade since he passed away. You've been a fucking tourist for God knows how long. You left your own mother here, alone. If it weren't for me moving back here, she'd be at a total loss. What is the matter with you?"

Bishop is pissed, and I haven't ever heard him this way. It takes everything for me not to open the door and put some space between the two of them before things go too far. But I can't stop listening.

"We all handle things differently, Bishop. Why don't you try to judge a little less, huh? You aren't one to talk. You run away from plenty."

Yikes, Benny. Even I know that is the wrong thing to say.

"Funny, it seems the only person running away is you. From your obligations, from your family, from life. But only when it's hard, though, huh? You always seem to pop back up when it's convenient for you. I've actually stayed put, right where I was supposed to. I took care of my shit."

"Yes, it seems like you've got yourself a pretty cozy situation here. Pretty girl, good job, a medical retirement from the military. You're just making yourself right at home, aren't you?"

"Oh yeah, because I asked to be retired, Benny. I didn't have a choice. They said I was unable to handle it anymore, remember? Or did you forget that part too? That the only thing I've ever known and wanted, the only thing I was great at, was taken from me! That was years ago. Why do you still bring that up, anyway? I honestly cannot believe you. You throw that in my face like it's something to be proud of. You know what? Maybe I am in a cozy situation here. NOW. Where were you when I needed you, as a father, all those years ago? Huh?"

Benny remains silent.

"Were you in Australia? Backpacking in Europe, perhaps? You know what, forget it. Don't answer that. All I know is I don't need you coming back here, screwing up everything I've worked so hard for. This bookshop means the world to Campbell. Don't go promising her things, only to take them away. I know how you are."

After a moment, Benny speaks again.

"Look, I know I've messed things up. Badly, depending on who you ask. But that stuff is between you and me. This here, this shop. This is something I know I just need to give up. I can't keep up with it. With all my traveling, shit has gone downhill and fast. I got an email the other day from my accountant. Seems I let a few things slip through the cracks. It doesn't sound good."

"Why am I not in the least bit surprised? You're always worrying about dumb shit and not caring at all about your actual adult responsibilities."

"Bishop, they are going to take the building away from me," he admits.

"What?! Who is they?" Bishop screams so loudly that I'm forced to open the door and face the two of them.

A pit in my stomach fills with bile.

"What are you talking about, Benny?" I question, and I'm scared to death to hear his explanation.

"Campbell, if I don't sell this building to you within the next thirty days, the IRS is going to put a lien on it, and I'll lose it for good. For all intents and purposes, if you want the shop, consider it yours."

S. C. Gray

THEN.

"When will you learn that all your daydreaming is a waste of time, Campbell? It's comical, actually," Nate says from the passenger seat of the car.

How I ended up here, I don't know. One day we're fighting, and I'm sure we both believe it's finally the end, but then the next day, we're together again even though we are obviously better apart.

This is how it always is—a constant back and forth. This battle of sorts. Shit goes down, only for me to end up taking him back. I get my "out" repeatedly, only for him to beg me to come home. This is the vicious cycle that is our disastrous relationship. It gets old as time goes on. There's only so much a person can take. And the weight of this world presses down on my shoulders like the mountain I'm crushed under.

Breathless and embarrassed, I continue like I'm trying to convince him the world is, indeed, not flat.

"All I was saying is I love books. Maybe one day, I could own a little shop of my own. It could be fun and amazing. Something I could call my own. That's not too far of a stretch I don't think. People open businesses all the time. It's nothing new," I offer.

"It's new to you. And we all know you never follow through with anything you do, Campbell. Come on. You barely finished college. If it weren't for me, you'd still probably be there, moping, making horrible decisions for yourself. Just barely getting by."

Maybe it's because you were keeping me down...

"You're lucky you have me to keep you grounded. Otherwise, who knows where you would be."

I sit and stare at the road. Maybe he's right. Who am I to think I could open a bookshop one day? I probably don't have the money for that. Or the means to keep the doors open. I wouldn't know the first thing about opening a store.

In one more attempt, I say, "There are classes I could take at the college for business. I actually looked it up the other day. Enrollment is just a few weeks away. I think it should be easy to get in since I've already taken classes there before."

"Are you kidding me? Ha! What a joke. Good luck with that."

Nate rolls his eyes. I'm used to this, although I know deep down, I shouldn't be. I think of how disappointed my parents must be in me—seeing me end up with someone like Nate. He only drags me down. I've only recently started to notice this for myself, especially after I learned about his rendezvous with someone who was supposed to be our friend. My friend. Better late than never, I guess.

At this point, we are moving closer to the end of this God-forsaken relationship. I just need one more reason to leave. One more. Inwardly, I roll my eyes at my pathetic self. I'm old enough to realize this is not love.

"Your dream is a joke," he says from beside me.

"Why are you so negative?" I ask.

At this point, I'm so fed up. He turns in his seat toward me. I wait for him to raise a fist. But it doesn't come this time.

"I'm just being real with you, Campbell. You'll never own a bookshop. Hell, you'll probably never own anything other than this lame-ass car."

He motions to his surroundings. Little does he know that I've been saving up every penny I can. I'll own something one day, mark my words. I'll do better for myself. I know I shouldn't have waited, but this is where I am.

"Better quit while you're ahead. You'll only keep disappointing everyone around you."

I look out the window as I pull up to a red light, begging tears not to fall from my eyes, my emotions deceiving me, letting him win this round of "who can hurt the other the most."

Maybe one day I'll find someone who won't think my daydreaming is a joke. Maybe, just maybe, I'll find someone someday who encourages it.

S. C. Gray

Rule Number Twenty-Three

Work hard for the things you want, and the rest will fall into place.

"So… when you say I can have the shop, do you mean, like, really *have* it?" I ask, inwardly freaking out.

From the tone in Bishop's voice and the look of concern on his face, I know not to get my hopes up. I'm not an idiot. I'm just excited and shocked.

Benny doesn't seem like someone I can trust from the sounds of that conversation I heard while he and Bishop were on the sidewalk. But, if it *is* true, then maybe this is my chance. I'm going to get what I've always wanted, what I've worked so hard for. A place that is mine. A place that's Piper's too. No strings attached to anyone or anything.

"I've already spoken with my lender. I've taken the proper actions to have everything switched over to you, Campbell. Electric, water, and I've got recommendations for the insurance. The whole bit. That is if you still want it."

"Well, of course, I want it. It's all I've ever wanted!" I basically scream.

And I mean it. No matter the circumstance as to how it's acquired.

I've waited for this moment my entire life.

Just then, Bishop moves over to me. He looks me in the eyes and puts a gentle hand on my elbow. He guides me a little deeper into the shop, leaving Benny near the front, shuffling his feet.

"Campbell, you deserve this. This is where you're supposed to be. Here, in this space. If what he is saying is true, and the legality is there, and don't worry, I'll make sure it is. Then, this was all meant to be. My grandfather would have wanted you to have it. He would have wanted this place to be taken care of and for it to be in the hands of someone who actually cares deep down. He would have loved for you to be the one in here, in the bookshop."

He gives me the slightest kiss on my lips. They're still cold from being outside in the dead of winter, duking it out with Benny.

"Thank you, Bishop. For looking out for me. For being here. I'm so thankful for you."

"There's no place I'd rather be."

He places his hand under my chin, lifting it for one more kiss. He and I turn back around.

"Benny, I think if it's arranged properly, then yes. I would like to move forward with the sale of the building. I'd love to buy the shop from you."

It's a quick, split-second decision. But, based on the amount of money the building is worth, how much I'm bringing in, and what I'm actually paying for rent, I would end up saving money in the long run. The monthly payments owning the building would be less than leasing it from Benny. And as I've said before, the shop has gained some amazing customers. Loyal ones. Ones that will help me keep the doors open. When it comes time to sign the papers, I will know in my heart that this is where I am meant to be. Here, in Salter's Ridge. Here, in this bookshop with Piper. And here, with Bishop by my side.

"Okay, great!" Benny doesn't even hesitate one second. "I'll have my accountant settle everything up. My lender will be in touch after drafting up a contract for sale. Congratulations, Campbell. You just became the owner of a bookshop."

S. C. Gray

Rule Number Twenty-Four

Coffee is always a good idea.

"A little to the left, I think?" I ask Bishop from outside the bookshop.

Benny has left the shop, off to meet with his "people," he says. The front door is wide open, and Bishop and I work together to get the tree in the middle of the shop, front and center of the window. Plain lights crawl up its branches. It sparkles from the street, and the ice on the ground creates a calming feeling that lingers in the air.

"I think that looks great!" I yell into the shop and jog in, out of the cold.

"I think it looks amazing," he says, placing his hand under his chin. "Now, what kind of wrapping paper should I pick for underneath?" he jokes.

I playfully knock into him. He grabs me, picks me up, and twirls me around the shop.

"Careful! You'll knock something over!" I giggle as he sets me down.

He still doesn't let go but keeps one hand on my hip, the other in my palm. He starts to slow dance with me.

"What are you doing?!" I continue to laugh, but he's not.

"No matter what happens, promise me you'll always be around."

"I'll always be here, Bishop." I scowl a bit, looking up at him. "You okay?

He looks deeply into my eyes. I can tell there's something on his mind, but he remains quiet.

"You know, when I first moved here, I had no idea what I was doing. I had no idea if the shop would work out. I felt like I had nothing to lose, you know? I mean, I packed my car and came here with a one-year plan. In my heart, I knew it was the right thing for me at that moment. I needed to get away. I needed an escape."

I take a breath and let out a sigh.

"Now that I know this whole bookshop thing might actually work out, I guess I need to start thinking about what I plan on doing going forward. What is my next step? I'm just renting the place I stay in right now. Maybe I need to find a more permanent home.

Now, I also have you, and I have us. And the thought of this, whatever this is, with you... it just all feels like, for once, I'm where I'm supposed to be. I feel good about the possibility of Salter's Ridge being a forever home. Although, the cold is really hard on my bones." I look down, laughing.

"I'm happy that you're happy here. You know, I saw Anders the other day. His neighbor is moving out of his duplex in a few months. I think it's just a few streets over from your place, actually. It might be a two-bedroom, a little bigger than what you have now. But maybe you could talk to him about it. I think they might be looking to put it on the market soon."

"Hmm... that would be idea. I would definitely want to stay close to the shop, that's for sure."

"How about this? Let's finish up here, get this mess cleaned up, and head over to Luca's for a cup of coffee? We can catch up with Anders, see if he has any information he can pass along about his friend. Maybe they'll want to meet up tonight for dinner or something. After all, we have so much to celebrate."

Bishop smiles, but by the look in his eyes, he's contemplating something else.

"What? Why are you looking at me like that?" I ask.

He's smirking as I reach down to pick up some of the bigger pieces of the tree that had fallen off during the setup. Christmas trees are so messy, but you've got to love them.

"Campbell, listen, I'm so scared..."

He pauses for the briefest of moments. "I have this crazy, intense feeling, like a sense of urgency. And being with you, it just feels right. Campbell, I think I'm falling in love with you." Then, in something lower than a whisper he asks, "Is that okay?"

This admission causes me to stand up straight. I look at Piper lying in her bed. She's lulled herself to sleep, cozy as can be in her own little world.

"That is perfectly fine with me, Bishop Graham. As long as you take me to dinner tonight... okay?" It causes him to smile, his cheeks reaching his soft eyes.

"Well, I think I'm learning quickly what makes you happy—dogs, books, and food."

"You already know me so well..."

Rule Number Twenty-Five

There is a right place|wrong time for everything.

"Anders, dude! Where have you been?" Bishop shouts as we storm into Luca's laughing.

Anders turns around and looks over at us from behind the coffee bar, his tan and caramel-colored apron tied neatly around his waist. He clears his throat.

"Ew. I've been right where I always am, you jerk-offs. Question is, where the hell were you two? Off playing hooky?! And you, Campbell Harrison. I have a bone to pick with you. I've been trying to text you since you got back from your mom's house. I have been worried *sick* about you. I went by your house... the shop even. Maybe we keep missing each other, but dang! Rude. Just plain rude!" Anders says, fed up with my crap.

Can't say I blame him.

"I know! I'm the worst. Let us make it up to you! We have some celebrating to do. I just bought the bookshop from Benny."

I raise my hands because I know what's coming.

"I know, I know! You're out of here in, what? Ten minutes? Want to go to The Bodega? Grab a few cocktails? We have a lot to process, and I hear their lounge area inside is to die for!"

I haven't made it inside yet. Our last time there was spent entirely outside. Not that I'm complaining. It was lovely back then. But now, there is fresh snow on the ground. We will be bundled up inside for the next few months. The bitter and unbearable cold hit me out of nowhere. There will be no outdoor dining experiences for a while. Bummer.

"Well, twist my damn arm. I do not forgive you, but... yes! Of course, I could always use a drink with you. I'm starving, though. I'll have to eat something before I turn into you-know-who when she gets hungry."

Bishop and Anders both turn to look at me. Now, *that's* rude.

———

All three of us hop into Bishop's truck and drive a couple of blocks to the restaurant, and as we enter, a large crowd can be heard on the opposite side of the dining area. Someone from the group motions over to Anders, the popular one in town. We can't go anywhere without someone knowing him from Luca's.

Upon further inspection through squinted eyes, I realize it's the same guy I saw Anders talking to in Luca's a while back at the coffee bar. They both come over to me and Bishop standing at the hostess stand as we wait to be seated.

"Lounge area, please," I smile and say to the teenage girl as she reappears from sitting a group down that arrived before us.

"Of course, and how many do you have dining in tonight?" she offers kindly.

I look around and am about to say three when Anders jumps in front of me before adding, "Can we make it four?"

He looks to his friend, then over at us like he's asking for permission.

Bishop says, "There will be four."

We walk through the dining room as one group to be seated in the back. There are colorful couches, low-lying coffee tables, and a few decorated Christmas trees in a corner. It's festive with the Christmas music playing overhead. I love it.

It brings me back to the first time I came here with Bishop not that long ago. A few months later and it feels just like it was yesterday that he swept me off my feet on the outdoor patio. I look at him now as we walk to our table. His low-hanging jeans, his cozy Adidas hoodie, his hair swept off his forehead but for a couple of strands that have fallen over his eyes. He catches me staring, and a hand moves up to sweep the strands from his face.

He moves in and says, "How did I get so lucky to have you?"

He leans down and kisses me on the cheek, then straightens up again to pull my chair out when we reach our table. I sit across from Anders, Bishop beside me, and Anders' friend across from him.

In this moment, the way Bishop makes me feel is unlike anything I've ever had. Are we the only two people in this room? It's like the moon shining in one corner of the night sky on an evening walk. It's like the waves in the sea, continuous, unable to be held back, no matter any force that tries. His appreciation for me being his is just like a puppy sitting in the humane society, with a new family waiting there at the front of the gate. He knows he's going home. He has love waiting on the other side.

The waitress interrupts my thoughts, standing over the table with a kind smile on her face, waiting to take our drink orders.

"I would love a blueberry mojito with some fresh lemon juice, please."

I jump in first, eager for something to calm my jittery nerves.

"We will each take a whiskey on the rocks!" Anders answers for himself and his friend.

"It's been a long day. Can I please have a coffee?" Bishop asks the waitress.

"So, guys! This is Oliver," Anders starts to explain. I can tell by their chemistry and body language that they seem quite comfortable with each other.

"Hi, Oliver! Nice to see you again. Sorry, the last time I saw you at Luca's, I was kind of in a weird space. I couldn't stay long. How do you two know each other?" I tilt my head, curious.

"Well, now that you ask..." Anders starts, but then he goes quiet. I can sense his hesitation.

I lean toward him ever so slightly.

"You know we love you, right?"

I reach over to touch my hand to him and whisper that it's okay. "I saw the look between you two that day I came into Luca's after Bishop "tried" to seduce me in my bed… he didn't get too far. We all know how that turned out." I turn to give Bishop's leg a squeeze.

"So, you're still holding strong, huh, Bishop? She hasn't driven you crazy yet?" Anders teases.

I pick up a chip from the basket in the center of the table and throw it at him. It lands with a thud on the ground and breaks into a few pieces.

"Hey, it's a legit question." Anders winks at me. "You can be a handful."

"Oh, believe me. She is," Bishop says.

They all laugh, and I mock hurt feelings even though I know this to be one hundred percent true. I am such a handful, and I have zero idea how he puts up with me.

"So, what is it we are celebrating, exactly? You bought the bookshop? Like, the entire building? Like, you're stuck with us? How the hell did that happen?" Anders asks, genuinely intrigued.

"As you may know, my dad is a piece of work. Long story short, he can't afford to keep up with the building anymore. Campbell just inherited the shop of her dreams. She's got the man of her dreams too. She's just all-around lucky her finger landed on Salter's Ridge," Bishop explains.

Even though he's joking, the way he says it gets my insides turning upside down because he's right. I *am* so lucky my finger landed here on this random, sleepy harbor town.

"I guess, all in all, it's you guys that are stuck with me. The shop is here to stay, and so am I."

I smile.

Our drinks arrive, Bishop's coffee steaming, and we order a few appetizers for the table. Appetizers for dinner. Sign me up. I'm here for it.

"What are everyone's plans for tomorrow? Everyone going to the Christmas tree lighting at Mrs. Graham's?" I ask.

I've been looking forward to it ever since Eleanor invited me the other day. I can't wait to see the decorations and the carolers. I pause to wonder if they will be taking requests. I love a good show.

"What kind of question is that?" Oliver shouts over the increasing noise in the room. "It's Salter's Ridge tradition. A long-standing one. It's super fun. We all have this understanding that you must show up. If you told Mrs. Graham you couldn't make the tree lighting, she would singe your soul with her death stare, and there would be nothing left for you in the world."

He says this completely straight-faced. We burst out laughing, but then he says, "What? I'm dead serious."

Our food arrives, and we chow down like none of us have eaten all day. We all order one more drink, and we talk about Christmas plans, now that it's just two days away. Everyone is staying in town, it seems. I turn to Bishop. He puts his hand on my thigh, and he softly runs his thumb over my jeans. In front of everyone, he casually asks, "What are you and Piper doing? You two should come over to my house for Christmas. I have a little something for you."

"Bishop, you don't have to get me anything."

I say it, and I mean it. I have never been one to want gifts at Christmas.

It's not about that for me. But I do love giving them.

"Oh no. I'm no expert at relationships, but I think it does go without needing to be said that everyone knows when someone says don't get me anything, it's a trap."

"Yeah, you're probably right."

We laugh.

But honestly, just spending time with him would be plenty enough. Maybe we can finish out our little sleepover that got all messed up last time.

I turn to Bishop, completely facing him. "We have zero plans." I smile ear to ear.

"Great! We can go to Grandma Graham's for a late breakfast. Then, we can go to my house. You haven't been there, yet. Have you?" I shake my head no. "That's kind of weird," he observes.

I hadn't even noticed. The way we feel about each other is in no way listed out in a clear-cut way. It doesn't follow any special guidebook to the perfect relationship. It's been all but a mess. I think between the guys at the table and us, it's all a little weird. It's all been so short-lived, our relationship. But there's still so much more to it. There's more to it than we've gotten to. That's the beauty of it. All we know is how we feel about each other, and that has to be enough, for now. If there is one thing I've learned in life, it's that no one has to understand the life you're living. If it makes sense to you, don't let other people's opinions get in the way of being happy.

I'm taken back from my thoughts and pulled back to the present when Bishop removes his hand from my leg to reach into his back pocket to pull out his phone. It's going off like crazy, vibrating, and after a couple of rings,

Bishop answers. It's unlike him to use his phone, period. So, when he answers it during our dinner, it unsettles me.

He takes the call, a look of vicious concern on his face, and quickly stands up from the table, hitting the side and rattling everyone's drinks, almost spilling one sitting too close to an edge.

"Campbell, get up. We've got to go."

"What? We're in the middle of dinner, babe." I laugh, giddy inside.

I'm two drinks in. He's still sober.

"There's a fire. Get up, Campbell." He looks over to Anders and Oliver, then back to me. "It's the bookshop."

Rule Number Twenty-Six

Seek the chaos. It fuels the fire that is your soul.

Thankful to have driven to the restaurant in Bishop's truck, he and I hop in and race a few blocks to Main, leaving Anders and Oliver at an otherwise empty table. My heart races the entire way, turning what is usually an almost three-minute drive into an eternity. I look at Bishop sitting in the driver's seat, one hand on the wheel, the other hand urgently adjusting the straps on his uniform overalls he keeps in the backseat for moments like this. An emergency that could come at any time. As we arrive, I notice the bellows of white smoke against the backdrop of the moonlit night. It's almost poetic. Almost beautiful.

Emergency vehicles with flashing lights block the way of us getting any closer than we already are. I see police talking with a group of people off to the left, holding back what looks to be Mrs. Leo. But I can hardly see with all the smoke and no glasses on. She's screaming, her arms up in the air as someone urges her to stand back. That someone looks like Sienna's husband, Evans.

Bishop haphazardly pulls onto a curb, slamming his shifter into park. Before he hops out of the truck, I reach for my door handle.

"No, Campbell. Stay here! It's too dangerous," he screams. The sirens, the crackling of the fire... It's so loud and hot, and we are still a block away from it all.

"Bishop, please. I need to see if the shop is okay!"

I can feel my entire body shaking uncontrollably, the adrenaline a fierce river coursing through my veins. He reaches over and holds my hands in his as if to still me. I'm crying so heavily, I can barely see his face in front of mine.

"Trust me, Campbell. You have to stay here. It's not safe to get any closer. Promise me you won't get out of this truck. I'll be okay. I'll come back for you. Just stay here. Please."

The look of worry on his face is what causes me to stay put. I'm not going to argue with him. I'm in too much shock to say much more than, "Please, be careful."

He kisses me once on the lips, harder than he has all the other times before. He holds both hands to my face to make sure I'm looking right at him. "I really love you, Campbell."

My eyes snap up to attention as he continues. The admission shocks me.

"I know it might not make sense right now to both of us, but I have loved you since the moment I first saw you coming out of your bookshop that night. This short time I've had with you has been what my soul has needed for the past ten years. You're the best moment of my life so far." I wanted to tell you that night at The Bodega when you asked me, but I thought that would make you run away. It was too soon."

He looks down.

The finality of his words causes a sense of alertness in me. Why is he telling me this now? He turns away from me. He gets out of the truck to run toward the smoke, a pillow that seems to have doubled in size since we pulled up, and all I can do is sit there and watch as he disappears into the raging madness that's screaming poetic beauty. It's so bright that if you couldn't smell the smoke, one might think it's daytime, not evening. He fades off into the gray.

I don't even have time to tell him how much I love him too.

S. C. Gray

Rule Number Twenty-Seven

Believe you deserve the best. Because, you do.

When I was younger, I think I always knew I would do great things. Maybe it was because of my upbringing and my ability to survive in situations when I needed to. Maybe it was my over-confidence in every circumstance I found myself in, however minor or significant. Like all those times I found myself in a concert. Me, the star of the show. I'm thrown back to my Christina Aguilera performance at my teenage birthday party all those years ago.

Do you ever notice a bit of foreshadowing in your own life? Have you ever had a feeling like you knew years ago that you would be right where you are now?

As I sit back and watch numbly at the scene before me, I'm startled when I hear a banging on the truck's window. By now, the fire is just a matter of smoldering. Everything seems to be at a standstill, and an hour has passed, although I feel as if it's just been fifteen minutes.

"Campbell! What are you doing here? Where is Bishop?" Sienna yells through the glass window of the truck.

She has worry and years' worth of stress on her face. "I've just gotten back from talking with Evans. Jesus Christ. Are you okay?"

She waits for me to answer, but I sit still, saying nothing at all.

"He says they are still working on getting everything taken care of, but for the most part, it wasn't as bad as it could have been," she shouts.

I attempt to roll down the manual window. My hands and arms have a bit of trouble, the weakest of moments if I've ever experienced one. I just look at her, still in disbelief as she continues.

"They think the fire started in Mrs. Leo's shop. They think she left a heater on under her desk, too close to some clothing she had stashed underneath. Or maybe a wire overheated or something. She's freaking devastated. But the fire was pretty contained to her building. Terrible for her but, you're so lucky, Campbell." She reaches in and barely touches my shoulder through the window. "Did you hear what I said?"

I can barely get past her saying the fire was contained to her building.

"What? What do you mean 'contained' to her building? The bookshop's okay?"

I'm horrified for Mrs. Leo, but a minuscule spark of hope raises in my chest, my breathing labored.

"I think for the most part, yes. There may be some smoke damage on the outside of the building, but the brick really did a good job of keeping the fire from spreading. They still need to check the ventilation and the structure stability, but because the firehouse is right there, they were able to contain everything pretty quickly. I think all the smoke, combined with the cold weather, made it look worse than it really was. Thankfully, the building itself held up pretty well, it seems."

All I could think about for the past hour was how my entire years' worth of work, in a matter of minutes, was gone, quite literally up in flames. I sat here for what seemed like an eternity, useless, waiting for Bishop to come back. To let me know the shop wasn't able to be saved. From my standpoint, what could there be left to do? Everything inside is paper.

I hop out of the truck, and a newfound focus is instilled in me.

"I need to find Bishop. I need to make sure he's okay. He told me to stay put. I tried a little while ago to get a closer look, but the police turned me away. So, I came back."

"Yeah, Evans usually says they have to hold everyone off until at least the flames are contained and until the smoke is fanned out," Sienna says.

I shut the door, and we begin walking together toward the row of businesses that house the bookshop, Mrs. Leo's thrift store, and another office beside hers. Even though it's night, some sort of halogen lighting is shining on the building like it's a construction site. It's late, but I can easily see the extent of the damage.

"Oh my God, Sienna. I cannot believe this is happening. Is everyone all right? Have you seen Bishop?"

Never mind the shop. I just hope the firefighters are okay. This is an actual nightmare. And, I haven't seen Bishop since he left me alone in the truck.

"Evans said no one had been injured in the fire. Like I said, it was pretty minimal, considering."

I look at the front of the bookshop. But still, for the most part, it looks like it did the day I moved in. Almost like there wasn't a fire at all. Eerie. Before I can say anything else, I hear Bishop come up behind me. I turn around to see a man who looks like he's been through another war. The image is startling. I think of him and Foster. What was meant to be a forever friendship, cut short.

"Campbell, are you all right?" I can feel an overwhelming pressure in my heart like it's about to explode.

"Am I all right? Are *you* okay?"

I rush over to him with a sigh of relief, thankful he's in one piece, but he holds his arms out in front of himself, keeping me at arm's length. I halt where I stand.

"Let's wait until I'm home and get showered. I don't want to get soot and grime all over you. This stuff is really nasty. It can get you sick."

"Oh, of course," I say.

But try as it might, I can't help it. I have to at least know he's still here. That I'm not hallucinating. I have to know he's still mine. I reach out a hand and touch his face covered with the leftovers of the fire. I give him the gentlest of kisses, his face covered in dirt and sweat.

"I love you," I whisper in his ear so no one can hear except for him before pulling away.

I notice Sienna staring from off to the side, and she quickly looks away, pretending to mind her own business, but I know her curiosity is piquing.

"I love you more," he says as he steps back. "Listen, we still have some work here to do. Once the area is cleared for safety, you can go into the bookshop and make sure everything is okay, but I think you lucked out. There should be very insignificant and minor damage to your side of the building. We were able to put the fire out pretty fast."

He tries to reassure me everything is okay, but I'm still so flustered. I'll believe him once I get inside the shop and see it's well enough for myself.

"Thank you, Bishop. For everything."

I think the shock is still taking over my ability to rationalize just how bad this could have been. At least everyone is okay, and the building seems to have taken a hit but is still standing.

"No need to thank me." He puts his gloved hand onto my shoulder. "Hey, why don't you go home, get some rest? From our standpoint, there isn't much you can do until the building is cleared. Sienna, would you be able to take Campbell home? Once I finish up here, I'll come by to check on you, and we can come back together to see how everything fared once we have some daylight."

His suggestion is more than enough to get me the hell out of here. The stress from the evening's events has done a number on me, and without some sort of stability in the form of Piper, I might not make it.

With Sienna by my side, we walk the short distance back home. Within a few minutes, we are standing in front of the walk-up, and I see Piper in the window waiting for me. She must have been wondering where I was.

"Sienna, thank you for being here for me tonight."

These small-town friendships mean everything, and tonight, I learned there's no use in trying to hide the fact that this town is where I am meant to be. With people who show up for me without having to ask.

"Stop it, Campbell. You are so welcome. We are all here for you, and when the morning comes, we will still be here for you. The entire town. We love you."

It's all I can do to stop crying. I turn around and walk into my home, bone-weary. Piper is already at my legs, begging for kisses. I walk into the kitchen and pour myself a glass of wine. I start a steaming hot bath. I light a candle. Piper lays on the towel right beside the bathtub on the floor. And I cry into the water for what seems like a lifetime.

––––––––

When the water is as cold as the night outside, I get dressed and make a cup of hot tea to gain my warmth back. I fall into bed with a book in my hand, even though I'm too exhausted and worn to read it.

Before I know it, I roll over to see Bishop lying next to me, and Ghost and Piper are at the foot of my bed. I must have passed out from the evening's events. Everyone is in a peaceful sleep. This looks familiar. Like it's right where we left off that fateful night of Bishop's nightmare. Only now, the nightmare has been replaced with mine. He stirs awake and catches me watching him.

"Hey, you creep. Watching me sleep? Isn't that what horror films are made of?"

He giggles a little, but I'm still too worn out to joke.

"What time is it?" I ask.

He taps his phone beside him to illuminate the time. It's 3 am. I rub my eyes. I'm so drained. I'm sure Bishop is too.

"Have you slept? I just got back. I hope I didn't wake you. After I grabbed Ghost, we drove over, and I took a shower here."

His hair is still wet. He's on top of the blanket with gray joggers on.

"Your shirt is missing," I say.

And by God, everything else just disappears. He laughs and rubs a rough hand up and down my arm before pulling me in to be closer to him. I lay my face to his bare chest.

"That was so scary, Bishop. We pulled up to the shop, and I thought I lost everything."

I rest my hand on his chest near my face, his breathing easy and calm. Once again, how right could this feel?

"Campbell, you have to stop thinking all of the good that has come your way is going to disappear. This life is yours. It's here to stay."

I'm still, and his words settle into me.

"Once you left and we fanned the smoke out of there, we realized her building didn't fare out too badly. I mean, Mrs. Leo is definitely going to have to clean everything out of the shop because of the water damage from the hose, and she'll have to start over, but since it was very clearly an accident, insurance should be quick to help her out. She should just have some renovations to do—new floor, new walls, new paint. She'll need to get some new merchandise back in there, which might not be a bad thing. But at least the building is stable and secure."

I know this should give me the biggest breath of relief. I know I should feel so thankful for this news. But, for a split moment, I thought I was about to lose everything. I thought about having to start over from scratch again, and the thought of it nearly killed me to the core. My life is tied up in this bookshop.

"Bishop, I can't lose you. I can't lose Salter's Ridge. Tonight, I realized just how much everything means to me. Even though I have so much gratitude, I don't want another day to pass by without you knowing how much you mean to me. I don't want another day to pass by where I don't tell my family how much they are wanted and needed in my life." I look over at Piper. "She already knows how much I need her, so..." Bishop smiles as Piper's ears perk up. She knows we are talking about her.

"Campbell, we all know what we mean to you. You show us how you care for us. You show us in your concern, in your efforts in our relationships. Everything is hard right now but trust me when I say this town needs you as much as you need the town. Do you know how important your shop is? People love it. Everyone talks about it. It's a staple... like Luca's, but coffee kind of gets the upper hand if you ask me."

I pinch his arm.

"Ow!" he shouts.

"I think we should get some rest. Your grandmother's tree lighting is tomorrow."

"See, proof that you're a Saint. Your bookshop just almost caught fire tonight, and you're worried about my grandmother and the town's Christmas tree lighting." He lifts my chin to meet his face. "Honestly, how did I get so lucky?" he asks again.

"Well, it is Christmas after all. I wouldn't miss this for the world."

"I know you wouldn't."

"Hey, do you think the carolers will sing me some Bublé?

And with that, Bishop turns over and tries to fall asleep.

S. C. Gray

Rule Number Twenty-Eight

Traditions.

Forever is composed of nows.

-Emily Dickinson.

Standing in the middle of the bookshop, the smell of smoke is acrid. It's angry—a harsh, bitter slap in the face. But, the shop still stands. The books still remain unbelievably untouched. It's incredible to see in person. In my mind, I thought so easily that it would all be gone. Disappear from these four walls. In my mind, this morning, I thought I would walk in to see a bunch of nothingness.

But, here I am. And there they are. The shelves. The tables. The rugs.

The spool of natural ribbon. The small Christmas tree on top of the counter. The faded books in the front window. The beautiful vintage Dutch door, without its squeak. The table lamp. It all stayed put.

Like an American flag standing in the midst of a hurricane.

You can blow wind my way, but I'll remain unmoved.

Remarkable.

To get the smell out, I'll have to consult mother nature. And a specialist. I glance over at Bishop, who is assessing the shop as well.

"I think for starters, we'll have to prop open the front door, push the smell out with a fan, and get an industrial vacuum in here to get out any odor we can from the rugs. We have a fire restoration team a few towns over. I'll contact them, and they'll get some folks over here to help with the rest. It'll take some time, but once the odor is out, you'll never know a fire happened next door."

I want to believe him. It's reassuring, yet unconvincing at the same time. The smell is just so overwhelming, and it's hard to imagine a time when it won't smell so bad in here. It's heartbreaking, nonetheless.

"I'm just happy it's all still here. I can replace the books. I can replace the rugs. I just didn't want to have to start over, you know?"

I'm overcome with a blanketed sense of good fortune. I breathe lightly, knowing this is the best possible outcome. And although I'm going to have to presumably close the shop for the time being while I get this place cleaned up and back in order, I know the town will be here when I open back up. Whenever that may be.

Now, it's my turn to ask—How did I get so lucky?

Rules for Dating a Bookshop Owner

———

The Christmas tree is much larger than I had anticipated. The lights are woven through the tree, which towers dozens of feet into the sky, and people from every surrounding town can be seen littering the area here in front of the Thomas L. Graham House.

The streets have been cordoned off with fancy rope strung from telephone poles. Instrumental music is coming from somewhere nearby. Carolers in large velvet shawls with red and green plaid dresses underneath are crooning *Deck the Halls*. Their bonnets tie underneath their chins, wrapped around their heads.

Unsupervised children run haphazardly, zigzagging around the wide and expansive tree, although they are careful not to touch the fragile bristles of its branches. I have a quick thought of *where are your parents*?

I look all around for a familiar face among the sea of festive event-goers, everyone dressed in beautiful coats, and just when I think it would be impossible to spot anyone, I see Anders and Oliver across the way, hand in hand. I smile and give them both a wave. When they see me, they begin to head over.

"Oh, my goodness, I'm so sorry, Campbell. Are you okay?"

Anders hugs me, and I hold onto him like a lifeline.

"I'm good, guys. Okay? I promise. I can't go all day with people asking me that question. Run around and tell everyone, please."

He laughs, but I'm serious. As soon as I got here, I caught the looks and stares from everyone because as we know, in a town of this size, nothing is kept secret for too long. News here spreads like wildfire. Pun too soon?

"But thank you. I'm glad it wasn't as bad as it could have been. I should recover just fine."

Can I say the same for poor Mrs. Leo? Let's hope so.

Anders beams and takes it upon himself to shout to the crowd, "Got it. Everything is fine! Everyone, pretend like nothing has happened! Everything is so fresh and so clink, clink."

I look at him with amazement.

"You know it goes, 'so fresh and so clean, clean.' Right?"

I laugh out loud so hard, I double over as Oliver slaps Anders on the back. Outkast would be so disappointed.

"I'm sure he doesn't say 'clink, clink,' Anders. What the hell does that even mean?" asks Oliver.

I can see the wheels spinning in Anders' head.

Mind. Blown.

"Hmm, maybe you're right. Anyway, the lighting should be starting any moment now. Mrs. Graham normally does a little speech near the front before the lighting. Let's go find a spot."

We follow Anders over closer to the tree, where it expands at least twenty feet wide. Where did they find such a beautiful tree? The air is crisp and chilly. My gloved hands try to find warmth inside the pockets of my coat.

Just as we settle in, I wonder where Bishop is. As if reading my mind, he hustles over with someone in tow behind him. In shocking disbelief, I almost collapse to the ground.

It's Priscel.

"Campbell! Baby, are you okay?" She all but runs into my chest to grasp onto me.

"Mom! What are you doing here?" I look around at everyone in amazement, willing someone to answer for her.

"Bishop called me last night. He said there had been a fire. I came as soon as I could. I got the first flight out to come to be with you."

"What? Bishop. Oh my God. Thank you. And mom, thank you for coming. I can't believe you came all this way." Of course, she showed up, unannounced, but the surprise is welcomed in this circumstance, I guess.

"Why wouldn't I? My goodness. I'm so sorry it's taken me this long to come here. I know I should have come sooner. But, when Bishop called me, I knew I had to come to be with you, make sure you had everything you needed. You shouldn't be alone right now."

"I'm fine, mom. Just a little bit of smoke in the shop has it smelling like I burnt bacon on the stove, but other than that, I think I'll make it out all right. Maybe even better than before."

She sighs a large breath of relief.

"I just needed you to know I'm here for you, whenever you need me. I already spoke with Bishop. I know you've got plans with him tomorrow, so I won't impose on those. I'll explore the town and just catch you at dinner or something. I'll stick around a few days and head home."

She gives an understanding smile.

I look over at Bishop and the fresh green tree filling in the sky behind him. I hug him so tight. It's all I know to do. Everyone I need is right here with me. The town. My friends. My mother. Bishop.

In life, I've learned you can't control the unexpected. I have no power over the events that may occur in my life, Bishop's life, or the actions people may take against us. But, when I think back on my life and the moments leading up to the now, all the roads leading here are simply beautiful—meant to be, predetermined. Nothing here was expected. Just when I wasn't looking, when I was hardly trying, life happened in the best way possible. No matter the circumstance.

What was my goal a year ago moving to Salter's Ridge? I thought it was just me running away. I thought it was me looking for a place where no one knew my name. I thought that I would have nothing to strap me down or take up my time except for this bookshop by coming here. In the now, I find I have a lot strapping me and holding me down. And it's the best outcome. This is the goal. This home. This family. The meaning of life and our purpose. The traditions I start on my own.

I want that for Anders. I want that for Bishop. I want that for my mom.

I'm reminded here, in the now, that time cannot be wasted. It can't be rewound and played back. We don't get a do-over of the time already passed. We have to take our lessons learned, and we have to make the best of the now.

Although if we could, it would be nice to bring back the times when me, my sister, and our childhood best friend all lived together for just one summer back in North Carolina when we were younger. Our first summer, on our own.

Yet, they both took a job at Blockbuster. A job they took for the team.

They each got to pick ten free movies a week to watch. Back before Netflix and Hulu. We were too poor to afford cable. I think about that summer very often, as much as I love movies. Kind of how I imagine Bishop thinks of his last summer with Foster.

It was just the three of us in our small townhouse in the middle of the city. Naive. Young. Spending hardly any time in the sun at all, just cooped up on the couch in cozy blankets with all the snacks, watching movie after movie.

Life was so simple back then, and we didn't even know it. The memories made back then, are compiled of our amazing *nows*.

S. C. Gray

Rule Number Twenty-Nine

The best gift is a memory. Give those.

For many reasons, Christmas morning has always been sacred. It's instilled in me. It's in my blood, in my bones. When I was younger, my happiest memories centered around this day.

So, when Bishop asked if Piper and I would spend the day with him today, I have to admit... It made me slightly nervous. New traditions are what I wanted a year ago when I moved to Salter's Ridge. They are still what I want now. So, then, why do I feel this way this morning?

I think deep down it's that it seems to be a serious step in the relationship department when you spend the holidays with someone new. It's all so final. Although it really isn't. It's a mind screw. People can break up any time they want to. This is not final. It's not that big of a deal.

Although it kind of is.

Sitting in my closet trying to figure out what to wear, I become overwhelmed by a minimal sense of aggravation. I align it to that feeling when someone asks what we should eat for lunch. That is such a horrible question. Perhaps, the worst question of them all.

"Piper, what do you think of this outfit?" I ask as I hold up a cozy knitted sweater with a pair of faded blue jeans. "Too casual?"

She looks at me, remaining silent. I've lost my damn mind. She doesn't wear pants. She's a dog. So, what does she know... It's way too cold outside to wear a nice dress. Cozy sweater and jeans, it is.

As I finish applying a light dash of makeup, pull my hair into a low bun, strands falling carelessly this way and that, I give myself a once-over in the mirror, content with what I see. I hear a knock at the door.

"Hello, hello..."

Bishop pushes his way in, grabbing me up and pulling me a foot off the rug.

"Well, hi!"

I squeal as he sets me down. What's gotten into him? Here I am, in need of a serious dose of Imodium, and he's giddy like it's, well... Christmas Day.

"You look beautiful. Are you ready?" he asks, showing his smile of straight, white teeth permanently glued to his handsome face.

The five o'clock shadow from not shaving for a day is a look on him I'm in serious appreciation of. Another thing I appreciate is him not caring what outfit I'm wearing today, or any day. He sees right past it, unaware of the time I spent worrying for nothing.

"Yes, I just finished getting ready. I just need to grab a sweater for Piper, and we'll be all set."

I grab one from a basket sitting by the front door. I turn off all the lights, grab my bag with Bishop's Christmas present in it, and we start the four-block walk to Eleanor's house.

"Grandma Graham always makes these delicious cookies for the holidays. The powdered sugar ones are my favorite. I'm sure she'll try to make us stay all day, so when I wink at you twice, it's time to go. Okay?"

He's talking a mile a minute, the excitement written clear as day on his face.

"Okay, sounds like a plan."

We walk hand in hand the entire way. Piper is in the middle of the sidewalk, careful not to get too close to the icy edge. Outside, it's a picturesque Christmas Day. Snow is on the ground. Every house has been decorated with wreaths and fresh garland hanging from porches. Some Christmas lights are still on from the night before. After a few moments of silence, Bishop slows us both down when we are halfway to his grandma's house.

"Campbell, thank you for spending the day with me," he says.

"Are you kidding? Thank you for inviting me. I'm looking forward to it."

I smile. He's quiet then, deep in thought about something I can't quite put my finger on. Insert unnecessary self-sabotaging doubt.

"You okay? If it's all too soon, me spending time with you and your family like this, I'll understand. I know how weird this must be."

"Are you crazy? No, it's not that at all! Stop it. I am more than ready for this."

"Okay."

I know he's got something on his mind. I can see his wheels spinning.

"What is it? Is there something going on?" I ask, nervous.

Maybe this is happening too quickly. Christmas with his girlfriend and his grandmother? In the same room. My stomach is all of a sudden in knots. I feel sick.

He stops us both and pulls me into his warmth, and I'm so thankful.

"Campbell, I've been waiting my entire life for you," he says in the middle of the walkway, just a block from his grandmother's home now. I can see her large white columns from where we stand. He pulls me even closer.

"Can I give you your gift now?" he asks, smiling big.

I laugh.

"What? Why?" I ask. "No, why can't it be a surprise?"

"I can't wait any longer."

"Are you sure? I mean, yeah... If you insist."

Jesus, please do not get down on one knee... I adore you, but...

He reaches into his back pocket and pulls something out, revealing a piece of paper. I reach out, thankful for a moment that it's not a damn ring, and take it cautiously from his hands.

"What is it? Not Pepto, huh?" I offer nervously.

He doesn't miss a beat.

"Benny is halfway to Machu Picchu by now, I'm sure, but before he left, we had a meeting with his accountant and a real estate team. After some lengthy talks about a bunch of mortgage terms and some negotiating on my part, we came to a solid conclusion. He wanted me to give this to you."

Confused, I unfold the long piece of paper and find what looks to be the sale deed to the building for the bookshop. On the left, Benny's authorization to sell the building to me. And, at the bottom on the right-hand side, a single line waiting for my signature.

Upon further inspection, I see a second name and additional signature on the left I wasn't expecting to see. My heart begins to race, and emotion threatens to spill from every crevice of my body.

"Bishop."

"Yes?"

"Why is your name on this deed?"

"Well, the building is, or was, half mine. My grandfather left it to both of us."

"Are you kidding?"

"I know, another something I could have let you in on... but I didn't want to tell you and then have you believing you couldn't take it or buy it or whatever."

I look down at the deed in my hands. The shop is mine.

"The shop is completely mine? Already? That fast?" I ask because even though I'm thrilled it's happening, I still just can't quite believe it.

He laughs a "yes." He looks me in the eyes. "Well, once you sign the papers. The shop, the building, albeit a fire just occurred, and we need to get that shit odor out. But yes, everything. It's yours, babe."

I'm threatened with a weakness in my knees. The only thing to keep me up is the strength in Bishop's arms as he grabs hold of me, wrapping his arms full force around me, and pulls me up to the blue sky. He sets me down and looks me in the eyes, a gentle touch placed under my chin, forcing me to look up at him too.

"No matter our pasts, Campbell, I'll never hurt you. You're safe with me here. You always will be."

And his words have never held such meaning.

"I know. Thank you. For everything. Thank you for this. For supporting me throughout all this craziness. Also, thank you for being very good-looking, and for loving dogs, and books, and good food."

We laugh, but I'm so thankful in this moment, out here in the elements, Piper shaking like a Polaroid picture.

"Today is going to be the most memorable Christmas ever," I say.

And I've never meant it more.

———

After the loveliest meal with Eleanor, we move into my favorite spot in the house, her library.

Bishop and I are positioned directly across from her on the brown leather sofa, melting into the seats like butter. An exquisitely decorated tree, presumably the one used for the tree lighting, so it didn't go to waste, stands behind us at least twenty feet tall in front of the expansive window. You can see the lights and the garland from the street. It's just beautiful.

"You two together remind me of Thomas and me when we were younger. I remember he used to sit in this room, right where you two are. Feet up for hours upon hours, just reading. You couldn't get him up from the couch some days. And, with good reason."

She smiles a kind smile, reminiscing. I turn to Bishop, excited.

"Okay, okay. Time for you to open your gift," I say.

"Ugh, I hate gifts. You didn't have to get me anything, Campbell. I thought we said no gifts?"

He looks at me, accusatory, while I try avoiding his eyes. I reach down into my bag and pull from it a wrapped rectangle. A simple ribbon is tied around it, and I'm anxious as I lift it and hand it over to Bishop.

"Well, you'll love this one, I think. And, technically, I didn't have to buy anything," I say slyly. "Open it."

Bishop takes his gift, glancing over to his grandmother, who also has a devious look on her face. He begins to unwrap the paper, revealing a vintage wooden frame. The matting is split into an upper and lower section, leaving space for two things to be placed into the frame. After removing all the paper, Bishop is left holding his gift. His eyes become glossy. He stares at the frame but remains silent.

"When I went through the box we found in the back of the bookshop, I saw these." I point to the frame. "I believe this photo is the last photo you ever took with your grandfather before you left for your last deployment. He had it printed for safekeeping. It's a bit worn, but still. And then..." I point to the bottom of the frame, which holds a piece of paper with creases in it. "I also found this letter. I asked Eleanor if I could have them framed for you. If you look at the date, it was written right before you came home. Right before he passed away."

I move closer to Bishop, touching his leg with a gentle hand. He looks at me, eyes on the verge of letting go of the tears that build at the edges, as I say, "The letter was written to you, Bishop."

He looks over to Eleanor, then back to me again.

"I know it may be hard to read it now, with us here, but in time, maybe it'll help to heal some of the parts of you that are hesitant to move forward. Maybe, if even just a little, it'll ease your mind and bring you peace, knowing how he felt about you."

He looks from the frame to me and back to the frame.

In barely more than a whisper, he says, "Campbell, thank you." And he turns to kiss me with soft, full lips. "This is amazing." He lets out the deepest breath.

"Okay, you two, way to make me cry on Christmas!" Eleanor smiles from across the room. "If you'll excuse me, I'm going to go get some cookies."

She stands up from the couch, walking toward the kitchen, leaving us alone.

"Merry Christmas, Bishop," I whisper.

He places his forehead to mine.

"This is the kindest thing anyone has ever done for me," he says.

I'm so relieved.

"Well, I'm glad you love it. I thought it would be meaningful to have this memory hanging up somewhere. It couldn't be stuck in a box forever. It's too special."

"Yeah, I agree. Thank you," he says.

He reaches over to kiss me one more time, this time, much longer than if his grandmother were still sitting here with us. He pulls back after a moment and begins to read the letter, written in weak but legible handwriting, that has been ten years in the making.

Bishop,

Time is a thief, but to live in hearts we leave behind is not to die.
I read this line somewhere, a long time ago. And the line, it stayed with me.
Because it's so true, isn't it? Time being a thief. We never know how much time
we have left, yet we waste so much of it on things that don't matter. Most of all,
I think we waste time wallowing in sorrows we cannot help.
Before you left for Afghanistan the first time around, it was like my heart had
stopped. Because I knew, from experience, you would come back a changed
man. But no one could have stopped you, and you would have stopped for no
one. So, we let you go because it was your call to duty as it was mine
all those years ago.
We're men. We're tough. We're Marines. We persevere.
I'm writing this to you now, Bishop, because here I am wallowing in a sorrow I
know cannot be helped. I don't have much longer, and I know you're on your
way home already, and I won't be able to see you one last time.
If by chance I don't, please know this, what I wish someone would have
told me when I was your age:
Don't harbor in the past, as it robs you of the time you have now.

S. C. Gray

*You did good. You did everything right. By God, you gave it
everything you could have.
You're brave, smart, intellectual, and most of all, a good man.
You're a good man, Bishop.
Most of all, you deserve a peace that I know you may never find because you
feel you must carry the weight of the world now. Hell, I still have yet to find
that peace, so I understand. War changes a person, most of the time, not for the
better. But, in your case, I hope you realize the lives you changed in your specific
circumstance. The people you helped, the friends you'll have on
your side for the rest of time.
No matter how thankless you feel that job was, people are thankful for you.
People love you.
I love you.
I know it hurts not being able to see me now. But, when you read this, every
time you read this, know that I am in your heart because that's where I'll live.
Until the end of time.*

-Grandpa T.

Rule Number Thirty

Take the risk. In every sense, the reward is so plentiful.

"Are you ready?"

Bishop turns and asks me as I lean back in my seat, hair pressed tightly up against the headrest.

"I love flying. The thrill of take-off is exhilarating," he whispers beside me.

At times, I feel the same. But right now, my nerves are at a fever pitch.

"That glass of wine at the gate should have been enough, but I think I need another."

It's spring, the weather is warming up, and the sun is shining through the plane's cabin. The time has come, the moment I've waited my entire life for.

I liken this feeling to the anticipation I had when my parents bought me and my sister tickets to the NSYNC PopOdyssey Tour back in 2001. Back when I cried so hard during the entire concert from the excitement that my eyes had been swollen shut for exactly four days afterward.

Norah Jones is waiting for us in Boston, those tickets burning a hole in my tote pocket for months. It's been four months since the tree lighting. What? A year since Bishop ordered the most pretentious book on the planet?

Our hotel is booked, the concert is tonight at six at the Orpheum Theatre.

"I cannot tell you how excited I am for tonight," he says to me, a hand on my knee as the plane evens out in the sky 35,000 feet up. "This date is going to be epic. I have something planned for you." He always has something for me.

He has mischief written all over his face as he rubs his hands together, wiggling his eyebrows up and down.

"You know, for someone who hates surprises, you sure are full of them, Bishop," I say, looking out the window, blinded by the light.

I inhale the stale cabin air, feeling hot at my neck. After fifteen minutes of thinking in silence as he reads a book next to me, I say out loud what I've been thinking for months.

"You know, before I met you, Bishop, I remember just coasting along. Simply just being there. Before you came into my life, I was just trying to get by, day after day. I was searching for something, although I had no idea what that something was. I was messed up. I was wandering aimlessly. Just running for my life."

I continue to look out the window.

"I realize now that taking that risk, opening up the bookshop when I had nothing else to live for, and nothing else to lose revealed so many doors that I didn't even know existed."

I turn to him now.

"Then, I met you. You've shown me how to live, Bishop, and I don't even think you realize it."

I look down to my lap, overwhelmed by the life I'm living. Overwhelmed by the love and happiness that radiates from him. It's been a long road for both of us, but together, we're okay.

"I love you," is all he says with a smile on his face.

And today, I have everything I'll ever need.

S. C. Gray

THE END

HELPFUL RESOURCE LIST FOR OUR
WOUNDED SERVICE MEMBERS

- *American Military University: 1-877-755-2787 / www.amu.apus.edu*

- *American Foundation for the Blind: 1-212-502-7600 / www.afb.org*

- *Amputee Coalition of America:1-888-267-5669 / http://www.amputee-coalition.org*

- *AMVETS: 1-877-726-8387 / www.amvets.org*

- *Army Emergency Relief: 1-866-878-6378 / https://www.aerhq.org/*

- *Blinded Veterans Association: 1-800-669-7079 / www.bva.org*

- *Brain Injury Association of America: 1-800-444-6443 / www.biausa.org*

- *Brain Injury Resource Center: 1-206-621-8558 / www.headinjury.com*

- *Coalition to Salute America's Heroes: 1-888-447-2588 / www.saluteheroes.org*

- *Computer/Electronic Accommodations Program (CAP) 1-703-614-8416 / http://www.cap.mil*

- *Defense and Veterans Brain Injury Center: 1-800-870-9244 / http://dvbic.dcoe.mil*
- *Department of Veteran Affairs: 1-800-827-1000 / www.va.gov*
- *Disabled Veterans of America: 1-877-426-2838 / www.dav.org*
- *Give an Hour: www.giveanhour.org (Provides donated mental health services and counseling)*
- *Gov Benefits: 1-800-333-4636 / www.benefits.gov*
- *Guide Dogs: 1-818-362-5834 / www.guidedogsofamerica.org*
- *Helmets to Hardhats: 866-741-6210 / www.helmetstohardhats.org*
- *Hire Heroes USA: 844-634-1520 / https://www.hireheroesusa.org/*
- *Homes For Our Troops: 1-866-787-6677 / www.hfotusa.org*
- *Job Fairs/Possible Employment 800-226-0841/ www.recruitmilitary.com*
- *Marine 4 Life: www.marineforlife.org*
- *Military One Source: 1-800-342-9647 / http://www.militaryonesource.mil*
- *Military Severely Injured Center: 1-888-774-1361 / www.military.com/support*
- *National Center for PTSD: www.ptsd.va.gov*
- *National Family Caregivers Association: 1-202-454-3970 www.caregiveraction.org*
- *National Military Family Association: 1-703-931-6632 / www.militaryfamily.org*

- *National Resource Center on Supportive Housing and Home Modification: 1-213-740-1364 / https://www.homemods.org/directory/nrcshhm/index.htm*
- *National Resource Directory: www.nrd.gov*
- *National Spinal Cord Injury Association: www.spinalcord.org*
- *National Veterans Legal Services Program: 1-202-265-8305 / http://www.nvlsp.org*
- *Navy Marine Corps Relief Society: 1-800-654-8364 / www.nmcrs.org*
- *Operation Family Fund: 1-760-793-0053 / https://operationfamilyfund.org*
- *Operation First Response: 1-888-289-0280 / www.operationfirstresponse.org*
- *Operation Home Front: 1-800-722-6098 / www.operationhomefront.net*
- *Paralyzed Veterans of America: 1-800-424-8200 / www.pva.org*
- *Project Return to Work: 1-720-359-1541 / www.return2work.org*
- *Red Cross Emergency Communication Services 1-877-272-7337 / https://www.redcross.org*
- *Sentinels of Freedom Scholarship Foundation: 1-925-380-6342 / www.sentinelsoffreedom.org*
- *Safe Harbor: 571-970-6369 / http://www.safeharborfoundation.org*
- *Serving Those Who Serve: 347-360-0729/ www.stws.org*
- *Soldiers Angels: 1-210-629-0020 / www.soldiersangels.org*
- *Suicide Hotline: 1- 800-273-8255 / www.veteranscrisisline.net / Or TEXT to Chat: 838255*

- *Swords to Plowshares: 415-252-4787 / www.swords-to-plowshares.org*
- *The American Legion: 202-861-2700 / www.legion.org*
- *The Brain Injury Information Network: 707- 544-4323 http://www.braininjurynetwork.org*
- *The Military Order of the Purple Heart: 703-642-5360 / www.purpleheart.org*
- *The National Amputation Foundation: 1-516-887-3600 / www.nationalamputation.org*
- *Tragedy Assistance Program: 1-800-959-8277 / www.taps.org*
- *Traumatic Brain Injury Survival Guide: 1-231-929-7358 / www.tbiguide.com*
- *United Spinal Association: 1-718-803-3782 / www.unitedspinal.org*
- *USA Cares: 800-773-0387 / http://www.usacares.org*
- *Veterans of Foreign Wars: 816-968-1128 / www.vfw.org*
- *Vets4Vets: www.vets4veterans.com*
- *Wounded Soldier and Family Hotline: 1-800-984-8523, Mon-Fri 0700 - 1900*
- *Wounded Warrior Project: www.woundedwarriorproject.org*
- *Wounded Warrior Regiment Call Center (Sgt Merlin German Call Center): 1-877-487-6299 / www.woundedwarriorregiment.org*
- *Tips/Help for Spouses/Families: 1-405-535-1925 / www.veteransfamiliesunited.org*
- *USO: 1-800-876-7469 / http://www.uso.org*

Printed in Great Britain
by Amazon